CW00520824

Stress City

A Fairy Tale Gone Wrong

Emer Bruce

Emer Bruce

Published by Stress City Headquarters Ltd.

ISBN number 978-0-9576325-0-9

A CIP catalogue record for this book is available from the British Library.

Editor: Steve Lockley

Cover Design and Photography: Dave Brown ApeInc.co.uk

In memory of my mother

Jean Pyper Malcolm

Scotland the Brave

Emer Bruce

Stress City

CONTENTS

1 No Ordinary Doll

2 One for Sorrow

3 Who's the Fairest

4 Heroes, apply within

5 The Wilde Blue Yonder

6 *Hell and High Water*, Falias

7 Way out West

8 The Path of most resistance

9 The Fianna

10 The Amazons

11 Scathach Island

12 Donn of the Dead

13 Donn's TV - Flashback

14 The Gods have their own rules

15 The Best of Dreams

16 I'll get you my pretties

17 Suicide Bridge

18 Dreams Refined or Replaced

19 Aife, Queen of the Amazons

20 The Last Ray of Hope

Emer Bruce

Stress City

CHARACTERS

Jack	Lead character, idiot
Dundee	Lead character, idiot
Mrs D	Problem Solver
Mrs Snarlington-Darlington	Jack's guardian
Duggey	Book shop owner, pal
Brian	Manager of pub, pal
Echtra	Otherworldly doll
Echraide	Otherworldly messenger
The Cormacs	Dundee's cousins
Sharon	Gossip, neighbour
Ann Angel	Head of Human Resources
Villains	Aife, Queen of the Amazons
	Addison Bruce – Governor*
	Black Witch of Bad Luck
The Gods/semi-divine	Angus, God of Love
	Donn, God of the Dead
	Manannan, God of the Seas
	The Fairy Queen of dreams
	Scathach (Aife's nemesis)
Mythical heroes	Finn, Leader of the Fianna
	Diorruing, the Seer
	Diarmait, stepson of Angus
	Fergus, poet, wise counsellor
	Mac, the giant
	Keevan - Jack's former self
	King of the Cormacs - Dundee's former self
Seven Mortal Chiefs	The Adventurer
	The Wings
	The Rev
	The Spirit
	The Heart
	The Guardian Angel
	The Shadow - Addison Bruce's alter ego*

Emer Bruce

Prologue

Everything about Mrs D was big. Her body, her bouffant hair style, her hat with the very large hat pin, her dress, her coat, her shoes, even her handbag was big. But these were minor accessories compared to her demeanour which was so large the trees were forced to pull back their leaves to avoid the swing of it as she made her way purposefully along the narrow path in the woods.

She was on her way to *Emma's*.

Emma's was a quaint little yellow café. It had appeared, as if by magic, in the middle of a clearing in the woods that morning. Heaven knows how it got there. Mrs D would later tell the inhabitants of Stress City that it was the perfect spot for a café, and it was difficult to argue with someone who knew so much about catering.

Emma's ran like a dream. The tea was always hot and accompanied by a tea cosy. The drinks were always as cold as they should be and never filled with lemons, limes, brolly sticks, or cherries that you hadn't asked for. The food arrived without you having to raise an arm for it, and never interrupted a conversation. There were never any queues, or people standing around anxiously waiting to pay. And if anyone had a problem there was a bucket provided at the door.

As a hugely successful Problem Solver Mrs D knew that if problems were given too much attention they grew, and so she insisted that all problems were left outside the café, in a large yellow bucket. The bucket had *'for customer use only'* on it, but if you had thrown an unwanted problem into the bucket on your way past without purchasing anything no-one would have been any the wiser.

'What do you see, you people staring at me?
You see a doll on a music box that's wound by a key.
How can you tell, I'm under a spell?
I'm waiting for love's first kiss.
You cannot see how much I long to be free;
turning around on this music box that's wound by a key.
Yearning, yearning,
while I'm turning around and around.'

"Doll On a Music Box" Words and Music by Richard M. Sherman and
Robert B. Sherman © 1968, Reproduced by permission of EMI Unart
Catalog Inc, London W8 5SW

Emer Bruce

Chapter One

No Ordinary Doll

'You can see from the chart there is a direct correlation between the number of problem letters coming into the department, and the rainfall in the City.' explained the young woman, whose name was Echtra, casting her eyes around the large oval table in the board room.

'Our records show that when the majority of inhabitants are forced indoors, the urge to write in to us increases.'

Twelve bored men shuffled around on the Executive chairs, desperately trying to stay awake. There was nothing unusual about that. It happened every week. The man with the colourless tie sitting closest to the screen raised his head, and for a moment Echtra thought he was about to say something, but he just stared at the opposite wall for a few moments before turning his attention back to the agenda.

Nothing stirred the Senior Team, particularly during the 07.00 updates, the longest toughest meeting of the week where the Executive were always an apology on the agenda. The updates began at basement level and

1

continued up through the building until every Head of Department on every floor had been seen. By the afternoon each session began to blur into the next which meant the actions for the upper floors were always carried forward and never carried out. This had a huge effect on moral which was at its highest in cleaning, its lowest in finance, and is the reason why none of the windows at Stress City Headquarters open on the fifth floor.

Stress City Headquarters is one of the most important buildings in Stress City, second only to City Hall. It holds a prominent position on Main Street between the Bank and the Library and is the only building in the City to have a grand entrance and a carpeted walkway. Everyone wants to work there - apart from the employees.

They stopped putting the clocks back inside Stress City Headquarters in 1973. Everyone was getting up and going home in the dark anyway and so there was no need. In the early days there had been set hours of the day – nine to five. But these were gradually phased out by the people who wanted to get into work early. Then everyone followed suit. The competitive people got in even earlier. Everyone followed. And soon you were running late if you got in at seven am. Then people started to brag that they had been in since six thirty. Others arrived at six, saying they would leave at four pm, and go to the gym. But they never did. Then people started to work weekends. Not the whole weekend, just a few hours here and there, in order to catch up. Then everyone else did the same until everyone at Stress City Headquarters was at work almost all of the time.

Time is of the utmost importance in Stress City and there are clocks everywhere to prove it. The clocks are there, according to the people in charge at City Hall, to ensure the City always runs like clockwork. But it never does. There is always a problem. And whenever there's a problem it's the responsibility of the people in charge at Stress City Headquarters to solve it.

Every day the inhabitants of Stress City can be seen dashing around the streets with never a moment to spare, despite the clocks which loom overhead – at the corners of the lanes, which run to and from the houses, above the office buildings on Main Street, in the square, the park, and even on the avenue, around the City wall.

The wall encircles the City. The only way into the City is through a four pillared gateway which lies open, the gates having rotted away thousands of years ago. To the right of the entrance there is a welcome sign for visitors, which are rare - given that the City is hidden in the middle of an Island, surrounded by a dense forest. There are outsiders in the North, but they tend to keep to themselves. There is a Bridge at the edge of the Island, but there is nothing at the end of it. No land on the other side, just swirling coloured mists.

A City that is cut off from the outside world, and yet

it seems to mirror it perfectly.

'Message for Ann Angel,' said the City Hall courier, speeding along the corridor of the fourth floor at Stress City Headquarters.

He drew to a halt outside the door marked 'Ann Angel, Head of Human Resources.'

Ann's assistant Sharon was standing at the door barring his way. She held out her hand for the official looking envelope but the courier ignored it, pushing past her impolitely into Ann's office.

'She's not here,' said Sharon, noticing the look of disappointment on the courier's face when he realised the lovely Ann was nowhere to be seen. He passed over the envelope with a scowl and left the office.

Sharon crossed over to the desk, took the phone off the hook, and settled herself down into Ann's fancy leather chair. She opened the envelope with a yawn, expecting to find yet another boring memo from City Hall. Instead she found a handwritten letter, covered in flour, from a woman who had signed herself off as Mrs D, Problem Solver.

Sharon was up and out of the chair before she'd even had time to read the contents. This was news, big news. In fact it was better than news. This was gossip, and Sharon was the biggest gossip in Stress City. She paced around the desk with the letter in her hand in the same way she had seen Ann do whenever she'd received something important, stopping to check the clock on the way round, wondering if she had time to tell anyone before Ann arrived. Then she sat down and read the letter, twice.

It was more a *fait accompli* than a request for interview. In the letter Mrs D had explained, quite forcefully, that as a woman of the world she had experienced every problem there was to have:

'Big ones, little ones, lots of tiny ones that seem big, huge ones that need a team of people to solve, unexpected ones, expected ones that you try to hide from, problems you didn't know you had until someone else told you, and worst of all - other people's problems.'

Mrs D went on to say that she would be arriving in the City that morning, would be conducting her problem solving from a café in the woods, and would be popping in to Stress City Headquarters at nine o'clock to discuss her requirements for an assistant.

'Nine o'clock!' cried Sharon, checking the clock on the wall which said eight twenty-five. And there was still no sign of Ann. If she didn't arrive soon Sharon would have to interview Mrs D herself!

The inhabitants of Stress City had never had a Problem Solver before. They had a Problem Solving Department. It had a desk, an Executive chair, a filing cabinet and an assistant - Sharon's friend and neighbour, Echtra - who was, at that very moment, in the board room trying to justify the Department's existence to the Senior Team.

The Problem Solving Department had been set up

several months ago following some research into the excessive levels of noise in the City. The research had shown, according to some bright spark in Marketing, that if the inhabitants of Stress City were given the opportunity to write in about their problems, it would reduce their need to talk about them.

It didn't! And the problem was - no-one wanted the Problem Solver's job. It was an impossible task. The people of Stress City didn't want to solve their problems. They just wanted to talk about them. They were quite happy to listen to endless solutions of how they might follow their dreams, fulfil their purpose in life, and take the appropriate action.

It all sounded quite marvellous, like an incredible adventure. Yes, they would do something about it. Change their lives forever. It was all making perfect sense. But first they really must buy some new curtains for the back bedroom.

And so the job of Problem Solver had remained vacant, until now.

Sharon made her way into the tiny kitchen which was tucked away on the left behind the filing cabinets, and opened the window above the sink, even though it was against the rules. She stuck her head out, surprised to find that the sunny showers which had been plaguing the City for weeks, had suddenly come to an end. She checked the streets for signs of Ann but it was almost impossible to see what was going on beneath the stream of commuters who hadn't realised the rain was over, and still had their brollies up.

She was about to pull the window shut when she spotted someone outside the grand entrance. It was a man. A tall dark handsome one, dressed in overalls from the 1970's standing next to a black Scottie dog, which had eighties side burns.

'Dundee,' cried Sharon, recognising her neighbour at once. 'Dundee!'

Startled by the call from above Dundee looked up, saw Sharon dangling out of the tiny window, and gave her a casual wave as if there was nothing unusual about him being there.

Sharon waved back overly enthusiastic. 'What are you doing here?'

Dundee raised a hand to his ear to indicate he couldn't hear her.

'What are you doing?' screeched Sharon, determined to make herself heard.

'Here!' she cried, pointing towards the carpet.

Dundee came forward onto the carpeted walkway and pointed to a small window cleaning box at the front of the building.

Sharon edged a little further forward out of the window to get a look at the window cleaning box. Then she turned her attention back to Dundee, gazing dreamily down at his dark shoulder length locks.

She was about to ask what he was doing cleaning windows outside Stress City Headquarters, but it was too long a conversation to have four storeys up and so instead she asked.

'Where's Jack?'

Dundee heard that, and shrugged his shoulders.

Dundee had been waiting outside the grand entrance for Jack since seven o'clock that morning, arriving early in the hope of catching sight of some of the beautiful office girls, who worked inside the building, and were hardly ever seen. But he was too late. Almost every employee at Stress City Headquarters had been in since six thirty, even the secretaries. Dundee checked the gigantic clock above the grand entrance for the umpteenth time that morning. It was eight thirty. They were supposed to have started on the windows an hour ago.

'Where *was* Jack!'

Jack was in the middle of an extraordinary dream which was about to be cut short by his guardian, Mrs Snarlington-Darlington, whose early morning calls were so loud they reverberated through the walls of every cottage on the bank.

The bank was located at the edge of the Island on the outskirts of the forest, and was home to seven identical cottages which sat huddled together with their back doors overlooking the Bridge, and their front doors facing into the woods.

Mrs Snarlington-Darlington lived at number two. A formidable force in the City who, having taken Jack under her wing as a small toddler, felt duty bound to follow him around for the rest of his life in order to tell him where he was going wrong. He skipped breakfast to try and avoid her, but as soon as he opened the front door she was behind him in the hall, with her hat, coat, brolly and gigantic shopping bags.

Jack dutifully picked up the bags and followed Mrs Snarlington-Darlington out of the front door, turning right onto the communal pathway, which ran between the front doors and the trees. At the end of the pathway they turned left, along a narrow trail through the woods that led out onto the visitor's road, which ran through the forest all the way into the City. In the middle of the visitor's road there was a natural crossroads with a sign post, and they waited there for the bus. The bus was late and so Mrs Snarlington-Darlington took the opportunity to say a few words, and Jack tuned out.

It was then Jack heard the song. It seemed to be coming from the overgrown path to the left of the signpost, which was odd because the path didn't lead anywhere. He tried to interrupt Mrs Snarlington-Darlington to tell her about it but like most mother hens, intent on the welfare of their chicks, it was almost impossible to divert her. When the bus arrived she bustled him on to it, insisting on sitting next to him and then budging him up several inches to allow for her huge hips and shopping bags until Jack's face was squashed up against the window.

The bus sped along the visitor's road. It flew past

9

Mrs D who had just left the café in the clearing, and was making her way into the City on foot. The driver gave Mrs D a beep to indicate she should give the bonnet a wide birth, but Mrs D didn't appear to hear the beep because of the song, and the passengers didn't hear anything either because Mrs Snarlington-Darlington was drowning out the lyrics.

Jack was two stops away from his intended destination when the bus pulled through the City gateway and into the square, but he slid himself up the window, and before Mrs Snarlington-Darlington could get to the bit about him not getting any younger, he had climbed over the seat and jumped off the bus.

'You can't hide under the covers forever Jack,' Mrs Snarlington-Darlington called out after him but her voice was drowned out by Frank Sinatra telling him to 'wake up to reality' which was much the same thing.

As Jack arrived at the bus stop the song hit a big band crescendo and he twisted around, looking up for the source, which was how he managed to collide with the Governor of Stress City, Addison Bruce.

Addison Bruce couldn't hear a thing because he was on a teleconference on his Executive head phones. He went head to head with Jack at a terrific speed. There was a short outraged silence, followed by a tirade of abuse. Then a clatter of brollies as the inhabitants attempted to swing out of the Governor's way.

Addison stormed off through the square, with a

hanky pressed to his bleeding forehead, disappearing into a narrow side street that led through to Main Street. He was closely followed by Jack, who was also bleeding but didn't have a hanky, Mrs D, who had just entered the City gateway, and the song.

Sharon was at the window with a cup of tea in her hands when the song flew into Main Street. She leapt back, shocked to see Addison Bruce appearing out of the side street, the sea of commuters parting to allow him through. Seconds later she moved back to the window, assuming it was safe to do so. Then her boss, Ann Angel, finally appeared on the opposite side of the street, and so she jumped back again, completely missing Ann's arrival on the carpeted walkway.

But Dundee saw her - a dark haired beauty in a rose coloured rain hat and raincoat emerging from a sea of black suits, and she was heading straight for him. Encouraged by Frank Sinatra and oblivious to the fact that Ann was clearly running late, he leapt forward, trying to impress her with some light Scottish banter. Ann was extremely polite, sparing him a few valuable seconds of her time, but the conversation turned into more of an interview than a chat and the commiseration handshake she gave him at the end told him he had fallen well short of standard.

In Human Resources Sharon was back at the window,

determined to spend her last few moments of freedom in a cool breeze. The air conditioning had short circuited again, the sun had been blazing in through the windows since early morning, and the temperature in the building was becoming unbearable.

There was no longer anything to see on the streets down below, apart from a few late comers, and Sharon was about to pull the window to, when Jack appeared on the opposite side of the road.

'Jack!' she screamed, almost swooning out of the window.

Jack was just as tall and handsome as Dundee, with dark curls that fell just short of his shoulders.

He bounded onto the carpeted walkway, looked up at Sharon, and waved, as did Dundee before dragging Jack off towards the window cleaning box at the front of the building.

'It's such a shame they're both idiots,' thought Sharon, ducking back inside the kitchen.

She quickly washed her tea cup, placed it back in the cupboard, had one final look at Jack and Dundee, who were arguing over which one of them was going up in the box, and raced back into Ann's office putting the phone back on the hook. It rang almost immediately. When Ann entered the office Sharon was on the phone, smiling angelically, as if she had been there all along.

Ann read the contents of Mrs D's letter, shocked but pleased by the turn of events.

'We'd better keep this to ourselves for now,' said

Ann. 'Mrs D may not be suitable.'

'Yes of course,' said Sharon, intent on telling everyone as soon as possible.

The phone rang again. 'She's here.'

Jack, having lost the argument with Dundee, was on his way up to the top of the building in a window cleaning box that had seen better days. The box made it as far as the fourth floor then shuddered and ground to a halt. Jack checked the pavement below to see what was happening. Then wished he hadn't. Dundee was way below him fiddling around with the controls. The box shuddered again. Jack panicked and put his hands on the glass, making even more marks on the windows. Then he realised there was someone inside the room. He peered in, expecting to see one of the beautiful office girls, but instead he came face to face with a big woman in a green suit. The woman, who appeared to be in the middle of an interview, gave Jack a look that suggested he shouldn't be peering at people through windows, and Jack dove back into his box. Jack yelled down at Dundee. Dundee yelled back. The box was stuck! Jack shrieked. Then the box suddenly swung towards the board room window, with Jack still in it, clinging to the sides.

Inside the board room the temperature was high, and rising. The Senior Team had dispensed with their jackets and ties, even though it was against company policy, and were clinging to the large oval table as though it were an inflatable dinghy in danger of drifting off. Every so often someone would lunge for the water, but for the most part they remained immobile, keeping their shuffling around to a minimum.

At the front of the room, beyond the hazy wave of the projector, Echtra continued on through the slides, as if they were still with her.

Outside the window, the window cleaning box juddered to a halt. As it did, a cloud fell over the sun. It was a welcome relief for the Senior Team. For the first time that morning they sat up and turned their attention towards the front of the room, and that was when they saw her. *Really* saw her. Lit up in the gloom under the light of the projector - like a doll - tall and narrow, with dark silky hair, cut short like a child's, and ebony eyes that were holding them spellbound. No-one moved.

Oblivious to what was going on inside the board room Jack took a rag out of the window cleaning bucket and gave the glass a quick wipe. Then he peered in to see twelve men sitting perfectly upright around a large oval table, motionless and transfixed - and he followed their eyes towards the light.

Echtra must have sensed Jack was there because she turned towards the window and at that very moment she seized up, like an automaton doll, one hand pointing at the screen, the other across her middle, her head tilted slightly to the right at an awkward angle.

Frank Sinatra was still going strong outside the

14

building, and it could have been an incredibly romantic moment if it wasn't for the fact that Jack was stuck in a box, four storeys up, outside the window. Then the tea lady burst into the room, breaking the spell. Jack automatically stepped back and flew out of the box!

Moments later the City's newly appointed Problem Solver left the building. The song, which by that time was coming to an end, followed Mrs D until she was safely outside the City wall, and then it disappeared off into the woods.

Chapter Two

One for Sorrow

It was a simple service, just the Reverend, an organ player and two onlookers. That was the trouble with funerals. You were wholly reliant on kin. And if you had outlived your kin then close friends or admirers, or perhaps someone you had done a good turn, even fans. But the deceased had none of those and so it had been a little awkward. The Reverend struggled with the eulogy. Usually he had something to work with. A rose coloured view of the life of the deceased from one of the grieving relatives. Nothing fancy, 'favoured aunt,' 'beloved grandmother,' 'respected colleague.' But there was no-one to vouch for the young man in the box and so after a grim hymn through the valley of darkness the Reverend cut to the chase, and in no time at all the coffin was heading through the curtains into the eternal fires. A period of silence followed, to give the congregation time to reflect, and then it was on to the final hymn which was usually something cheery like all things bright and beautiful, but when the Reverend turned his attention back to the pews the onlookers had gone.

'We've got to do something,' said Jack, as he and Dundee sped through the gardens of the church.

'With our lives!' he added, stating the obvious.

'Aye,' said Dundee, opening the church gate, and they stepped out onto Cemetery Road.

Cemetery Road was the longest road on the Island, located several miles away from the City in order to accommodate the huge numbers of graves that ran along both sides of it. There were thousands of headstones and very little room. New arrivals were being pushed back all the time further and further into the forest. The plots on the left of the road behind the church wall were huge but had been taken a long time ago. The plots on the right, with a watery view were small, but popular. The dead had already been crammed in, all the way up to the water's edge. Some of the headstones had slid off into the water where the bank had come loose, causing the remaining headstones to lean to the left or the right, giving the impression they were constantly jostling for position.

The envious dead looked on, momentarily disturbed by the shadows of the tall dark handsome strangers as they passed along the church wall that separated them. One dressed in black, in a suit that had seen better days. His head tilted forward, his left hand in his trouser pocket, his right hand dangling free. The dark shiny locks that fell heavily over his eyes pushed back on occasion by his free hand, a habit he had picked up in his early years as an avid reader.

The other bounded ahead of his friend, forced to walk backwards on occasion to maintain the gap between them. He was dressed in a clean white shirt. His hands in and out of his overly pressed trousers, undecided. His hair as dark as the other's but wound into curls that bounced up and down a lot and refused to stay still.

'That was grim,' said Jack, relieved to be back in the sunshine.

'Aye,' said Dundee, his head firmly fixed on the path, his thoughts still back at the Church.

'Imagine having only two people at your funeral. The church was empty, apart from us.'

Dundee said nothing, determined to stay where he was, in the gloom. But Jack just kept on tapping.

'I wonder what made Brian do it…throw himself off the Bridge like that? Something must have pushed him over the edge.'

'Aye.'

'Is that all you can say…aye?'

Dundee pushed the hair back out of his eyes, looked up, and grinned at Jack, who was walking backwards along the bumpy road.

Jack grinned back, forgot where he was, and hit the wall on his right. Dundee burst out laughing.

Jack stayed where he was until Dundee had caught him up and they walked together for a while.

'The Rev didn't have much to say for himself did he?'

'He was hopeless,' said Jack, relieved that Dundee was finally joining in the conversation.

'He didn't even mention Brian's name. '*A young man who met with an unfortunate end*.' That could have been anybody. It could have been me yesterday!'

'Aye, so you keep saying,' said Dundee, who was fed up discussing Jack's near death experience of the previous day outside Stress City Headquarters. He quickly changed the subject back to the deceased.

'It was a bad turnout, especially for a man Brian's age.'

'Why, how old was he?'

'Aboot twelve years older than us.'

'Twelve years!' cried Jack. 'He looked miles older than that.'

'Aye, well. He had all those lines on his forehead.'

'Yeh - from frowning at all the customers.'

Dundee laughed. 'Aye Brian was dour alright…and pale. I've never met anyone as pale as Brian. I first met him when I was up North, and he was managing the *Hootsman*. Brian was always in a bad mood, even with the regulars. He was a hard worker though. Ten years I knew him. Ten years. And he never left that bar. It was no life for a man in his early thirties…'

Jack nodded along, his attention wandering. He had heard all this before.

'…Then, when I left the North, and came doon here to stay, there he was again! Behind the bar of the *Hell and High Water* pub. I don't think I ever saw his body at full

19

length.'

'Well it's at full length now,' said Jack, feeling guilty as a picture of Brian's coffin popped into his head.

They continued along Cemetery Road side by side, stopping when they reached the half mile point to take a look at the Heroes Graves – giant stones which had been placed there thousands of years ago to honour a band of warriors who had drowned defending the Island. There was a gap in the wall where children had forced their way through and Dundee clambered in to get a closer look, but there was nothing to see, the names of the Heroes having faded away long ago. There were lots of other tombstones and odd looking sculptures. Dundee attempted to wander around them, but there was hardly any room, and moments later he was back where he started, in the shadow of the giant stones.

Jack stood in the sun watching him. He knew instinctively that Dundee wanted to be like them, to die a hero's death. He felt a sudden chill and an urge to pull him back.

'Come on.'

Dundee turned, and headed back along a narrow patch of grass towards the wall. Half way there he hit the side of something, lost his footing and had to grab hold of a stone angel to save himself.

'Careful.'

As Dundee reached the gap in the wall Jack held out his hand. Dundee took it, even though it wasn't necessary and Jack, who was slightly broader, pulled him up and over the fallen stones with ease.

They continued their journey in silence, quickening their pace, the sun at its peak, anxious to be in the shade of the forest which they could clearly see up ahead, and were almost at the end of Cemetery Road when Jack opened his mouth again.

'You don't think Brian will go to hell do you?'

'Whit for? For managing the *Hell and High Water* pub?' said Dundee, amused.

'For killing himself,' said Jack, being serious for a change.

'It's hard to say, I don't know what the criteria is these days. You'd have to go back and ask the Rev.'

'I'm not going back there on my own. You can't see his eyes!'

Dundee burst out laughing.

'He never has those shades off. He even wears them for christenings!'

'If you ask me he's hiding something,' said Dundee, who had seen a lot of horror films. 'Imagine bumping into him on Cemetery Road in the middle of the night in his long dark coat and straggly hair. You'd think he was the 'ghost of things to come,' there to give you a warning.'

'Which one's he?'

'The one with the hood and no face…'

'Whoooo!' wailed Dundee, pointing his finger at one of the graves in an attempt to spook Jack.

'I don't need a warning like that thanks,' said Jack, backing away towards the forest. 'I'm going to do something with my life.'

'Aye, so you keep saying,' said Dundee, catching him up and together they entered the forest, leaving the dead behind.

Jack and Dundee are the talk of the town in Stress City. Everyone has something to say about them - none of it good, which is a pity because they do have some redeeming qualities.

Jack is compassionate and kind, charming to everyone, whether they like him or not. Dundee is studious, high minded, and fiercely loyal to his friends.

Dundee had arrived in Stress City from North of the border a few years earlier in search of a distant relative, Duggey, and had remained. Duggey, who lived at number one, 'the bank,' and was one of Jack's neighbours, had been delighted. Dundee was well liked - 'King of the stories,' able to recount scenes from almost any book or film making him a popular choice at parties.

For the first few days Jack had skirted around Dundee like an excited puppy. Then, after an extended drinking session at the *Hell and High Water* pub, they emerged, the last two out of the door at sun rise, like magnetically bonded soul mates.

The younger females of the City, who still put good looks and charm before career prospects, can't get enough of them. They adore Jack and consider themselves lucky if they catch his attention. He takes them away to a dreamy place where they forget themselves, and their virtue, and then he is off again before they can get a proper hold of him.

Dundee has a similar draw. Passionate when roused, something he is particularly good at, with a fiery temper and unpredictable mood swings which find him cheery one minute and dour the next - but this simply adds to his appeal, the lion must be tamed.

The older ladies of the City however go out of their way to avoid them. Mrs Snarlington-Darlington's companions for example say 'they are neither use nor ornament,' whenever her back is turned. The well to do ladies of the City, whose husbands have important jobs at the Bank, say 'no good will ever come of them', in the hope that it comes true, and the 'off with their heads' brigade whose husbands work at City Hall want them exiled.

Mrs Snarlington-Darlington was not to blame. She had done her best. Somehow she had managed to instil an element of common sense into Jack in the early years by threatening him with a big stick she had hidden in the cupboard, which he later discovered was just a pole for closing the curtains. But by the time Dundee arrived from the North any common sense she had instilled in Jack was promptly thrown out of the window. When Jack turned thirty two in March Mrs Snarlington-Darlington, who couldn't get either of them out of the house at that point, threatened them both with a job at the Bank courtesy of her cousin Eric who worked in Finance. They refused, saying they didn't want to spend the rest of their lives like Eric watching the clock. Eric, who was an accountant and liked to carry things forward, would bring the jobs up every time he saw them, and then they would disappear off to see Duggey who owned the local book shop, and would find them some odd job that always ended in disaster.

The forest was full of tiny butterflies, flitting in and out of the shade, and it cheered Jack and Dundee up no end as they walked the remaining mile and a half to the crossroads. They stopped for a rest at the signpost. Dundee parked himself down at the bottom of the post which said they were three miles from the church, half a mile from the City, two minutes from the Bridge if they took the right fork, and going nowhere if they took the left, although someone with a sense of humour and an inability to spell had scribbled 'Wilde Blue Yonder' in blue felt tip on the wood.

Jack sat down in the dirt in the middle of the crossroads, with no concern at all for his trousers which had been cleanly pressed that morning.

Dundee pulled a small flask out of his jacket pocket and threw it towards him.

Jack caught it in mid-air with his right hand, and as he did, a lone magpie flew over and parked itself on the post above Dundee's head.

'One for sorrow,' said Dundee, who was incredibly

superstitious, particularly about birds.

He searched the sky hoping another magpie might join it but nothing came and when he drew his eyes back to the crossroads Jack had a bloody hanky pressed to his forehead.

'I keep telling you, you need stitches in that,' said Dundee, referring to the cut Jack had incurred in his collision with Addison Bruce in the square.

Jack ignored him, took a drink from the flask, poured some water onto his hanky, pressed it onto the cut on his forehead, and attempted to throw the flask back to Dundee. It missed, hit the signpost and flew off into the bushes. Jack grinned. Dundee sighed and went off to retrieve it.

With the hanky still in place, Jack stretched his free arm out behind him, to prop himself up, and threw his head back. It was hot in the dirt. A bee flew by, followed by a couple of butterflies, but there was no sign of any birds and the lone magpie on the signpost seemed to have settled in.

Dundee had some funny ideas about birds, and lots of other things – signs, omens - things that Jack paid no attention to, and whilst Jack's imagination was equally as fantastical as Dundee's, in Dundee's imaginary world, which was full of grim myths and fairy tales - things always ended badly. Recently however even Jack felt his sunny day world was constantly being overshadowed - by something.

Jack checked his hanky. The bleeding had stopped.

Emer Bruce

He checked the sign post. The magpie was still there.

'That looks bad Jack,' said Dundee, emerging from the bushes. 'You should go and see Doc Spoc.'

'I'll go later,' said Jack, who had no intention of going at all.

'What did *she* say when she saw you?' asked Dundee, referring to Mrs Snarlington-Darlington.

'She said, *'I've had enough of you two and your cartoon capers. Every time you leave the house it ends in disaster,'* said Jack, who did a good impression of his guardian.

'She's right though.'

'She's right, alright. If we're not careful we'll end up killing ourselves, like Brian! We've got to *do* something.'

'Aye, with our lives, so you keep saying.'

Dundee leant his head back against the post and sighed heavily. 'It's not as though we haven't tried.'

'No-one tries harder than us,' agreed Jack.

'It's like every time we turn a corner, we hit a brick wall...'

Jack smiled knowingly, the bloody hanky still in his hand.

'Nae matter what we do, trouble finds us. Bad luck follows us around,' continued Dundee, ranting on.

Jack nodded, carefully.

'It's like, it's like…'

'It's like the Universe has got something against us,' said Jack, without thinking.

'That's it Jack, that's exactly what it's like!' cried Dundee, sitting up straight. 'The Universe has got

26

something against us.'

Jack smiled, pleased he had come up with the answer. He waited patiently in the dirt whilst Dundee came up with their next move.

'We should go and see Duggey aboot this,' said Dundee finally, clearly in a better mood.

Jack was up and shaking the dirt off his trousers before Dundee could get to his feet.

The thought that some Universal force was responsible for them lagging behind in their lives had cheered them up. They were not to blame. They were innocent! And at any rate, whatever the cause of their predicament it would be up to Duggey to solve it. Duggey had almost as many books as a library, and a wisdom that was beyond his years.

'Your heed!' cried Dundee suddenly, pointing towards Jack. 'It's bleeding again...there's blood all over your good shirt.'

'She'll go mad!' Jack tore off the shirt, almost losing the buttons. Then, leaving Dundee at the post, he sped off in the direction of the cottages on the bank, naked from the waist up, his shirt in one hand and his hanky in the other, pressed firmly to the cut on his forehead.

Just before he disappeared into the bushes Jack spotted a second magpie heading in Dundee's direction and he swung around.

'Two for joy!' he called back, but the original magpie had gone and so it didn't count.

27

Dundee leant back against the signpost and lifted his face towards the sun. He could hear Jack rustling through the bushes as he made his way out towards the bank. Then there was silence, apart from the birds, and the music. Dundee sat up. It was the same song that had been playing outside Stress City Headquarters the previous day when he had bumped into Ann Angel, and it was coming in the direction of the Wilde Blue Yonder path.

Dundee picked himself up and headed towards the sound, hesitant at first, recalling that bad things usually happened to people investigating strange sounds alone in forests, but the music was cheery and his curiosity got the better of him. The path was narrow and incredibly overgrown, his height a disadvantage, his hair getting caught up in the brambles and low hanging branches, but eventually he stumbled into a tiny circular clearing. And in the middle of the clearing, stuck between two giant trees, was a small yellow café.

Dundee stared at the quaint little café which looked oddly at home in the woods. The door and the windows were shut. The sign above the door said *Emma's*. There were two windows either side of it, and a large window on the right, which he assumed was an adjoining room. It had a roof, that had been painted yellowy cream to match the walls, and there was music escaping from the tiny chimney.

Dundee was about to step forward, when suddenly the door and the windows flew open, and a dozen tiny birds flew out. He staggered back, almost toppling over.

Then he turned and ran - out of the clearing, along the overgrown path, left at the crossroads, and was soon speeding along the visitor's road towards the safety of the City.

There were two ways onto the bank from the visitor's road - along the proper trail that Jack and Mrs Snarlington-Darlington had followed dutifully that morning, or straight through the bushes following the fork at the crossroads.

Jack took the direct route, arriving on the embankment with his hair tangled up in leaves. There was a footpath that ran along the top of the bank, separating the immaculate back lawns of the seven cottages on the left, from the grassy slope on the right, which curved steeply up from the water's edge. Jack strode along the footpath until he came to the back lawn of number two. Ignoring the tiny shell lined pathway he strode straight across the lawn, placed his key in the back door, and was about to step into the back kitchen, when he sensed someone behind him on the Bridge.

The Bridge is incredibly unreliable. It is not just the fact that it is old and worn and full of holes. It is rootless, undecided, as though it had been dreamt up in the morning and might choose to skip off again in the afternoon.

Opinions about the Bridge are mixed.

Some say, 'Stay away from that tatty old thing it's a

death trap.'

Others say, 'It's the most beautiful Bridge in the world.'

It does have a certain feminine charm - pale blue in colour with gold trim around its delicately crafted railings and spiralling towers, the raging winds having battered against it for the past thousands of years giving it a certain shabby chic - the sort of Bridge that would go well in a bedroom with a couple of old French armoires and a freestanding mirror. One of its most unusual features is the golden pillar box which is set deep into the stone in the middle of the archways, and is almost unreachable from the Bridge itself, unless you are prepared to lie down on the wooden planks and dangle your arm through the railings.

Despite that fact, every year, at the end of October, the inhabitants of Stress City come to the Bridge to post their dreams there. A quaint little tradition from the past which is still observed, and on days like these, with the flowering vines from the forest wrapped around the railings, and the sun's rays reflecting up from the waters below, you might be tempted to post a dream there yourself.

Jack knew it was Echtra on the Bridge. They were neighbours and she lived at number seven with her guardian, who was incredibly small, the smallest woman in Stress City.

Jack headed straight towards Echtra with no concern

at all for the neighbouring lawns. He stopped a few yards in to wait for her, and was leaning over the railings watching the sun on the water when she came up behind him.

'Is it you?' he asked, a childish game.

'Who?' she smiled.

He turned to face her, temporarily blinded by the sun in his eyes. Then she came into view and he stared at her, lost in the moment.

She stared back, the first to turn away, intent on leaving him behind at the Bridge.

'Don't go,' begged Jack, conscious of the fact that she was always pulling away from him.

'I'm late for a meeting,' said Echtra, already at the foot of the embankment.

'What sort of meeting?' said Jack, now at the top of the slope.

'A meeting about the new Problem Solver,' she replied, suitably excited.

'What new Problem Solver?'

'She arrived in the City yesterday.'

'Arrived?' said Jack, surprised. 'Where did she come from?'

'I'm not sure,' said Echtra, vaguely, her eyes on the forest, clearly anxious to be on her way.

'Where is she now?' Jack was keen to see the visitor for himself.

'She's at her café in the woods.'

'A café? In the woods! Where in the woods? Are you

going there now?' Jack was full of questions. 'I'll come with you.' He began moving towards her.

'I told you. I'm on my way to a meeting at the office to pick up the problems,' said Echtra, backing away.

'What problems?'

But she had already disappeared into the woods.

Disappointed Jack returned to number two, 'the bank.' He stumbled into the kitchen, through the sitting room, and out into the hallway through a door on the left, stopping when he caught sight of himself in the hall mirror.

'No wonder she ran away.'

Jack had forgotten he was naked from the waist up with blood all over his forehead and wondered why Echtra hadn't mentioned it. He flew up the staircase and into his bedroom, grabbed a t-shirt from the ironed pile, and walked into the bathroom. Using one of Mrs Snarlington-Darlington's best flannels he tried to mend his head but he was unable to stop the flow of blood. Then he heard the rattle of a key in the back door and was down the stairs and out the front door in a flash, leaving the bloody flannel behind him.

'Is that you Jack? Jack!!!' screeched Mrs Snarlington-Darlington, stepping into the kitchen followed by her Wednesday ladies.

'You've left your key in the back door again,' she continued, making her way through the sitting room and into the hall.

'I'm telling you that boy will be the death of me,' said Mrs Snarlington-Darlington, stopping in front of the hall mirror to take off her hat, her ladies reflected in the glass behind her.

'One minute he's here, the next minute he's gone. This may sound a little odd,' said Mrs Snarlington-Darlington, turning to face her ladies who had crowded around her, hoping it would be something of interest.

'But I can tell you this, in confidence,' she raised her eyebrows for dramatic effect.

'If I didn't know any better I'd say someone had dreamt him up.'

'Good heavens,' said the ladies, who had never heard of such a thing, but they nodded their heads in agreement. Mrs Snarlington-Darlington was hardly ever wrong.

Jack emerged from the bushes, disappointed to see that Dundee had left his post, relieved when the bus pulled up. He hopped on, hoping to catch Dundee up, but by the time the bus had arrived in the square Dundee was already lost in the throng.

It was lunchtime in the City and there were queues of people everywhere. Some people were queuing for sandwiches. Some people were queuing for teas and coffees. Some people were queuing for other people. Sometimes the queues overlapped and people found themselves queuing up for the wrong thing which was incredibly frustrating. There was hardly any room in the square which was jam-packed with tables, chairs and café owners who were constantly popping in and out, arguing over a few extra inches of pavement - and people were still streaming in, along the narrow passageways and lanes. Some sought refuge in the park which sat to the left of the square but this was already full, as was the avenue, which ran parallel to the park, along the City wall.

There are no historical records as to why the City wall was ever built, and from time to time City Hall officials considered knocking it down, but then they always voted against it. The general view being that the early ancestors must have built it for a reason. In fact some were quite superstitious about it. Others were quick to point out that they were not the only inhabitants on the Island. There were others in the North who might become unfriendly. And there were other reasons. The wall provided an ideal shelter from the forest which sprawled around untidily outside. This was largely unexplored. The majority of the inhabitants preferring to stay within the much neater confines of the City - the cardboard trees, the painted scenes, the fake grass - which was not to everyone's taste.

Oblivious to City Hall's attempts to improve it, nature continued to run wild outside, with no interest at all in what was going on at the other side of the wall. Whenever it got too close the 'men in blue,' who looked after the park, would appear at the entrance with giant hedge trimmers and try to cut it back, but as soon as the men had gone it was back again, climbing the wall.

Whatever the reason for its construction the wall had clearly been built to accommodate the inhabitants of that time, but the population of Stress City had grown considerably since then, and their entertainment needs had changed. The inhabitants were no longer interested in tipping hot coal onto the heads of their enemies. The modern citizen wanted shops, fancy cafes, cinemas and leisure centres. That left City Hall with the problem of space. There was very little room in the old square which was full of ancient buildings and temples that were never used, but were far too important to tear down. And so, in order to meet demand, City hall had built a new square around the old square.

The problem is, the squares overlap. The sharp corners of golden temples jut out dangerously close to pedestrian walkways. Scary ghouls loom over the canopies of fancy cafes, scaring the children. Shoppers have to pass by a crowd of fallen angels just to get to the dry cleaners. And in the middle of all the chaos stands City Hall - the only building in the City with a clear view of the gateway and plenty of room at the back and sides to make sure no-one ever challenges its decisions. It is also the tallest, and the longest. Theatrical in design, its entrance door half hidden by two stone curtains draped back around two giant pillars. Godlike figures adorn the heights. Statues of actors and actresses play their parts on the steps below, steps wide enough to accommodate half the population, and yet no-one is ever allowed inside. Like a grandiose Theatre, once vibrant and alive, where everything suddenly stopped.

Dundee pushed his way politely through the queues until he found himself in the shadows behind City Hall. He swung by the fancy shops and cafes with expertise, and disappeared behind a wall which hid a cobbled road that sloped downwards, into the older part of the City. The road bent to the left. Dundee followed it, passing the giant doors of the ancient Halls of Learning on the corner, and along the widened streets of the old square. Scary ghouls overshadowed him from the rooftops of the ancient buildings, but he did not look up. Sculptures lined the route, like scenes from a play, and he skirted around them. When he reached the centre he passed by the front of the white marble Temple of the Gods, which held pride of place, took a sharp left at the crowd of fallen angels, and headed down into Old Street.

Everything on Old Street was on a downward slope, including the shops which were too old to stand to attention for the entire day and bent forwards, sideways or backwards depending on the weather and the weight of the building next door.

Duggey's book shop was in keeping with the rest. It had been young once. The wooden sign above the front step had been pale blue and it had a purpose. It said *Books for sale* and had once swung neatly back and forth

36

in the wind on chains that were well maintained, and
didn't keep breaking off and hitting shoppers on the
head. The front step and entrance had been solid and
level. It didn't feel as if you were sliding out on your way
in. The bookshelves were clearly marked. Customers had
been able to find their way around. If they were in the
middle of historical battles they stayed there and didn't
suddenly find themselves in the spiritual section,
learning how to turn the other cheek.

But sadly, over the years, the shop had been bent out
of shape. The walls leant inwards, the floors were
wonky, and the book markers kept falling off the aisles.
But the customers didn't seem to mind. They expected
Duggey's to be old and bent. Duggey himself was young
but he had an old head and an inquisitive nature. If there
was something on your mind, Duggey would find it.

'Duggey,' said Dundee, ducking his head to avoid hitting
the sign above the door.

'Oh…you've got to see this,' said Duggey, calling
him in, his eyes on the screen of the dusty old television
on the counter.

You could tell straight away that Duggey was odd.
Even with his back to the door. He was sitting on a chair
that had been bent out of shape, low in the seat with his
arms folded and his heels high up on the counter. He was
funny looking. Like a bird, tall and lanky, with a long
beaky nose and round spectacles which slid forward to
the end of his nose when he was searching for something.

37

His hair was light brown, and slightly straw like, short at the back and sides with a fringe that fell to one side. He had one pair of red cowboy boots which he wore come rain or shine, and a green knitted cardigan with deep pockets, which he liked to put his hands in when he was walking around the aisles. He was saved from being unattractive by his celebrity smile that threw you off guard. It was the sort of smile that looked as if it should come with a wave and it would appear whenever the mood took him, which was often.

Dundee slid into the shop and up to the counter, the television blaring away - an old Tom and Jerry cartoon.

'Look, here he is now,' said Duggey, bolting forward, his nose to the screen, as Tom ran off the edge of the cliff, hovered in the air, then plummeted to the ground.

'Aye that's Jack alright,' said Dundee, laughing. 'It's a good job we had him harnessed up.'

'You should have him on reins.' Duggey swivelled his chair around to face Dundee, his celebrity smile in place. Then he saw the look on Dundee's face.

'You're in love,' said Duggey.

Meanwhile, a few doors down at Doc Spoc's, Jack was having his head seen to.

'There ye are now Jack, as fit as a fiddle,' said Doc Spoc, who talked like a leprechaun and was always in high spirits.

Some said he was too cheery for a doctor but he was

extremely popular with the inhabitants who had a habit of calling round to see him whether they were ill or not. Doc Spoc simply loved a good story, especially a love story. He was obsessed with a woman in blue who he said could have been his wife if he'd ever had the courage to ask her. Everyone in Stress City had heard the story of the woman in blue several times over and as a result no-one ever mentioned their love life to Doc Spoc. Anything could set him off, even comments like 'there's something wrong with my heart' and so Jack surprised himself by spilling the beans as soon as Doc Spoc had finished sewing up his head.

'I think I'm in love.'

'It's probably just concussion,' said Doc Spoc, amusing himself at Jack's expense.

'Not with you. With a girl.'

'A girl you say. Ah well now, they're the best kind to be falling in love with. I remember the first time I saw the woman in blue…'

'But I'm not sure she *is* a girl,' said Jack, interrupting quickly.

'A girl that's not a girl. I see…'

'I think she might be a doll,' said Jack, amazed he had blurted it out.

'A doll ye say. Ah no, ye don't want to be falling in love with a doll. Look what happened to the Tin Soldier. He fell in love with a doll, a ballerina doll,' said the Doc, referring to the fairy tale.

'What happened to him?' asked Jack, suddenly

interested.

'Well now, let me see…' Doc Spoc tried to recall the story.

'As far as I can remember he only had one leg, so that may have put him at a disadvantage.'

'Yep,' said Jack, who was easily bored.

'And he was tin, so he couldn't speak. Perhaps if he had been able to say something things would have been different,' said Doc Spoc, clearly thinking of the woman in blue again.

'Yep,' said Jack, impatiently, still lying flat on the surgery table.

'But he couldn't. And so he was left in the hands of Fate who dealt him a terrible end.'

'Why, what happened to him?' asked Jack, sitting up.

'Well, first of all he was washed away down a drain and went on a great adventure. Then, by some miracle, he managed to return to the ballerina doll and then…' said Doc Spoc, pausing for effect.

'What. What then?'

'They were both thrown into the fire.'

'Great. Thanks,' said Jack, getting up from the table.

'No problem Jack,' said Doc Spoc, seeing him to the door.

Jack stepped out onto the wonky pavement and almost fell over. He leant back against the surgery door to steady himself, his eyes drawn to a notice pinned to the door of the *Hell and High Water* pub across the street. Curious, he let go of the surgery door and made his way cautiously over the cobbles.

The notice said, *Closed, in memory of Brian.* Then it gave the details of Brian's funeral.

Jack shook his head. Brian had managed the *Hell and High Water* pub for ten years, and yet none of his regulars had even bothered to turn up for his funeral. He sighed heavily, took the notice carefully off the door, and slipped it into his pocket. Then he headed back across the street and into Duggey's book shop but there was no sign of Dundee or Duggey, and so he slid out again and made his way back towards the square.

Seconds later Duggey and Dundee appeared out of the back kitchen, carrying three glasses and a bottle of whisky.

'She's not out of your league,' said Duggey kindly, referring to Ann Angel. 'Just out of your reach.' He filled up their glasses. 'She's like all the damsels in distress at Stress City Headquarters.'

'They're not in distress though are they,' challenged Dundee. 'They just work there.'

Duggey had several book shelves dedicated to heroic romance and had a tendency to get carried away.

'Not according to Brian,' insisted Duggey. 'He told me that the Governor's personal assistants never left the building.'

'How would he know? He never left the *Hell and*

High Water.'

'Yeh, at nights. In the mornings though he was cleaning windows.'

'Was he?' Dundee was shocked.

'That was his window cleaning round you were on yesterday. He was up there, on the top floor cleaning windows, the morning he...'

'Jumped,' said Dundee, helping him out.

'Yeh, jumped.' Duggey lifted his glass. 'To Brian.'

'Brian.'

They quickly emptied their tumblers.

'Was there many there, at the funeral?'

'Many there! There was naebody there, just me and Jack, and the 'ghost of things to come.'

'Who?'

'The Rev.'

'Oh,' said Duggey, filling up their glasses again. 'Where's Jack now?'

'I'm not sure. He was pretty shaken up by the funeral.' Dundee suddenly realized that Jack had been missing for several hours.

'You don't think he'd do anything stupid do you?'

'Like what?'

'Like throw himself off the Bridge.'

'Och no,' said Dundee, amused.

'You mean he wouldn't have the bottle.'

'He'd be brave enough to jump if he had a mind to,' said Dundee loyally.

Unaware that his friends were discussing his propensity for suicide Jack had just arrived outside Stress City Headquarters, with Doc's Spoc's words of wisdom ringing in his ears, determined to say something to Echtra about the way he felt.

He settled himself down on the pavement opposite, expecting a long wait, but it wasn't long before Echtra appeared on the carpeted walkway. She had two large sacks of problem letters with her, and to Jack's dismay, Addison Bruce, who was looking extremely dashing, even with the cut on his forehead, in his expensive suit and his cool winkle picker shoes.

Jack flew up off the pavement and before they had time to spot him he had disappeared into the narrow side street and was heading back the way he had come.

Back at the book shop Duggey and Dundee were on their third toast. Dundee was slouched on a stool in front of the counter. Duggey was even lower in his chair, his boots up, next to Dundee's head, his face hidden behind a large book.

'I'm telling you Duggey, it's like every time we turn a corner we hit a brick wall. Literally! I think we're jinxed or cursed or something. Like my cousins the Cormacs…'

Duggey stayed where he was behind the covers of his book. Dundee's cousins were a right bunch of psychopaths, and were one of the reasons why Duggey had left the North. He was relieved when Jack suddenly bounded into the shop, bringing the conversation to an end.

'Listen to this,' Jack announced, placing Brian's funeral notice on the counter and reading it aloud. 'And no-one even bothered to turn up.'

'It's a disgrace,' said Duggey, from behind the covers of the book.

'Aye, it's a disgrace, poor Brian.'

'Yeh, poor Brian,' said Jack, grabbing the third glass, which resulted in a fourth toast.

'Where have you been?' asked Dundee.

'Next door at Doc Spocs,' said Jack, between shots, trying to catch them up.

'What did the Doc say?'

'Stop falling off tall buildings.'

Duggey giggled. 'I was just saying to Dundee, we should have you on reins.'

Jack smiled graciously, then joined Dundee at the counter.

'Have you told Duggey about the Universe?'

'What?' Duggey came out from behind the covers.

'I was just getting there…'

'We think the Universe has got something against us…' said Jack, jumping in.

'I see,' said Duggey, who saw a lot more than they realised.

'What do you think?'

Duggey leant even further back in his chair to give the matter some thought. 'It *could* be the Universe. Then again, it could be the fact that you're always acting like clowns. Maybe the Universe thinks you enjoy bumping into things.'

Whilst Jack and Dundee reflected on his wise words Duggey returned to his book, an old annual he had found whilst tidying out the cupboards, entitled *Problem Solving for Beginners.*

'You could always try reinventing yourselves...' said Duggey, finally.

'What?'

'Change your characters. According to this book reinventing yourself is the latest thing.'

'It says here this book was published in 1973,' challenged Dundee, pointing to the back cover.

'It's making a come-back, insisted Duggey.

'How do we do it?' asked Jack, keen to try anything.

'I don't know. Someone's ripped a page out. I hate it when that happens.' Duggey checked the remaining pages were still intact and then placed the book on the counter. 'You should try asking the new Problem Solver. She's bound to know.'

'What new Problem Solver?'

'She arrived in the City yesterday,' said Jack, surprising everyone with his recently acquired knowledge. 'She's got a café in the woods.'

'Is it yellow?' asked Dundee, surprising everyone by knowing the café was yellow. 'I think I saw it yesterday, on the Wilde Blue Yonder path.'

'You should go there,' suggested Duggey.

45

Jack looked to Dundee.

'Aye, ok. I suppose we could wander over.'

'I might take a trip over there myself, after I've finished the book.' And with his celebrity smile still in place, Duggey topped up their glasses.

Mrs Snarlington-Darlington had given up waiting for Jack several years ago, but as he had left his key in the back door, and she wasn't the sort of person to be leaving keys in doors, she had been forced to wait up for him.

Jack was always wandering off, even as a young child. She often wondered whether he had crawled away from his parents and that was how he had come to be on her doorstep all those years ago. Of course she had alerted the proper authorities who had searched around the Island for days, but when no-one came forward Mrs Snarlington-Darlington had agreed to take Jack in. The inhabitants of Stress City had praised Mrs Snarlington-Darlington for her charitable act, but if truth be known, she was delighted. Mrs Snarlington-Darlington had lived alone, ever since Mr Snarlington-Darlington had mysteriously disappeared on a fishing trip, and she was glad of the company.

She had her curlers in, and was in her bedroom in the middle of putting on her night cream when she heard the front door slam. She dashed down the stairs, fussing over Jack who was in the mood to be fussed over and was quite pleased to see her. She was about to send him off upstairs, intent on racing into the kitchen to find him some supper when the intruder light came on outside. Mrs Snarlington-Darlington cautiously stuck her head out of the door.

At the end of the path a large woman in a green suit was standing outside the front door of number seven. The door opened suddenly and the woman was ushered inside.

'That's odd,' said Mrs Snarlington-Darlington, closing the door when she was sure there was nothing else to see.

'What's odd?' asked Jack, who hadn't been able to see anything at all from behind Mrs Snarlington-Darlington's body.

'A visitor in a green suit outside number seven…at this time of night…and with people in their beds.'

Jack rushed to open the door.

'She's gone inside. I can't imagine who it could be. At this time of night…and with people in their beds,' repeated Mrs Snarlington-Darlington.

'It'll be the new Problem Solver,' said Jack.

What!' said Mrs Snarlington-Darlington, more loudly than she had intended.

'The City's got a new Problem Solver. She arrived yesterday. She's got a café in the woods.' Jack delivered the startling news in a casual manner.

It took a while for Mrs Snarlington-Darlington to recover from the fact that there were things going on in the City that she knew nothing about. She took a couple of deep breaths. Then she gasped. 'A café…in the woods? Where in the woods?'

'It's on the Wilde Blue Yonder path, Dundee saw it this morning,' said Jack, heading up the stairs to bed. 'It's yellow.'

Mrs Snarlington-Darlington took out her curlers, wiped off her night cream, and with her telephone voice in place began the huge task of spreading the word. By the time she got to bed every lady in the City had heard the news.

Emma's was open for business.

Chapter Three

Who's the Fairest?

As far back as they could remember the 'well to do' ladies of Stress City had never stepped foot outside the City gates and yet there they were, traipsing through the forest in their fancy dresses, summer hats and wellington boots. They had agreed to meet at the crossroads at an alarmingly early hour to be sure of a good table, and had made an incredible din on arrival at the signpost, disturbing the bees and the birds who had been enjoying the peace and quiet. When at last they set off along the Wilde Blue Yonder path it was tougher than expected but they pushed on, using their summer brollies to flatten everything in sight until they stumbled into the circular clearing, slightly less fancy than when they had begun but in no way disappointed.

The first thing that struck them about *Emma's* was the colour which was a pretty primrose yellow and met with their approval, as did the curtains with yellow flowers at the windows and the matching bucket outside the front door which they assumed was for their umbrellas. They stood in a huddle at the edge of the clearing undecided and then moved forward, as one, and stood in a huddle outside the front door. There was no hint of activity inside the cafe even though the sign on the door said 'open.' They were just starting to panic when the door flew open and they were ushered in by Mrs D's helpers who all wore black dresses and white pinnys, and sped around so quickly it was difficult to tell them apart. In no time at all the 'well to do's' were settled down at table one with a gigantic pot of tea and some scones, where they stayed for the rest of the day observing the reactions of the incoming and outgoing customers.

Table one was one of the best tables in the house, on the right hand side as you entered the café close to the wall. There were only two other tables either side of it. Table two which had a clear view of the till and cake display case, but was too small to seat six, and table three which had the corner window and a triangular notice in the middle of it that the ladies assumed said reserved. On the opposite wall the tables ran two by two from the door to the till. The adjoining room was slightly larger with two tables of six and four tables of four. There was one large window, with a ledge wide enough to hold baskets of magazines and on the opposite wall there was a book case which hid a tiny corridor that led through to the ladies toilets, the back larder and the kitchen. The kitchen was so small there was only room for two people at a time and so, regardless of what was going on in the kitchen at *Emma's*, there was always a helper in sight.

Mrs Snarlington-Darlington arrived much later than

planned, a little shaken when she realized the café was already full, and the 'well to do's' had taken the best table. But she quickly recovered, informing her Thursday ladies who were following dutifully behind her, and the 'well to do's,' who put their conversation on hold when they saw her, that she and the new Problem Solver, Mrs D were soon to be neighbours.

'How exciting,' said one of the Thursday's, as they were shown into the adjoining room. 'What's she like?'

'She's big,' said the woman behind her, as they were seated at a table for six by the window. 'That's what I heard.'

'It's true, she is big,' said Mrs Snarlington-Darlington, self-consciously, who was very large herself. 'But she's smart. She was wearing a forest green suit when I saw her…'

The Thursdays nodded, approving the colour. One of Mrs D's helpers rushed in and took their order, then rushed away again.

The Thursdays waited patiently whilst Mrs Snarlington-Darlington adjusted the position of the table in her favour before imparting the news about Mrs D, who was fast becoming notorious.

'…She was on the front path,' continued Mrs Snarlington-Darlington. 'Right outside the front door of number seven…'

'Isn't that where you said the fairy queen lives?' interrupted the woman to her left.

'Don't be ridiculous. I never said any such thing. I

just said she was incredibly small, and had a strange taste in ornaments,' said Mrs Snarlington-Darlington, pleased to see that the surrounding tables had stopped their conversations and were listening to hers.

'But I can tell you this, in confidence.'

The ladies at the other tables leant in, hoping it would be something of interest.

'There have been some strange comings and goings at that house over the years, visitors at the door, at all times of the day and night. People appearing and disappearing…' said Mrs Snarlington-Darlington taking a break to finish off her scone.

'…and now she's gone and disappeared herself.'

'Who has?' said the lady on her right who was hard of hearing.

'The woman at number seven!! She's disappeared!!' yelled Mrs Snarlington-Darlington, loud enough for everyone in the café to hear. There were gasps from the other tables and lots of 'what's the world coming to's.'

'Then, last night the new Problem Solver appears, right outside the front door of number seven. In the middle of the night, and with people in their beds!'

There were more gasps from the tables and Mrs D's helpers took the opportunity to rush in and refill all the tea pots.

'But why would the City's new Problem Solver be staying with the woman at number seven?' asked one of the ladies at the other tables, addressing Mrs Snarlington-Darlington who was clearly in charge.

'They must be friends,' said the hard of hearing woman who was smarter than she looked.

'Exactly,' said Mrs Snarlington-Darlington, wondering why she hadn't thought of it.

'Perhaps she came to see the girl,' said a posh woman by the book case.

'What girl?' asked the lady next to her.

'The tall girl with the short dark hair - the woman at number seven is her guardian.'

Then everyone started talking at once.

'I didn't know there *was* a girl at number seven.'

'What's her name?'

'Echtra.'

'Strange name for a girl.'

'Strange altogether if you ask me,' said Mrs Snarlington-Darlington taking back control of the conversation.

'She spends most of her time at the other end of that Bridge. I keep telling her it's full of holes. It should have been demolished years ago.' The Thursdays' nodded, as did the ladies at the other tables.

'Of course she has Jack bewitched. I've told him to keep away from her but like most of my advice it falls on deaf ears.'

Everyone shook their heads but kept their thoughts to themselves. Mrs Snarlington-Darlington wouldn't have a word said against Jack unless she was the one saying it.

There was a pause in the conversation whilst the

ladies devoured their cakes. Mrs Snarlington-Darlington tuned in to the conversations of the ladies in the main room which were buzzing with rumours about *Emma's* formidable problem solving owner who had yet to make an appearance.

'My husband says she's from the North.'

'My husband says from the South.'

'My husband says she's from the Otherworld on the other side of the Bridge.'

'Don't be silly.'

'There's no such thing as the Otherworld.'

'She's too big for a fairy.'

Suddenly *Emma's* began to shake. The tables shuddered and the teapots shook. The cutlery rattled and the rolling pins rolled. The clock almost stopped, but then thought better of it.

She had arrived.

'It must be a Tuesday,' said Mrs D stepping over the threshold, fully intent on making as grand an entrance as possible.

'Always follow your destiny on a Tuesday. Most people choose Fridays but that's always a mistake.'

It was Thursday, but Mrs D had never quite gotten the hang of the days. With all eyes upon her she waltzed over to the large oval mirror which was hanging on the left hand wall, took off her hat and adjusted her hair, which was a wavy bob in Venus red. Then she took off her coat, revealing a voluptuous body wrapped inside a blue and white striped pinny which was straining at the hips and arms. She checked her orangey red lipstick was still in place, her nose and cheeks were suitably powdered, and her turquoise blue eye-shadow, which was the same colour as her eyes, was still intact. The customers looked on open mouthed. Then, seemingly oblivious to the fact she had attracted an audience, she dispensed with her hat and coat on the hooks attached to the adjoining wall, and disappeared along the corridor and into the kitchen. The ladies held their breath until they were sure she had gone and then returned to their conversations with renewed vigour.

Mrs D was the topic of conversation almost everywhere in Stress City that morning. At Stress City Headquarters Sharon, who had spent a frustrating afternoon the previous day with everyone worth talking to in meetings, had arrived at the office early. By ten o'clock news about the Problem Solver had hit every department from the basement to the fourth floor, and was just about to be shared with the fifth, courtesy of Sharon who was on her way up to the Executive meeting room with a message for Ann Angel.

Sharon entered the lift on the fourth floor where the corridors were narrow, the carpets were threadbare, the temperature was unbearable and everything was in need of a lick of paint. Moments later she was in open plan territory where everything was brand new, including the carpets and the air conditioning. Ordinarily a personal assistant from a lower floor would never have been allowed access to the Executive level, but Sharon, who had been on secondment ever since she had joined the company in 1997, had worked for almost everyone in the building, and she had a key.

Sharon turned right out of the lift and headed in the direction of Governor's domain, where Addison Bruce's personal assistants, eleven of the City's most beautiful damsels, were sitting behind their desks lined up along the wall like a chain of flowers en-route to his office. They gasped in delight when they saw her but as Sharon came towards them the door to Addison's office opened, an inch. He had been disturbed. Without missing a beat Sharon continued on through the double doors, and into the Executive lounge which had a refreshment area, and two meeting rooms either side. She made herself a decent cup of coffee and then placed her ear to the door of the meeting room on the right.

Inside the room, at a table that could easily have held up to thirty people, twelve members of the Senior Team were discussing the incident that had occurred the previous day in the fourth floor board room. The meeting was being chaired by Ann Angel who had been called in to referee. This time the air conditioning was on but the Senior Team were hot under the collar for a different reason. No one wanted to be held responsible for the previous day's fiasco and so they were passing the blame around the table like an unwanted parcel.

'The golden rule is...' said Bill, who had been

promoted to the Senior Team in 1982.

'Never mind the golden rule,' said Bob, who considered himself more senior.

'The golden rule is,' said Bill, determined to be heard. 'That the person nearest the exit should raise the alarm.'

'In the event of a fire,' said Bob, who had been the one nearest the exit.

'In the event of an emergency.' said Bill, raising his eyebrows to make the point.

'Now correct me if I'm wrong,' continued Bill, casting his eyes around the table by way of a challenge. 'But someone falling out of a window cleaning box four storeys up constitutes an emergency.'

'And correct me if *I'm* wrong,' said Bob. 'But the last time someone fainted in the board room it was the responsibility of health and safety.'

'But she didn't faint,' said Jim, who had recently been appointed Health and Safety officer.

'Well she wasn't on fire either!' said Bob, losing his temper.

And they were off again, passing the blame around the table.

A few hundred yards away in the fifth floor board room at City Hall another meeting was taking place.

The board room at City Hall was one of the finest in the City. It had a marble fireplace at the head of it, an antique table in the middle, a row of expensive cabinets on the left, and two large windows on the right, which had a perfect view of the square. The room was out of bounds to everyone, except for the Governor Addison Bruce, the tea lady, and the six City Hall Officials. It was an exclusive group. Positions at City Hall were hereditary, based on blood line rather than ability. They were positions that demanded the commitment of a lifetime, and had demanded the lifetimes of every one of their ancestors, including the original invaders of the Island, the ancient Chiefs. There were paintings of them on the wall to prove it, although there was very little resemblance between the ancestors and the men in charge around the table. The ancient Chiefs were like giants in comparison, and appeared to be looking on in anger at the current generation who they had risked their lives to spawn, and as far as they were concerned were making a complete hash of things.

Meetings at City Hall were held daily and the agenda was split into two parts.

First there were the major problems they could do nothing about. The wall, which the inhabitants complained was too high and blocked out the light on sunny afternoons. The old square, where the pavements were far too dangerous and the buildings moved with the wind. The new square, where there was never any room. The lack of leisure centres, shops and cinemas. The park to the left of the gates which City officials were accused of being obsessively neat about, and the avenue, which was home to the old wishing well, which City Hall had recently replaced with a painted scene. Some said they had gone too far. You can only paint over the cracks for so long. The forest was coming in over the wall again. The City gates were rotten. The visitor's sign wasn't welcoming enough, and the Bridge was on the verge of collapse.

Then there were the minor problems they could do nothing about. The weather, the birds, the bees, the height of other people's hedges, the days of the week, almost everything in Stress City was a problem.

And the problem under discussion at the moment was in the major category.

'I must say I hadn't expected the problem solving to be taking place outside the City wall,' said the man with his back to the window who sat on his chair as straight as a broom, as if he had been glued to the back of it.

They all did. The men in charge at City Hall knew how to conduct themselves in meetings. There was no slouching around, drifting off, yawning, doodling, or nipping home early. The men were hardly ever seen during the day. They wore grey in summer and dark grey in winter. They were a similar height and weight; paunchy, prematurely grey and balding. They all wore spectacles and spent lots of time nodding their heads which was what they were doing when the tea lady entered the room.

No one saw her come in. She was too small to be seen in the mirror above the mantelpiece, and was bent forward at an alarming angle, with a tight grip on the handle of her tea trolley, as if she might tumble forward onto the carpet without it. She took an age rolling the trolley past the extremely long antique table and even longer setting the cups and saucers out on the cabinet beside the mantelpiece. The men around the table didn't bother to look up, and would have been hard pushed to recognise her in a line up, which was a pity because the tea lady was a Witch - and a particularly nasty one - a shape shifter, known as the 'Black Witch of Bad Luck.'

'It's not *where* she's solving the problems that concerns me, it's the Problem Solver herself,' said the man who had his back to the Witch. 'Do we even know where this Problem Solver comes from?'

Everyone shook their heads, a lot. It was a good point.

'What's her name again?' said the man nearest the door. There was a shuffling of papers by the man nearest the mantelpiece.

'Mrs D,' said the man.

There was a loud clatter of cups and saucers causing the men to look up from their agenda.

'Funny name for a woman,' said the man with all the papers, returning them to the business in hand.

'Funny sort of business altogether if you ask me,' said the man with his back to the window, whose wife had been one of the first at *Emma's* cafe that morning. 'This woman appears out of the blue, and the following day half the female population is outside the City boundaries discussing our private affairs.'

'What do you mean outside the boundaries?' asked the man next to him.

'The area to the right of the crossroads is outside our jurisdiction,' replied the man at the window.

'Isn't that a security risk?' said the man by the mantelpiece frantically shuffling through his papers.

The nods were going ten to the dozen now and the Witch had stopped pretending to make the tea and was blatantly listening in.

'Perhaps we should try and persuade the Problem Solver to come into the City. Isn't there a Problem Solving department?' said the man closest to the tea trolley.

'No!' said the man in front of the mantelpiece, startling everyone with his tone of voice. Then he stood up, which was unheard of in the middle of a meeting.

'We'll get rid of her,' he declared, unaware that the Witch had forced the thought into his head.

The five remaining officials stared at him open mouthed, then almost jumped out of their skin as the tea lady left the room, slamming the door behind her.

Back in the Executive meeting room at Stress City Headquarters there was an urgent tap on the door.

'Message for Ann Angel,' said Sharon, smiling apologetically as she opened the door, holding up a telephone note as proof.

Before anyone could object, Ann was up and out of the room.

'News from *Emma's*,' said Sharon in a low whisper as she and Ann walked along the thick pile carpet, past the Executive secretaries whose ears perked up when they saw who it was. Sharon kept her silence as they passed by their desks, stopping when she reached the coffee machine.

Ann continued on into the Executive ladies cloakroom which was more like a boudoir than a toilet. It had a shower, a double wardrobe, perfume, make up and a huge dressing table mirror with pretty chairs that were hardly ever used because the ladies who worked on the top floor were always too busy to sit on them.

Ann collapsed onto one of the chairs, exhausted before the day had even begun. The pass the parcel meeting with the Senior Team had sent her head into a spin, and now her precious schedule was out of sync. Something would have to be carried forward – again!

Ann stared at herself in the mirror, unhappy with what she saw. Her face was paler than ever, her skin dehydrated from the amount of coffee she was drinking in order to stay awake, and her hair, which had been swept up into a high bun that morning, was keeling over to one side. She pulled out the clips and let her hair fall, intent on re-doing it. Then she took off her glasses to wipe them, her image now a hazy wave in the glass, as if she was fading away.

When Sharon appeared with the coffees she was taken aback. She had never seen Ann at ease before. She looked stunningly beautiful with her glasses off and her long dark hair sweeping down over her shoulders. Ann had the darkest blue eyes Sharon had ever seen.

She placed the coffees on the dressing table and, quickly avoiding a comparison between herself and Ann in the mirror, Sharon plonked herself down sideways on the chair next to her.

Ann took the coffee gratefully, perking up when she saw the look of excitement on Sharon's face.

'Well…' began Sharon, pausing for dramatic effect.

'It's definitely in the woods…and it's yellow.'

'Yellow!' cried Ann.

'Primrose yellow with matching flowery curtains at the windows,' declared Sharon, who had just received the news from her Aunty May who had been one of the first at *Emma's* café that morning.

'There's a sign above the door. It says '*Emma's*.' It has a roof and a chimney, and it's stuck between two giant trees…' Sharon took a breath, 'as if it had fallen out of the clear blue sky,' according to my Aunty May.'

'Really!' cried Ann, in delight.

'Really,' confirmed Sharon, pleased with Ann's reaction. 'It's yellow inside as well as out. It has a cake display case, and two rooms, with lots of tables, all the tables have numbers and…'

'What about Mrs D. Was she there?' interrupted Ann.

'She *wa*s there,' said Sharon, who had been saving the best bit till last. 'But she wasn't solving any problems. Apparently all the problems are kept outside in a large yellow bucket. Mrs D says we're giving them far too much attention.'

Ann began to laugh, out loud. Sharon didn't know what to do. She had never seen anyone laughing at Stress City Headquarters before. She waited until Ann had managed to compose herself before continuing.

'The problem is - we've had another two sack loads of problem letters this morning.'

Ann began to laugh out loud again. 'More problems…they won't all fit in the bucket.'

'What should we do?!' cried Sharon, in an effort to get Ann to take things seriously.

'Why don't you take the sacks over to *Emma's* now, give Echtra a hand going through them. I'll see you in the morning,' said Ann, in an unexpectedly generous gesture.

'Thanks!' said Sharon, who didn't need to be told twice and without bothering to look back at her reflection she was out of the building in a flash.

Sharon had never been one for looking in mirrors. Her mother always told her she was 'fine as she was,' which wasn't much of a compliment for a girl in her early thirties. It was her hair that was the problem. It was blonde but dull, short thick and square looking, as if it had been cut with a knife and fork, giving her a sort of tom boy appearance. But it didn't bother her. Sharon came from a huge family with a wide network of female relatives who already had their fingers on a number of bachelor candidates. When the time came Sharon would be packaged off like the rest of her cousins into marital bliss with a man who needed knocking into shape by someone practical who enjoyed being in the kitchen chasing after children.

Sharon had never been through the City in the middle of the morning before and it was quite eerie without all the people and the noise. When she was half way across the square she sensed someone watching her from the spooky windows above City Hall. There were attic rooms at the top of the building that ran beneath the rafters. The only rooms in the City high enough to breech the top of the City wall, but they were never used. Sharon reminded herself that the rooms were closed off, even to City Hall officials, something to do with the floor boards. Still, she quickened her step, and by the time she got to the gateway her thoughts had turned to more practical matters, like the fact that the bus had gone and she would have to drag the problem sacks all the way through the forest to *Emma's*.

The Witch drew away from the window.

The attic rooms above City Hall were pitch-black and the Black Witch inhabited them all. She liked to spread herself out. The room she was currently in was the largest one of all and was full of wardrobes and cabinets overflowing with clothes.

She headed towards her dressing table in the far corner which had all sorts of strange looking potions on it and sat in front of the large oval mirror. The Witch stared into the glass. The face reflected there was not her own. It was pretty. Then it changed, better cheekbones, quite stunning, but it failed to please. The Black Witch had hundreds of faces but never revealed her own. The sight of her real self would surely have killed her, for her soul was black as soot.

Her thoughts turned to her obsession, Addison Bruce. He had kept his distance of late. Now, at last she had an excuse to see him. News of Mrs D's arrival would surely bring out the worst in him. The side she liked the most. The face in the glass changed to reflect her thoughts. It was Addison's face. Sometimes Addison could be difficult to shed. There were nights when she would leave him on, take one of his lovers, and hide herself until the last moment, but then the heat would drive her talons out. It was a messy business.

Sharon tried her best to walk in the shade but it was hot work dragging the mail along the visitor's road. When she got to the crossroads she dumped the sacks at the signpost and headed for the bank, intent on picking up a cool drink from one of the cottages - preferably not number three which she knew would have her mother in it.

Sharon knew her way around all the kitchens on the bank. Number one belonged to Duggey who had lots of drink in the fridge but never any food and was always round at number two borrowing something from Mrs Snarlington-Darlington who had two back larders.

Sharon lived at number three with her parents and an assortment of visiting relatives where it was impossible to get any peace. At number four the cupboards were always bare. Eric worked in Finance and was hardly ever at home. Number five belonged to Miss Blunt, a retired school teacher who was forever at the back door sweeping something out. Number six was full of children and their mother, who was a terrible gossip, and was always in the back garden hanging something out to dry.

Number seven was the sort of thing you might expect from a fairy queen - full of enchantment and disarray. The door was always open - animals and birds wandered in and out from the forest as if they owned the place, amongst the rare and priceless things. Divine paintings lined the walls. Framed photographs of unfamiliar places filled the mantelpiece, cabinets and window ledges. There were strange looking ornaments everywhere. Some were quite scary. There were centaurs in the hall. Others looked harmless enough, misshapen pots in the shape of a kettle or an old shoe that moved around the house a lot, suddenly appearing out of nowhere, which some people found a bit sinister. The Deities were kept in the attic but that wasn't much comfort if you woke up in the middle of the night to find an old pottery boot under your pillow.

There was hardly any room in the sitting room because of the two huge sofas which sat next to the fireplace, taking up all the space. There was a real fire that was never out and lamps that were always in. The curtains were colourful and almost matched the rugs but you didn't notice the decor because of the pictures of the Gods. Seven huge paintings which covered the walls, and were so incredibly lifelike it was as if the battle between darkness and light was continuing to go on around you as you were sipping your tea by the hearth.

Echtra was unaware that Sharon had arrived on the bank. She was in her bedroom, sitting at her dressing table beneath the side window which overlooked the Bridge. The sun streamed in through the glass as she stared at her reflection in the mirror. Her hair was so dark it was almost black, and had kinks which stuck up whenever it was misty or damp. She was dressed plainly in a white vest and black slacks with nothing around her neck or ears. No need for adornments when you have a warrior's heart, which her guardian used to say was a mandatory requirement for heroines, and came in quite handy when you were facing a den of lions or the Senior Team at Stress City Headquarters.

She was well hidden, there was no doubt about it - although if you had an eye for such things you could see she was not of this world. And now it was time to leave. The thought scared her. She knew all about Deliverance and it was not for the faint hearted.

It was 4 o'clock when Mrs D rang the bell on the counter to indicate it was time to leave. The ladies of Stress City, who were used to conducting themselves in the proper manner, paid their bills and left the premises in an orderly fashion.

It was late afternoon when Addison Bruce crept quietly in through the door. Mrs D was busy in the kitchen, her helpers long gone. Addison had been hoping to catch Mrs D off guard but his vanity got the better of him. Unable to resist the oval mirror on the wall he stopped to preen himself.

Addison was unattractive, small and thin with blond hair and blue eyes, a sharp nose, and a small mouth. But he had the pull of the devil. He was still admiring himself in the mirror when his face began to change, revealing his darker side. It was a side he hadn't come face to face with before and it scared the hell out of him. But he was unable to look away. Then he saw a bright light behind him, turned around to face it, and there was Mrs D.

'I think you'll find I'm the fairest,' said Mrs D, with a smile.

Addison turned on her and scowled, his other side still on show. She flinched, a touch. He saw her reaction and stepped forward, which was a mistake.

Whack! The giant rolling pin winded him like nothing else he had ever experienced before. As Addison struggled to catch his breath, crumpled up on the floor between the tables for two, Mrs D began mopping the floor around him as if nothing had happened.

'We're moving back in,' said Mrs D, getting straight to the point.

'Wh…Wh…What,' said Addison, finally managing to get a breath.

'We're taking it back. The Island, the City. It's all there. In the Prophecy,' said Mrs D, waving a large envelope in his face.

'What Prophecy?' said Addison, attempting to grab the envelope but Mrs D snatched it back.

'The Prophecy of the God of the Seas. It predicts the return of the Gods. And so we'll need the Key to the City back.'

'The Key's gone,' said Addison, knowing he should have kept that information to himself but hoping it would take the wind out of her sails. He was right.

'What do you mean gone,' asked Mrs D, genuinely shocked.

'Your fairy friend from number seven has stolen it. But don't worry, she won't get far. Aife is arriving at dawn with her Northern army. She'll be delighted to see you,' said Addison, with a vicious grin.

This was bad. The impending arrival of Aife, the dreaded Queen of the Amazons, and her vast army was the worst kind of news. But Mrs D recovered well. She grabbed hold of a stiff broom and began pushing Addison towards the door like an unwanted parcel.

'There's no point trying to escape. No-one gets off this Island alive!' screamed Addison.

'Well. Thanks for the information,' said Mrs D, giving Addison a final push out of the door. 'Do come again.'

Addison picked himself up and dusted the flour off his expensive City suit. He wasn't feeling himself. The brief showdown with Mrs D had left him drained. He staggered out of the clearing and along the overgrown path towards the crossroads. His shadow stretched out ahead of him. It was eerie. He stopped dead in his tracks and his shadow drew back, but it took a while. He shivered in the heat, taking long deep breaths to steady himself. Then he saw her. The girl from the office he had met on the steps - the one with all the problem letters. He couldn't remember her name but he recalled his thoughts when he saw her. And now here she was again, alone in the forest.

'Lucky me,' the thought came unbidden, evil aroused, his dark side refusing to go back in the box. Addison's body broke out in a sweat. There was saliva on his lips. He grabbed a hanky from his pocket, still stained from the blood of yesterday and pressed it to his mouth for fear of what might come out.

She came towards him. He nodded and she continued on. She had her back to him. The urge to grab her by the throat with his free hand was overwhelming. He clenched his fist to his groin, and dragged himself off into the bushes like a grotesque creature in pain. Had he known who the girl really was he would have had her enslaved.

Echtra called out as she entered *Emma's* but there was no sign of Mrs D and so she made herself a pot of tea and settled down at the corner window on table three.

Table three had a mind of its own and did not take kindly to the company of the dull. It had been known, on occasion, to take a hand in the destinies of some of its customers usually resulting in their untimely demise. And so Mrs D had put a warning notice on the table stating that *Emma's* could not be held responsible for any valuables, including husbands, wives or elderly relatives left at the table. Most people assumed the table was reserved and so table three was almost always free.

Echtra was about to make a start on some of the problem letters when to her delight Sharon appeared in the clearing. She rushed to the door in surprise.

'What are you doing here?'
Sharon staggered towards her, too out of breath to speak, dragging the two huge sacks of mail behind her.

Echtra rushed forward to help and together they dragged the sacks up to the front door and dumped them next to the bucket.

'More problems,' said Sharon, by way of an explanation for her appearance. Then she spotted the cake display case through the open door and headed straight for it.

'So this is *Emma's*,' said Sharon, gazing around the room whilst filling a plate full of fairy cakes.

'Yes. This is *Emma's*,' said Echtra, delighted to see her friend who always had lots to say.

Sharon joined Echtra at the table and polished off a couple of cakes. Then she began talking ten to the dozen.

'Ann's losing her marbles. She laughed today, out loud. Thankfully no-one heard her. I think it's because of all the problems. They're pushing her over the edge. You wouldn't believe how many letters we've had this morning. Everyone's writing in. There's a rumour going around that some people are making problems up, just to see what Mrs D's response will be.'

'I'm sure the letters are genuine,' said Echtra. 'Some people find it easier to reveal their secrets to a stranger.'

'That's true...' said Sharon, wondering whether there was anything of interest inside the envelopes. 'We should make a start.' And in no time at all Sharon had grabbed a handful of envelopes and was opening her first problem.

'Great,' said Sharon, looking pleased. 'I've had this one.'

Twenty minutes later Mrs D appeared, looking rather dishevelled, her pinny covered in black marks having just cleared out the back larder.

'We must get a message to the heroes of Stress City,' she announced, addressing Sharon who looked alarmed.

'Heroes...but there are no heroes in Stress City.'

'Ah yes...of course,' said Mrs D, scolding herself for being so forgetful and without bothering to say goodbye she dashed away again, towards the back larder.

'We leave at dawn,' called Mrs D, her voice echoing as she made her way back along the corridor.

'Leave?' said Sharon, dismayed.

'For the Otherworld,' said Echtra, rising from the

table to retrieve her things from the coat hooks.

Echtra had once confessed to Sharon that she and her guardian were from the Otherworld, which was rumoured to lie on the other side of the Bridge. Sharon, who was unable to keep anything to herself for longer than five minutes, had tried to pass the gossip on, but no-one had believed her. The people of Stress City found the idea of the Otherworld difficult to grasp. Sharon herself came from a long line of non-believers. Sharon's mother said it was pure nonsense. Sharon's father refused to believe in anything he couldn't see, like God, and so there was no way he would have entertained the idea of Gods, in the plural. Sharon always imagined that at the end of his days there would be a struggle as he was dragged over the threshold of reality to a world that he was convinced did not exist.

But as the girls emerged from the woods onto the bank Sharon began to have doubts. Maybe it was true. Maybe Echtra was right. Maybe her father was wrong. And so when they got to the back door of number three Sharon threw her arms around her friend, and in an emotionally dramatic manner fit for the occasion, wished her good luck in the Otherworld. Then, in order to bring herself back down to earth she began taking in the freshly laundered sheets from the line, relieved that she was destined to be a housewife instead of a heroine.

Back inside *Emma's* larder Mrs D found what she was

looking for at the bottom of an old suitcase. It was a notice covered in dust. She brushed it off with the tail of her pinny until the words could be clearly seen, and then she took it and placed it in the window.

The notice read, 'Heroes, apply within.'

Chapter Four

'Heroes, apply within'

'I told you it was yellow,' said Dundee as they stumbled into *Emma's* clearing.

Jack could hardly believe his eyes. He rushed forward with childlike enthusiasm and peered through the cafe window.

'I can't see anyone,' he said, moving sideways to check the windows in the adjoining room. 'Maybe it's closed.'

'It says open on the door.' Dundee was now on the front step. 'Look, there's a note here on the window.'

'What does it say?' Jack bounded onto the step and flung his arm around Dundee's shoulder.

'It says Heroes, apply within.'

'That's us,' said Jack boldly. 'Try the door.'

'You try the door,' said Dundee, nervous after his previous experience outside *Emma's*.

Jack turned the handle and was in the adjoining room before Dundee had made it over the threshold.

'Hello,' said Dundee politely. 'Anybody in?'

'There's a corridor here!' cried Jack.

Dundee joined Jack at the beginning of the tiny corridor and they made their way cautiously along it, Dundee at the back having forced Jack to take the lead. The corridor bent to the left and then straightened out. There were two brightly painted toilet doors on the right and a back larder at the far end which was open, and had Mrs D in it. She was so intent on her task of clearing out the clutter in the larder she didn't hear them on the approach, and so Dundee took the precaution of clearing his throat before addressing her behind.

'Excuse me,' he said, taking his right hand out of his jacket pocket to push the hair out of his eyes.

'Yes,' replied Mrs D, without bothering to turn around.

'We've come about the advert,' said Jack, ignoring the dig in his side from Dundee.

'Advert?' said Mrs D, placing her hands on her knees, and hauling herself up to standing position before turning around.

It was quite a shock. There was a startling resemblance between Mrs D and Jack's guardian, Mrs Snarlington-Darlington, although Mrs D wore more make-up and seemed larger, and even more formidable.

'The advert in the window,' said Jack, pulling back, nervously. 'Heroes, apply within.'

'That's not an advert,' said Mrs D, coming out of the back larder and closing the door. 'It's a statement of fact.'

They drew back against the walls to allow for the swing of her hips as she passed between them, and followed her into the main room of the café where she drew out a chair from table three, and indicated they join her. Dundee worked his way around the table until he was as far away as possible from her and sat down. Jack did the same, glued to his side.

'Now then,' said Mrs D taking a large book out of her giant handbag and putting on her spectacles. 'Names?'

Jack and Dundee looked at each another in bewilderment before giving Mrs D their names.

'Qualifications?' asked Mrs D, after making a note of their names.

'Qualifications?' echoed Jack.

'Yes, heroic traits…courage for example. Do you have any?'

'Erm…' said Jack, suddenly realising they were being interviewed for the heroes' jobs. He looked to Dundee for help.

Mrs D wrote something down under Jack's name but he couldn't see what it was.

'No,' said Dundee, truthfully.

'Experience?' said Mrs D, moving on.

'Erm, to be honest we're not actually heroes at the moment,' said Dundee, owning up.

'But we'd like to be,' said Jack, hopefully.

'I see,' said Mrs D, giving Jack a quizzical look.

He drew back in his chair.

'Although that might be a bit of a leap from where we are now,' said Dundee, stepping in.

'And where is that exactly?' asked Mrs D, encouraging them with the sort of smile that made them want to tell her everything.

'Rock bottom,' said Jack, blurting it out.

'Aye, rock bottom,' admitted Dundee.

Mrs D smiled, sympathetically.

'It's not as if we haven't tried,' said Dundee, keen to ensure that Mrs D didn't think they were wasters.

'No-one tries harder than us,' added Jack.

'But no matter what we do, trouble finds us. Bad luck follows us around…'

'I nearly died yesterday,' said Jack, boastfully.

'This may sound a bit daft,' said Dundee, lowering his voice and leaning in, 'but we're beginning to think…'

'The Universe has got something against you.'

'How did you know!' said Jack, amazed.

'It says so here, in the book.' said Mrs D, pulling the book away as Jack tried to read the page upside down.

'But…why?' asked Dundee, looking seriously worried.

'Why?' said Mrs D, surprised by the question. 'Because of all the karmic debt you've managed to accumulate in the past.'

'Karmic debt?' cried Dundee.

'What past…we've hardly had a past!' cried Jack.

'Past lives,' said Mrs D, closing the book with some finality, as if that was that.

'Where I come from it's known as avoiding the call.'

'Where do you come from?'

'The Otherworld.'

They stared at her open mouthed again and she disappeared off into the kitchen to give the news time to sink in, returning moments later with a gigantic pot of tea, three tea cups, and a Victoria sponge.

'But what can we do,' said Dundee, unable to take his eyes away from the book on the table, his worst fears confirmed, in writing.

'Do?' said Mrs D, lowering her behind back onto the seat.

'To get rid of it. The karmic debt,' he prompted.

'Erm…' said Mrs D, tapping her fingers on the table, as though giving the matter some thought. 'It would have to be something hugely heroic.'

'Like what?' asked Jack.

'Like saving a life?' asked Dundee.

'Like saving a City,' replied Mrs D. 'Stress City.'

'Stress City!'

'Why, what's wrong with it?'

'Stress City is a jail.'

'A jail!!' they wailed.

'Simmer down,' said Mrs D, who enjoyed using vocabulary that was equally appropriate for people as well as pans.

'Stress City wasn't always a jail. It was once a treasured possession of the Gods. They built the City, a mirror image of the City of Falias, the first City of the Otherworld, and it was wound by a Key. The Gods used to spend their holidays here. Unfortunately the City was

80

stolen long ago by Aife, the Queen of the Amazons. She uses it to store her captives. Now the Key to the City is missing, along with my very good friend the Fairy Queen of dreams. The problem is without this Key the City will stop...'

'Stop?'

'Yes. You see the Key controls the City. Without it everything and everyone in Stress City will wind down, and eventually stop,' said Mrs D, pouring out the tea.

'What do you mean eventually?' asked Jack.

'How much time do we have?' asked Dundee, anxiously.

'Time,' said Mrs D. 'I've no idea. We don't have time where I come from.'

'Milk, sugar?' They nodded, stunned by the news.

'And so this Key must be found and Stress City returned to its rightful owners,' continued Mrs D dishing out the Victoria sponge.

'Of course it will mean taking a trip across the Bridge into the Otherworld...'

'The Otherworld!' cried Jack and Dundee, hardly able to believe their luck. 'We can do that!'

'...and there will be Shadowy forces trying to stop us.'

'Of course,' said Dundee, as if he was fully conversant with the nature of heroic quests.

'...and the characters you are playing now will have to go,' she continued.

'Of course,' said Jack enthusiastically, without

81

thinking.

'What do you mean go?' asked Dundee, cautiously.

'Die,' replied Mrs D, in a manner that suggested it was no great hardship.

'Die!'

'Will it hurt?'

'You needn't worry. A complete change in character is not the sort of thing that happens overnight, it can take several lifetimes to achieve. But we shall try and hurry things up.'

Mrs D rose from the table and retrieved her hat and coat from the hooks. Then she swept towards the oval mirror where she adjusted her hat and reapplied her lipstick.

'The trick is that before we let ourselves go, we must awaken the hero within,' she concluded, turning to face them.

Jack and Dundee were still sitting at the table, acting like idiots.

'Come along then,' she urged, half way out of the door before they realised they were supposed to be going with her.

They hurried after her like chicks to a mother hen, out of the front door, down the step, and onto the little path in the clearing. There was never any choice in the matter. Mrs D had come from a faraway place. They could sense it. She had found them in their hiding place, and dragged them out of their playpen, like an insistent grown up.

'Are we going to the Otherworld now?' asked Jack, wondering if he had time to nip home and pack.

'No. We're off to the cottage of the Fairy Queen of dreams, to rescue her abandoned charge, and before you ask she lives at…'

'Number seven, 'the bank.''

Mrs D twirled around to face him. She looked surprised, which didn't happen very often.

'You mean the girl at number seven don't you?' asked Jack.

'No ordinary girl,' said Mrs D, lowering her voice and looking around, as if the bushes were filled with spies.

'This may sound a little odd,' she continued, as if everything she had said so far had been the norm.

'But I can tell you this, in confidence.'

'That girl is a doll, with a very important destiny. She cannot be allowed to fall into the wrong hands.'

Then Mrs D disappeared out of the clearing leaving Jack and Dundee standing there stunned.

'Whatever you do, don't tell anyone!' she called back, from the bushes.

They followed her along the previously overgrown path, which had since been trampled and widened out by *Emma's* customers, stopping when she did at the crossroads to speak to a young journalist girl, who had been sent to the cafe to interview the new Problem Solver.

'I'm afraid the interview will have to wait. We're off

on a trip,' explained Mrs D, introducing Jack and Dundee as the heroes, who were delighted, taking care to shake the journalist's hand in a heroic fashion.

'Where are you going?' asked the journalist, swiftly grabbing her notepad from her handbag and scribbling down their names.

Mrs D stalled for a moment, reluctant to reveal their true destination, then her eye was drawn to the signpost.

'The Wilde Blue Yonder,' she declared, and they were off again, leaving the journalist scribbling away at the crossroads.

They chose the proper trail to get to the bank. Jack was at the front, keen to be the first through the door of number seven. But as he entered the familiar kitchen his heart drew back. He had always known deep down that he and Echtra were worlds apart. Now he knew just how far apart they really were he felt the urge to back away. But when he entered the sitting room and saw her by the fire, cheeks flushed, clearly relieved to see him, he forgot all about backing off and came forward. It was then he noticed the state of the sitting room.

'What happened?'

The room looked as if a tornado had flown through it. There was glass everywhere, ornaments smashed, books torn apart, lamps overturned, even the paintings of the Gods were lopsided.

'It was like this when I got here,' said Echtra. 'It must have been Addison Bruce.'

'Addison Bruce!' cried Jack, jealousy surging up

inside him. 'What's he doing here?'

'He's the Villain…' said Mrs D, by way of an introduction.

Jack and Dundee looked at each other in alarm, remembering Jack's collision with Addison Bruce in the square.

'He may still be here.'

A prompt to the heroes that it was their job to find out - and they were very brave about it. Brave in the knowledge that they had Mrs D on their side, who looked as if she could handle several Addison Bruce's no bother. They crept up the stairs side by side, checked the bathroom, and the two bedrooms, including the wardrobes, and under the beds. Then Jack quickly popped his head up into the attic, before racing back down the stairs again.

'There's nae sign of him,' said Dundee, as he and Jack returned to the sitting room to find Echtra alone, sweeping up the mess with a large broom. 'What's he after?'

'The Key,' said Echtra.

They suddenly realised there were keys strewn all over the floor. Wardrobe keys, dressing table keys, music box keys, keys for the windows, keys for the doors, every key in the house, apart from the Key to the City of course.

'Addison Bruce suspects the Fairy Queen has stolen the Key,' said Mrs D, calling through from the kitchen.

'And has she?' asked Dundee.

'I expect so.'

There were no clocks in the cottage but they could tell by the light from the windows that the day was drawing in. They sat by the hearth, surrounded by paintings of the battling Gods. Jack and Dundee on one sofa, Echtra and Mrs D on the sofa opposite, with the tea trolley in between them, as if it was just an ordinary afternoon.

'Are those paintings of the Otherworld?' asked Dundee, who had always been fascinated by the pictures in the sitting room.

'No,' said Mrs D. 'They are paintings of this world.'

Jack and Dundee looked at each other in surprise as Echtra passed over their cups and saucers.

Mrs D explained. 'A long time ago, when the Gods of the Otherworld frequented this Island, it was invaded by mortal Kings. They came overseas from sunken lands with their many Chiefs, and they were very powerful. They kicked the Gods out.'

Jack and Dundee looked suitably shocked.

'The God of the seas was furious. He separated the worlds with an impassable sea.' Mrs D turned to indicate the painting of a giant tidal wave near the kitchen door. 'The Gods simply love a good flood.'

'The Fairy Queen of dreams lived here at number seven, protected by the God of the seas. She was the one who built the Bridge, as a means of escape for the inhabitants. But then the Amazons arrived and stole the City. Since then no-one's been able to get off the Island alive.'

'Who are the Amazons?'

'The Amazons are warrior women, the most violent females in the Otherworld. They rule the air in some regions.' Mrs D shuffled forward on the sofa to refill their tea cups. 'There's a picture of them somewhere, coming in over the Bridge.'

'It's over here,' said Echtra, jumping up to close the door to the hallway, revealing a painting they had never seen before.

Jack and Dundee were behind her in an instant, desperate to get a look at the Amazon women. But they were disappointed. There was no detail to the painting. The Amazon army was vast and looked more like a black weather cloud hovering over the Bridge.

'They can fly,' said Jack, stating the obvious.

Dundee studied the painting of the Amazon invasion. Then he looked around. There were seven paintings in the sitting room, with hardly a space between them, and he suddenly realised that the paintings in the cottage were the story of their world.

He moved away towards the far end of the room, his earlier bravado waning by the minute. The huge pictures by the forest window, which he had seen many times before, had suddenly taken on a new meaning. It was true he wanted to be a hero - he didn't want to spend all his life at the dull end, but he wasn't sure he had the courage for it.

Jack didn't have the courage for it either but he used jovial alarm to hide it.

87

'What are these pictures of?' he asked, bounding towards Dundee at the window.

'They are paintings of the battles to come,' said Mrs D, watching them from the comfort of the sofa.

'Battles. What battles?'

'She means battles here. On this Island,' explained Dundee.

'Really?'

'I'm afraid so,' confirmed Mrs D.

If Mrs D was to be believed, and they did believe her, there was no escape - Villains at the window, fiends in the air, visions in the sitting room of battles to be won.

'What's this picture of?'

Dundee had drifted off towards the fireplace where the seventh painting was hanging in the dark, looking very, very scary.

'Deliverance,' said Mrs D.

Dundee left Jack staring at the painting and returned quietly to his seat on the sofa.

'As you can see, we're going to need some help.'

Mrs D retrieved her handbag from the hearth, and took out her fancy notepad and pen

'We could ask Duggey,' said Jack, racing over, assuming Mrs D was making a list.

'We need heroes, not librarians,' argued Dundee.

'What about your cousins, the Cormacs?' suggested Echtra.

'The Cormacs!' cried Dundee, horrified at the thought. 'Ma cousins are great fighters, there's nae doubt about that. But they'd never leave the North, and anyway, a good cause would surely put them off.'

Dundee looked at Jack who nodded his agreement. Jack had met Dundee's cousins once before on a trip to Dundee's home town. It was an initiation he would never forget. The Cormacs had been delighted to see them, insisting on a lock-in at the *Hootsman* where they had christened Jack, Jimmy with twelve cans of McEwans and then dumped them both in the dungeon of the spooky old Abbey in town.

'I meant Otherworld help,' said Mrs D, taking the note she had just written and placing it into an envelope. 'I need you to post a letter.'

Echtra watched from the kitchen window as Jack made his way cautiously along the Bridge, trying to avoid the holes. When he got to the middle he lay down on the planks and put his arm through the railings, swinging it backwards and forwards, searching for the golden pillar box.

Dundee directed him from the embankment, but he clearly wasn't very good at it, because Jack kept missing the slot.

It was almost dark when they returned to the cottage. Jack stormed into the kitchen in a rare huff, with Dundee grinning behind him.

'It's done!'

It was after midnight when they heard the cry from the

Bridge. The wind had picked up outside and was rattling against the windows, the beginnings of a storm. Jack and Dundee were settled down for the night on the sofas. Echtra was in her bedroom wide awake in the dark, and Mrs D was making her way along the landing from the bathroom to the master bedroom with her curlers in.

'Help! Help!'

Mrs D rushed into Echtra's bedroom, threw open the side window, and stuck her head out.

It was a man, and he was in serious danger of being blown into the water.

'Hold on! Help is on the way,' cried Mrs D, bellowing so loudly that the man almost lost his grip. She called to the heroes who were already behind her.

Jack and Dundee immediately threw themselves into their new hero roles. First, they saved the man by prising his fingers away from the railings. Then, they carried him down the embankment, across the lawn and in through the back door of number seven like a fallen king, plonking him down rather harshly onto one of the sofas. They took a break whilst Echtra and Mrs D fussed over the man with fluffy towels and a hot cup of tea which he gratefully accepted.

The man, who appeared to be in his late fifties, looked very 'well to do,' dressed in a pin striped suit, waistcoat and matching overcoat. He had thinning blonde hair, blue eyes and a pair of round spectacles which he kept pushing up to the top of his nose. He had a face that was kind but professional and when he smiled the bags underneath his eyes crinkled up like the neck of a tortoise. Echtra noticed that the man had a briefcase with him and she thought for a moment that he might be a jumper from the City. The Bridge was a popular spot. But then the man suddenly stood up and offered out his hand.

'I'm Mrs D's lawyer,' said the man.

They looked to Mrs D for confirmation and she nodded in the man's direction.

Dundee was the first to shake his hand and offer him a drink of something stronger.

'A drop of malt if you have it thanks Dundee,' said the man.

Delighted, but surprised that the man from the Otherworld knew his name, Dundee raced off into the kitchen, returning minutes later with a large bottle of malt whisky. Using the Fairy Queen's best crystal glasses that Echtra had retrieved from the sideboard, they toasted the visitor's good health.

Then Mrs D's lawyer got down to business.

'Now then,' he began, taking out two huge bundles of paper and his posh pen.

'I'll need you to sign these heroes' contracts. It's just a disclaimer against accident, injury and of course death...' explained the man, as if it was par for the course.

Jack and Dundee signed the papers without bothering to look at them.

The man placed the signed documents back in his

91

briefcase. Then he took out something far more interesting.

'…and you'll need shades.'

'Shades!' cried Jack and Dundee excitedly.

'They're supernatural,' said the man. 'You must wear them at all times, in order to see the Otherworld around you…' He passed over the sunglasses which were rectangular with thin delicate frames, almost weightless and very, very dark.

'I'm afraid the inhabitants of this Island are unable to see anything outside their own existence. There's nothing wrong with their eye sight, but the continual habit of shying away from anything that does not directly affect them has caused a temporary restriction in their vision.'

Jack and Dundee tried the supernatural shades on, expecting to see hardly anything at all in the dimly lit sitting room, but instead they could see everything, as it really was.

'Will there be anything else?' said the lawyer, to the lady in charge.

'We're a little short on heroes.'

'I can see that,' said the lawyer, as the newly appointed heroes raced around the cottage like children, staring at things.

'If you want my advice…' said the man, who's advice was worth its weight in gold and always preceded an invoice.

'Which we do.' she confirmed.

'Your best chance is Finn and his Fianna.'

'The Fianna!' cried Dundee, coming in from the hallway. 'You mean the mythical warriors?'

'There's nothing mythical about the Fianna,' said the man, standing up and fastening his overcoat in preparation for the weather outside, having completed his duties.

He switched his attention back to Mrs D who was ushering him out of the sitting room and into the back kitchen. The others followed close behind.

'Finn and his men are camped close to Falias, at Black Rock Lake,' he continued. Mrs D opened the back door which blew back from the force of the wind.

'Of course you'll have to get over the Bridge first.' Mrs D nodded, using the door as a shelter, the others standing behind her.

'Well good luck and cheerio,' said the man, standing in the doorway with his hair blowing forwards. He backed out into the wind and, with his head down, swivelled around and then headed out towards the embankment. When he reached the end of the Bridge he attempted a farewell wave but a freak wind caught hold of his briefcase and so he focussed his efforts on the crossing. Jack and Dundee stood at the door watching until Mrs D's lawyer had disappeared off into the Otherworld mists, and then they joined the ladies in the sitting room.

As Mrs D preferred a feather mattress to a forest floor she decided they would be quite safe there for the night, provided they left the Island before the Amazons arrived at dawn and so they retired, once again.

It was three in the morning before they fell asleep. Dundee was flat on his face, an open book on the Fianna warriors next to his head, an empty bottle of malt on the floor. Jack was by his side, on his back with his mouth open.

A bee woke Jack up at eight o'clock. Somehow they had slept through dawn and the alarm. He staggered into the kitchen for a glass of water, intent on going straight back to sleep, but the events of the last twenty four hours slowly began to make themselves known in his head and he remembered that his whole world had changed. Jack stared out at the lawn with an odd feeling of foreboding, but he couldn't see anything out of the ordinary, apart from a few broken branches and foliage that had been blown in by the wind. He remembered his shades and went back to the sitting room for them. Then wished he hadn't.

They were surrounded. By fiends! They were all over the lawns and the Bridge. Jack backed away from the window, reversing through the sitting room just as Dundee was coming round on the sofa.

'What…' said Dundee, groggily.

'It's….it's…' Jack was having trouble getting the words out. 'The Amazons!' Then he belted up the stairs two at a time.

Chapter Five

The Wilde Blue Yonder

They crept quietly out of the front door, eventually. Mrs D took an age to pull herself together. By the time she had taken her curlers out and powdered her nose it was well after nine o'clock.

She had been quite concerned when Jack burst into the room with news of the Amazon's arrival, but when she peered through the gap in the curtains she could see that it was only the Banshees who guarded the Island, and informed Jack and Dundee that it could have been worse.

They didn't see how. Jack and Dundee were unable to tear themselves away from the bedroom window. The Banshees looked demented. There were over a hundred of them - females with crazy white hair, dumb eyes and huge mouths that were red raw from wailing. Every so often one of the women would open her mouth and screech a portent of impending doom or death, and one by one the others would join in. Then they would quieten down again until someone else set them off. They would have no chance of getting over the Bridge now!

Thankfully Mrs D had a plan B which involved

95

entering the Otherworld through a secret door in *Emma's* back larder, but they had to get there first. With the heroes at the rear, Echtra in the middle, and Mrs D at the front they moved slowly along the communal path between the front doors and the trees, conscious of the fact that there were over a hundred fiends waiting for them on the other side of the cottages. They crept past the front doors of numbers six, five and four without a hitch, but when they got to number three the bathroom window was open. It was Sharon.

'Jack! Dundee!' she screeched, at the top of her voice.

The resulting cries from the other side of the cottages were deafening - swiftly followed by a rush of feet.

Leaving Sharon open mouthed at the window they flew along the pathway, swerved left along the narrow trail in the woods, and out onto the visitor's road. The Banshees might have caught them, but they were brainless and went off in the wrong direction at the crossroads. The four were half way along the Wilde Blue Yonder path before the Banshees caught them up. They would have escaped, if it hadn't been for the fact that Addison Bruce was blocking the way.

He was looking particularly dashing, having selected one of his most expensive suits for the occasion, and they didn't realize he was standing in front of *Emma's* door until they were almost upon him. The Banshees had found the clearing and were falling over themselves to get to them. They were trapped.

Inside, *Emma's* was full to the brim. Mrs Snarlington-Darlington and her Friday ladies had arrived at eight am that morning determined to get the best table. Other customers, who had the same idea, had started queuing up behind them, and by eight thirty the clearing was full of ladies desperate for a cup of tea. There had been no sign of Mrs D's helpers and so Mrs Snarlington-Darlington had taken charge. By nine o'clock everyone was seated at a table and the Fridays' were rushing around to the order of Mrs Snarlington-Darlington who was in her element, particularly when the 'well to do's arrived and had to be squeezed onto a table of four in the adjoining room.

At a quarter past nine the Fridays left the café to get extra milk. The lady with the extra-large bosom and the strength of ten thousand men was the first to the door and she hit it with such ferocity that Addison Bruce was thrown back, trapped between the café door and the window.

And they were in - saved by the Fridays!

Mrs D navigated her way expertly around the tables, Echtra following close behind. But Jack and Dundee made the mistake of slowing down to see who was in the café and they caught the eye of an old crone sitting alone at a small table in front of the till, pretending to read a *Woman's Weekly*. From behind their shades they could see that she was really a Witch - a seven foot tall Black Witch. And she knew it.

She was behind them in an instant. Jack and

Dundee fled into the corridor, crashed around the bend, flew past the ladies toilets and headed for the larder which they could see was open, the girls having already gone through. They were almost at the door, Dundee slightly ahead.

Jack had the Black Witch right behind him, too close for comfort. She stretched out her long bony arm, intent on grabbing his curls. Jack tensed up, sensing he was about to go down but nothing happened. He leapt into the back larder behind Dundee. Then he heard a familiar voice behind him.

'Is that you Jack.'

Jack turned to find Mrs Snarlington-Darlington, who had just come out of the ladies toilets and was standing in the corridor with her arms folded, inadvertently blocking the Black Witch's path.

With a big smile on his face Jack turned to face the void.

'Jack!!!'

And with Mrs Snarlington-Darlington's words echoing behind them Jack and Dundee took a leap of faith through the open door and they were through.

Chapter Six

Hell and High Water, Falias

'Ice and lemon?' asked Brian, out of habit.

The man at the bar said nothing. He grabbed his whisky and headed for his crew who were sitting opposite the bar at a large table beneath the only window in the room. He took his seat at the head of the table and threw his booted feet onto one of the empty chairs.

The sun streamed in through the window, casting particle beams across the room, and it was difficult to see the faces of the five men at the table but you could tell from the way they held themselves that they were not the sort of men you would want to upset.

The rest of the bar was empty apart from a pianist in the corner who was singing a song about the blues, which was the sort of song that resonated with the customers of the *Hell and High Water* who had, more often than not, fallen by the wayside.

The *Hell and High Water* pub was a well-known watering hole in the Otherworld, frequented by villains and heroes who would bump into each other on occasion and thrash out their differences. It stood as far away as possible from the shops, at the top end of Old Street, which had a wild west look about it. There were two steps up to the entrance, two pillars either side, and a pair of wide saloon swing doors suitable for throwing large numbers of people out. On the other side of the doors lay a large square room with a long bar on the right. Everything inside the pub was dark wood, including the bar, the walls, and the floor which was full of tables and chairs that had been thrown around a lot - some with legs and no arms, wonky stools and a few rockers. At the far end of the room there was a slight step up to the piano and the pianist, and on the right an open staircase that led upstairs to additional seating, which gathered more dust than customers.

The pianist rose from his stool, picked up the broom that he had left against the wall and began sweeping up, avoiding the table by the window. When he had finished he joined the manager, Brian at the bar. They were an odd looking pair. Brian, was as dour as they come - the dourest man in Falias - young looking but pale, with red hair that was matted together and stood up straight, as though he had fallen asleep flat on his face. The pianist had a hangdog face that had seen better days and was dressed like a dude in his twenties. He helped himself to a shot of rum and leant on the bar next to Brian who was wiping the top over and over, a nervous habit he had picked up in a previous life.

'Who are they?' asked the pianist, his voice was deep

and it echoed through the bar.

'That's the Adventurer and his crew,' whispered Brian.

'Don't they work for the Gods?'

'Shsst! They work for Angus.'

'The God of love?'

Brian nodded.

The pianist took a swig of his rum. 'They don't look very angelic do they?'

'They're not. Angus uses them for all the difficult jobs. They tour the Otherworld masked as entertainers, but they're really Liberators for Angus, and they take their work very seriously...' explained Brian, taking a bottle of malt off the shelf and joining the pianist in a drink.

'...The Adventurer's 'an eye for an eye' kind of guy.'

'Was that him at the bar, the one in black?'

'Yeh. He's the front man.'

'What about the guy on his left, in the cowboy hat?'

'That's the Wings - he's friendly enough - a big drinker. The one next to him with the white hair they call the Spirit. He never speaks. And the good looking one at the end with the dark wavy hair, they call him the Heart.'

'What about the guy at the window?' The pianist indicated with a flick of his head towards the man with golden curls, who was checking the street outside.

'That's the Guardian Angel. He's darker than he looks. Don't stare at him. He's knows magic.'

Brian and the pianist stood sipping their drinks from

the safety of the bar, fascinated by the crew of unlikely saviours.

'They're a tough looking bunch.'

Brian nodded. 'They're tough alright. You're looking at the Chiefs of the Kings who kicked the Gods off the Island of Destiny.'

'But that was twelve thousand years ago!'

'Yeh, it was.'

'How did they end up here?'

'When the Gods left the Island there was a constant feud between the mortal Kings, until there were none left alive. The six Chiefs of the South took the City. The seven Chiefs of the North came here. They've been trying to redeem themselves by working for Angus.'

'There are only five here. What happened to the other two?'

'They were all back on the Island the day the Amazons attacked. The Rev and the Shadow got left behind.'

'How come you know so much?'

'I was there,' said Brian. Then he disappeared into the back.

The pianist picked up his broom and dragged it over the wooden floor until he reached the bottom of the stairs. He stole a glance at Angus's famed Liberators, and then slowly climbed the stairs on the right, as if he had heavy weights in his shoes and continued sweeping up. He was still up above finishing off the corners when the saloon doors swung open.

It was a man in a dog collar, black suit and shades. He staggered into the room in an ungodly fashion, his hair parted in the middle, long and unkempt as if it hadn't been washed for days, his suit covered in dust and mud.

The Adventurer and his crew were on the alert, eyes at the door, but they returned to their drinks when they saw who it was.

Brian, who had heard the door in the back, came into the bar, and put his head down.

'What'll it be?'

'It'll be a bottle of red wine,' said the Rev.

Brian opened the bottle whilst trying to avoid his eye.

'Haven't we met before?'

Brian shook his head, his eyes still on the deck.

'Well then, I do declare, I buried your double yesterday,' said the Rev, thumping the bar.

Brian drew back and stared at the Rev who grinned at him like the devil.

Then the Rev turned away and joined his comrades at the table.

'What news from the other side?' enquired the Adventurer, as the Rev took the one armed seat next to him.

'Well hello there, so nice to see you….how have you been keeping these last twelve thousand years,' replied the Rev, swinging his head from side to side.

'How have you been keeping?' asked the Adventurer, impatiently.

'I've been jailed up…preaching to the non-converted,' said the Rev, pouring himself a giant glass of red wine.

He grinned at his favourite, the Wings, and nodded to the Heart at the end of the table, who looked pleased to see him. The Spirit, who was sitting opposite him, hardly batted an eye lid, and the Guardian Angel at the window still had his back to the table.

'What news of our comrade?' asked the Adventurer impatiently, leaning in.

'He's changed sides, got himself a fancy new job and a new name – he's calling himself Addison Bruce now.'

'Yeh, we heard. We met his alter ego.'

'Alter ego?'

'Addison's repressed self. The Shadow is over here.' The Adventurer let his shades slide, and eyeballed the black sheep who had suddenly returned to the fold.

The Rev frowned and dove into his wine glass.

The Guardian Angel drew away from the window, sensing his unease. He chose the chair next to the Rev and closed in on him, sitting far too close for comfort.

'You wouldn't recognise the Shadow now. He's gone mad. Like a mad pied piper…' He placed the fingers of his left hand, which were adorned with symbolic silver rings, firmly on the Rev's right shoulder, and gripped hard. 'and we're under orders to put him to rest.'

The Rev shook him off, picked up the bottle of red wine, and poured himself an extra-large glass.

'The Shadow's got his own crew now,' said the Wings, attempting to lighten the mood. 'And a crazy circus called Showtown. He's been touring the Otherworld selling immortality to the mortals.'

'Of course it's a trap,' said the Heart.

'Of course,' said the Rev, remembering some of his sermons.

'So, how did *you* manage to escape the Island?' asked the Spirit, who rarely spoke, and so it was a little unsettling.

The Rev took an annoyingly long time to answer. 'Someone's stolen the Key to the City.'

The Adventurer almost spat out his whiskey. The Rev grinned - pleased his news had hit the mark. The others leant in.

'Who took it?' asked the Wings.

'If I knew that brother I'd tell you,' said the Rev, hoping the lie would hold up behind the darkness of his shades.

They sat in silence for a moment contemplating the news whilst they finished their drinks. Then the Adventurer stood up and headed for the door, his crew following.

'Where are we off to?' asked the Rev, picking up the wine bottle and racing after them.

'We've got a gig, in Finias.'

'Great,' said the Rev, glad to be back in the fold. As

they hit the street the Rev took his old place in the line, on the Adventurer's right.

'Anything else I should know about?'

'No boss,' replied the Rev.

At that moment two young men appeared out of nowhere in the middle of the street and walked straight into them.

'Forgive us our trespasses,' said the Rev, a phrase he had picked up on the other side.

Then he saw who it was and was as startled as they were. The young men hurried off up the road and the Rev got back into his stride.

'Problem?' asked the Adventurer, who was no fool.

'Just two idiots from the Island.'

'How did they get here?'

'I've no idea,' said the Rev truthfully.

'Did they follow you?'

'Erm...I don't think so,' said the Rev, trying to remember.

'Find out,' demanded the Adventurer, and then he walked on with the others leaving the Rev alone in the street.

The Rev kicked the road in a temper and headed off in the direction of the idiots. He was fed up being at the right hand of the Gods. He wanted a seat.

Chapter Seven

Way out West

'Jings! Was that the Rev?' cried Dundee.

'It was either him or his double,' said Jack, still in a daze after their jaunt into the Otherworld.

Following their leap of faith through the back larder of *Emma's* cafe Jack and Dundee had found themselves in another back larder, which unbeknown to them, belonged to *Emma's* Otherworld double. After scrabbling around in the dark for an exit they took the wrong door and ended up on the back streets of Falias, by the bins, eventually finding their way onto Old Street.

The Gods of the Otherworld had four Cities: Falias, the City of Earth in the North, Finias the City of Fire in the South, Gorias, the City of Air in the East, and Murias, the City of Water in the West.

Falias was the place where people came to discover their destinies. The Druids had their Halls of Learning there. The Masters had their schools. The Gods had their white marble Temple. The Goddesses had their Theatre, and many sculptures which were to be found all over the

City, depicting scenes of honourable deeds and moral lessons, of which there were many.

Falias had lots of visitors. It drew in the tourists, and unlike Stress City, which had been built in its image, Falias had no wall around it. Yet it had managed to maintain its circular shape, despite the forest, which kept its distance most of the time, and steered clear of the four pillared entrance. There was plenty of room inside the City for citizens and tourists. The buildings, the square, and the streets were kept in good order and so there had been no need for a new square. There was no such thing as Main Street. No banks, or office buildings, and no need for telephones, or computers. If you wanted to communicate with someone in the Otherworld you paid them a visit.

'This looks just like Old Street,' said Jack, stopping in the middle of the road.

'Aye, a wild west version,' said Dundee, quite taken with the theme.

The street was much wider than the one in Stress City, with fancy pavements that had been stepped up, away from the dust of the road. The buildings were the same in number, shape and size, but they were standing upright. All of the shops looked newly painted. Some had additional windows, coloured rooftops and chimneys. Others had white wooden canopies, with stilted pillars to shade the passing trade.

'Come on,' said Dundee, keen to explore. He strode

up the street with Jack dawdling behind him, quickly reaching the top end, where the pavements ran out, but the street ran on, disappearing off into the forest.

'There's no end to it...' said Dundee, who hadn't realised he was talking to himself. Jack was several shops behind him, his attention caught by a pair of red cowboy boots in one of the shop windows.

'There's a pub up here, on the left.' Dundee was forced to use his hand to shade his eyes from the sun overhead, despite the fact that he had his supernatural shades on. 'It's the *Hell and High Water*!'

'Dundee!' yelled Jack.

Dundee swung around to find Jack with his back to him, on the opposite side of the road, pointing at one of the shops.

'Dundee!'

'What!' Dundee headed over begrudgingly, his hands in his pockets.

'It's Duggey's!' said Jack, who felt like the world was turning upside down, with him in it. He grabbed hold of Dundee's arm to steady himself.

'That's weird,' said Dundee.

'You're telling me it's weird! You don't think he's in there do you?'

'I don't know. It's definitely his book shop.'

'Look,' said Jack, pointing to the sign above the door which was newly painted. 'It looks different.'

'Maybe Duggey's different!'

'What if it isn't him?'

Emer Bruce

'What if it *is* him?'

'Have a look through the window.'

'*You* have a look through the window.'

Jack looked. It was Duggey, the original. They stood at the entrance and peered inside.

'Oh, you've got to see this,' said Duggey, beckoning them in with his left arm without bothering to turn around. He had his red cowboy boots up on the counter and his eyes glued to the television set.

Jack and Dundee tried to slide into the shop but the floor was level and so they had to make the effort to walk up to the counter.

'How did you know it was us?' asked Jack.

'I could hear you talking outside. Look,' said Duggey excitedly as Dundee leant on the counter. 'They're showing Laurel and Hardy again. It's *Way out West.*'

'Brilliant,' said Dundee, leaning in towards the television, the crazy situation they were in temporarily forgotten.

'I love this bit,' said Duggey, as Stan and Ollie entered the bar. 'They end up telling the barman everything - and he's the Villain!'

'Idiots!' said Dundee, laughing.

'I hate to interrupt,' said Jack. 'But what are you doing here Duggey?'

'I've got a book shop in both worlds,' said Duggey, managing to tear himself away from the screen.

'Why didn't you tell us?'

'What would you have said?'

Whilst they were thinking this through Duggey headed off into the kitchen returning with a dusty old bottle of malt whisky which he had been saving for the occasion and three glasses.

'It's good to see you,' said Duggey, who was slightly emotional as he raised his glass towards his two pals. 'To freedom.'

'Freedom,' said Jack and Dundee, feeling quite heroic already.

'So what's it like in Falias?' asked Jack, after a couple of shots.

'Full of beautiful woman with long legs.'

'Really!' cried Jack. Duggey laughed out loud as Jack raced to the window.

'We're nae staying,' said Dundee, taking charge. 'We need to get to Black Rock Lake, to find the Fianna.'

'The Fianna!' exclaimed Duggey, suitably impressed. 'So you're heroes now are you?'

'Yep,' said Jack, returning to the counter.

'No,' said Dundee.

'We signed the heroes' contracts,' argued Jack.

'Aye, that's aboot it.'

'And we escaped the Island,' insisted Jack. 'Everyone's chasing us. The Amazons, the Banshees, even a Witch.'

'Sounds like a bad dream,' said Duggey, filling up their glasses like a barman. 'Why are they chasing you?'

'Because the Key to the City's been stolen…'

'Yeh, I heard,' interrupted Duggey.

'How did you know?' asked Dundee.

'You hear most things in this shop, it carries,' Duggey pointed to the ceiling.

'Mrs D thinks that the Fairy Queen has....' continued Jack.

Dundee gave him a thump.

'What?' cried Jack, rubbing his arm.

'We can't just go around spilling the beans, like Laurel and Hardy.'

'But I'm on your side,' said Duggey, looking hurt.

'How do *we* know you're on our side?' Dundee's paranoia was kicking in.

'I'm the mentor! Every story has one!'

Dundee was unsure. He looked at Jack. It was two against one.

'Ok, tell him.'

'Mrs D thinks the Fairy Queen has stolen the Key. She's...'

'I know who *she* is,' said Duggey, getting annoyed. 'I know more than you do!'

Jack thought about this for a moment. Then he said. 'Did you know Echtra was a doll?'

For the first time since they had met him Duggey looked alarmed. He jumped out of his chair, swung around the counter, and bolted to the door. He checked the streets outside for passers-by. Then he returned to the counter where he opened the top drawer and put his shades on – which was a rarity.

Dundee looked worried.

'Do you mean,' whispered Duggey, leaning forward onto the counter, addressing Jack in a serious manner, 'one of the Dollmaker's dolls?'

Jack looked confused. 'Who?'

'The Dollmaker. He built Stress City, and he created the dolls at the same time. There were twelve of them, thought to have been destroyed when the Amazons took the Island. The dolls have an important destiny - they cannot be allowed to fall into the wrong hands. Whatever you do don't tell anyone about her - and don't lose her.'

'We already have,' admitted Jack. 'You see we were delayed by a Witch. Echtra went through the larder before us with Mrs D and then...'

'They'll be at *Emma's*,' said Duggey. 'It's two doors down.' Then he returned to his former position in front of the set. It took a while before he realized that Jack and Dundee were still standing at the counter.

'You'd better get going. You're heroes now aren't you.'

'Aye...I suppose we are. Well, cheerio then,' said Dundee, reluctant to leave the comfort of Duggey's shop. He backed slowly out, one hand in his trouser pocket, the other pushing the hair back out of his eyes.

'Yep, cheerio then,' said Jack, following Dundee's lead, reversing out of the door. 'And thanks.'

'No problem,' said Duggey, giving them one of his celebrity smiles before returning to Laurel and Hardy.

In the spiritual section of Duggey's book shop the Rev replaced the hymn book he was pretending to read back on the shelf of aisle five and headed for the door. On the way out he bumped into an old crone who was tiptoeing out of aisle two. The Rev recognised her immediately as Addison's spy, the Black Witch of Bad Luck. He tried to back away from her but she gave him the evil eye, then left.

The Black Witch returned to her seven foot form and swept swiftly out of the City, through the four pillared entrance, and into the forest. She flew along the visitor's road until she came to the Bridge, which was now on her right, and called in seven of her nastiest Banshees.

As they headed back towards Falias the Witch's thoughts were on Addison Bruce - as usual. It would go down well with Addison if *she* captured the doll herself. Maybe then he would break off his unholy alliance with Aife. She was looking forward to the day when she would rip her head off.

The Rev headed out of Falias in the same direction as the Black Witch. He passed through the four pillared entrance, and along the visitor's road, but continued on at the crossroads, heading south in the direction of Finias.

His comrades were way ahead of him but he had plenty to think about, and the person foremost in his mind was Addison Bruce. In the mortal world Addison was powerful, but spineless. He would never leave the confines of the Island. There was something about freedom that bothered him. The Rev, however, couldn't wait to get out of there. When the Key to the City had been stolen he had been delighted, and in the chaos that ensued he had headed over the Bridge to freedom. Unfortunately Addison had come to wave him off – he almost hadn't made it. The Rev convinced Addison that *he* should be the one to retrieve the Key from the Fairy Queen - with the intention of switching sides when he had been reunited with his old pals, the Chiefs of the North. But now he had discovered that the Shadow, Addison's darker side, was alive and kicking, and more powerful than ever. So he decided to keep this new information about the doll to himself.

The Rev had always swung both ways, depending on who was winning.

Back in Falias the door to *Emma's* café swung open to reveal two slightly dusty, tall dark handsome young heroes.

'Ah, there you are,' said Mrs D, looking up from her custard cream.

Chapter Eight

The Path of Most Resistance

Far away from the hustle and bustle of Falias nature ran wild, safe in the knowledge that it would be largely ignored by the City's inhabitants. The trees raised themselves up towards the heavens, so high the birds were forced to dance around them. Plants and flowers abandoned their regular shapes, covering the landscape in great blankets of colour. And at the centre, there since the earliest beginnings, the sacred mountains, home to the falls which ran through the forest at a tremendous pace creating rivers, ponds, and the Lake at Black Rock.

Black Rock was a huge formation of giant boulders that looked as if someone had thrown it together in haste. Each boulder balanced precariously on top of the next, some so far away from the core, they appeared to be suspended in thin air. Some of the heavier rocks had broken away, falling close to the base. Others had tumbled into the forest, or had rolled on towards the edge of the Lake.

The Lake was hidden from view by dense undergrowth on every side, forged from the force of the falls, which had, over the years, unearthed a basin of black hematite crystal. Huge curtains of vines had wrapped themselves around and above it, creating beautiful fairy-like bridged ceilings, the sun having to force its way down through the gaps, the rays like spot lights on a stage of black water.

This wild untamed land that nature had created in the highest of spirits had yet to be explored by the citizens of Falias, and so visitors who had the urge to venture in were warned to keep their wits about them.

Thankfully Mrs D always kept her wits securely fastened about her person.

'Hurry along,' called Mrs D, who was leading the way along the forest path with Echtra.

The path was wide enough for four but Jack and Dundee had been lagging behind, distracted by the scenery.

They had left Falias over an hour ago, following Old Street through the woods until the street ran out. Now they were in the wilder part of the forest where the trees were gigantic and everything was mad and colourful, including the wildlife and the birds, which were so loud Jack and Dundee could hardly hear what Mrs D was saying to them.

'What did you say?' asked Jack, as he and Dundee caught them up.

'I said hurry along. We're not out of the woods yet,' warned Mrs D, stating the obvious.

She was wearing an old yellow flowery dress and an

oversized summer hat. They stood in the shade of it as she explained. 'We must find Black Rock Lake, and the Fianna, before the Amazons find us.'

'I thought you said the Amazons were on their way to the Island?' queried Dundee.

'You forget. Falias is only a bridge away. It won't take them long to find us.'

'What about the Banshees?' asked Dundee.

'And the Witch. A Witch tried to grab us in the café,' added Jack.

'The Banshees will stay where they are,' said Mrs D, confidently. 'It's their job to guard the Island. The Witch is Addison Bruce's spy. She is known in the Otherworld as the Black Witch of Bad Luck and she can be difficult to shake. But you needn't worry. She hardly ever leaves the Island.'

Dundee looked concerned.

'Try and keep your thoughts bright and cheery,' she instructed, 'Mind creates, and in the Otherworld it creates a lot quicker than you're used to.'

Then Mrs D twirled around, and was about to step forward onto the path, but instead she fell back causing Jack and Dundee to stumble.

'Oh my goodness!' she cried, her hand to her bosom.

'What is it?' cried Echtra. 'Is it the Amazons?'

'Is it the Banshees?' cried Jack.

'Is it the Witch?' cried Dundee, looking up at the sky.

'It's the path,' said Mrs D. 'It's fading away.'

'What do you mean fading away!'

118

'Where's it going?'

Ignoring the panic behind her Mrs D began rummaging around in her giant handbag for her special spectacles which were forest green like the woods. She put them on and bent over to examine the path.

'Hmm…I haven't seen anything like this in a long time,' muttered Mrs D. She moved to the left. The path wobbled a little and then moved with her. She moved to the right. It caught her up, eventually. 'It seems to be having trouble following us.'

'Following us!' cried her brood, huddled together on what was left of the path. Being in control of where they were heading was a completely new experience for them. It was far easier leaving it in the hands of a path they had never met before.

'It's a beginner's path - the path of most resistance. It won't move forwards until you stop looking backwards,' explained Mrs D straightening up, and turning around to face them.

'If we're not careful, we'll end up back where we started - in the ordinary world.'

She put her special spectacles back into her handbag, and adjusted her hat which had tilted forward.

'You must keep your thoughts away from the past,' she instructed. 'And look forward. Look forward, look forward, look forward. *Never* look back, at the beginning of anything, or anybody.'

Then she stepped out with such conviction that the path was forced to reappear.

119

Diorruing watched the approaching strangers with interest. He stood a little too close to the edge of Black Rock, the water from the falls racing past his feet. The air was filled with spray from the force of it descending into the Lake below causing thick clouds of mist to rise up, occasionally blocking his view of the surrounding forest.

He was more like a prince than a warrior, dressed in the finest of clothes. Unlike any other member of the Fianna his hair was as black as coal, and his dark green eyes, when shielded from the light, caused his mind to pull back into an infinite darkness, enabling him to see events that were happening elsewhere, and also events that may occur in the future. It was this visionary gift that had earned him the exalted position of Seer to the Leader of the Fianna, and he did everything he could to live up to that honour, as did all of Finn's warriors. For Finn they said, was like the sun.

Finn had a powerfully warm nature which he wore like a radiant cloak lifting the spirits of all around him. His men, and there were many of them, say there was no better man than he. The few that had ever set eyes on him outside his own band of warriors say he was more godlike than mortal.

Finn stood with his back to the falls in the silence, the three warriors at the Lake not given to idle chatter in his presence.

His poet and wise counsellor Fergus was close by, sitting under the shade of a tree, his head down, engrossed in a book. Fergus was at his happiest in the forest. It was said he had the beauty of the day in him. He was tall and slim, with wild wavy hair that was dark brown like the earth, and never grew past his shoulders. He was well liked. Nothing bothered Fergus - and so, when the pages of his poetry book were suddenly soaked to ruin by a huge wave of water, courtesy of Mac the giant, he took it in his stride.

Mac was the most fearsome of all Finn's soldiers. He was more bear than man, easily recognised for the black fleecy hair on his back, his shorn head, colossal belly, and cold unwelcoming eyes. The best time to approach Mac was just after he had slept, and Mac always slept with the horses. It was his responsibility as Protector to watch over the Fianna day and night, but that didn't stop him dozing off on duty. Mac enjoyed his sleep better than any man, and so he relied on the sensitive nature of the horses to alert him to any danger.

Occasionally his comrade Diarmait would test this by launching an attack. Mac was always ready for him. At the moment he had him in a head lock and was dragging him towards the Lake. Mac was not in the best of moods, having been woken up from a deep sleep by a low flying dagger, and was intent on ridding himself of Diarmait once and for all. Blindly, and in a fit of great temper, he butted Diarmait's head against his own, rendering him unconscious and then hurled him into the black waters. As Diarmait's body sank down into the depths of the Lake Mac turned away towards the falls, intent on leaving him to drown. But Finn was by the falls, watching him, and seconds later Mac was back at the Lake, trying to save the man he had just sunk.

Like a bear with a fish Mac hauled Diarmait out of the water by his hair and threw him face down in a puddle of mud. Diarmait stayed where he was until he felt sure his spirit had returned, then he pulled himself to his feet and staggered away, rather ungratefully Mac felt, towards the falls.

Diarmait emerged from the falling waters and shook himself like a dog before climbing onto one of the rocks and spreading himself out. The sun shone directly onto the back of his naked muscular body, his long wavy red hair running almost the length of it. When his back was almost dry he turned around, revealing himself. There was none more handsome than Diarmait, foster son of Angus the ever young, God of Love. He placed his hand on the flat of his taut stomach, which had been badly grazed on the rocks, and the other on the huge cut on his forehead. Then he closed his grey blue eyes – undeterred. Giants were good practice.

Up above his head, Diorruing the Seer was making his way cautiously across the current, intent on making his descent to the left of Black Rock, where the boulders were more stable. At one point he almost lost his footing. Mac immediately went to his aid, but Diorruing had already steadied himself and so he dismissed Mac with an ungrateful wave, continuing with caution across the water drenched boulders until he reached safer ground.

Diorruing tried to clear his mind for the climb down

but all sorts of images kept sailing past his eyes. It was most distracting, and was one of the reasons why he found it so difficult to see, his vision blurred by pictures flying in from all over the place. He wished, not for the first time, that he had a different part to play. This role, played in the shadows, didn't suit him at all. He didn't even look like a Seer. Seers were short and bent, with tired looks and old ways. Diorruing was tall and straight, with high looks and a grand manner. He was completely lacking in humbleness, a trait considered necessary for a part which was predominantly earth facing. Diorruing, like the rest of the Fianna, preferred to face the heavens.

He did however have an inquisitive nature and loved to delve into other people's life stories. To him the whole script was foreseeable - a play, where even the slightest change in character could dramatically affect the storyline, and for this reason he was very much looking forward to meeting the approaching strangers.

Before he began his descent he paused to check on their progress and what he saw almost caused him to fall over again.

That was no stranger. He knew that lady very well. The one in the summer hat covered in flour.

They tried. They really did. But Jack and Dundee were unable to keep their thoughts away from the past for longer than five minutes. The path swung around, this way and that, until it was impossible to tell which way they were heading. At one point Mrs D lost her summer

123

hat and they were hugely disappointed when they found it again on a giant toad-stool, and discovered they had been going around in circles. The forest grew dark, in line with their thoughts. The width of the path began to narrow, and they were forced to walk two by two, which was when Jack and Dundee started lagging behind again.

'If only Duggey could see us now,' said Jack, trying to stay positive.

'Yeh, stuck in a dark wood going nowhere.' Dundee stopped suddenly.

'What is it?' Jack was right behind him.

'The path…it's come to an end.'

The path had split into two.

Mrs D and Echtra who had their thoughts on the future suddenly found their journey a lot easier. Their path lengthened and widened out, the sun flew in from behind the trees, and everything was a lot more cheery.

The heroes' path on the other hand had given up altogether.

'Mrs D! Echtra!' yelled Jack, over and over. 'Great. They've disappeared. What should we do?'

'Keep moving,' said Dundee, urging Jack off the end of the most resistant path.

Jack stepped out onto the forest floor, expecting something dreadful to happen. It didn't. Dundee joined him, and they moved on, calling out every so often.

'What was that?' said Dundee.

'What!'

'That wailing.'

124

This time Jack heard it to. It was the wail of the Banshees in the distance. They were searching the forest for them. 'That's all we need!'

'Try not to think about it,' warned Dundee.

'I can't help it!' cried Jack, as pictures of the Banshees kept popping into his head. 'I thought they were supposed to stay guarding the Bridge.'

'Tell *them* that, when they find us.'

They quickened their pace. Jack took a tumble over a tree root that he was convinced he had hit before. 'Those wails are getting louder.'

'We could be heading back, towards them,' said Dundee, unhelpfully, pulling Jack to his feet.

For some reason they looked up, expecting to see the Black Witch cackling away on a broom. Thankfully the skies were clear, but when they drew their eyes back to their surroundings it was as if someone had nipped in while they weren't looking and changed the scenery.

'Is it me or has it suddenly become a lot gloomier?' asked Dundee.

The birds had been replaced by huge fat ravens. The trees were black and singed, the branches looked like scary arms, and their roots seemed intent on tripping up their heels. The sun had run off behind a cloud, and they were unable to get their bearings.

'Great. Now we're completely lost.'

The man under the tree was unexpected. They didn't see him until they were almost on top of him. He was like part of the scenery - his grey beard and long hair blending in with the mossy ground. It looked as if he had begun in a sitting position with his head a fair way up the trunk, but then he had slid down, so that his head was now resting on the roots, and the rest of his body flat on the ground. His eyes were closed and he had a jolly look on his face, as though he had fallen asleep at a bus stop instead of in the middle of a scary forest.

Jack stepped towards him, intent on shaking him awake, with no thought at all for the consequences, but Dundee pulled him back just in time.

'What are you doing?' he whispered.

'I'm waking him up.'

'What do you mean you're waking him up?' asked Dundee, incredulous.

'We need directions.'

'We're not on a picnic. We're in the Otherworld now. You can't just go around shaking people awake. He could be anybody. He could be the Witch! She's a shape shifter.'

'What's a shape shifter?' asked Jack.

Dundee ignored him and tried to pull him away by the arm but Jack refused to budge. He had found something of interest that wasn't a tree or a bush and he wanted to savour the moment for as long as possible.

They stood side by side staring at the man, wondering what to do for the best.

'He's old isn't he,' said Jack.

'He looks like Rip Van Winkle.'

'Who's he?'

'The guy in the fairy tale. He goes off into the forest as a young man, finds these leprechauns, has a drink with them and then falls asleep for a hundred years. When he wakes up he looks like him, but his beard was much longer than that,' said Dundee, pointing to the man's beard.

'Was he carrying fish?

'What?'

'Fish. This guy's got fish. Maybe he'll cook some for us. I'm starving.'

'You're not waking him up,' insisted Dundee

'We have to, or we'll never get out of here,' argued Jack.

Dundee grabbed Jack's arm. 'Come on.'

'He just an ordinary man,' said Jack, fed up with Dundee's paranoia. 'I'm waking him up.'

'You're not.'

'I am.'

They scuffled around at the man's feet for a while and when they turned back the man was sitting up with his eyes open. They flew back in surprise, hitting the tree opposite.

'I'm terribly sorry. I must have dropped off,' said the man, as if they had been visiting him in his sitting room and he had fallen asleep in the middle of a conversation.

Jack and Dundee stared at the man wide eyed and open mouthed, as if one of the trees had spoken to them.

'Are you a witch?' asked Jack, boldly.

'No. I'm a man,' said the man, indicating that he

could do with a hand up. They rushed forward and helped him to his feet.

The man stood perfectly straight which was a surprise. They had expected a man of his age to be bent in some way but he was not. He was of medium height and build, and had no distinguishing features, apart from his silver grey hair and long beard. He looked as if he had once been someone of importance in the City who chuckled a lot at home.

'I'm from the other side,' said the man, dusting himself off.

'The other side of what?' asked Jack.

'The Bridge,' said the man.

'You mean Stress City!' cried Jack.

'Yes. Do you know it?'

'Know it! We live there.'

'Oh, thank goodness,' said the man, with a sigh of relief. 'I'm back.'

He picked up his rucksack full of fish and stepped out onto a path, which looked just like an ordinary path. The sun came out, and everything around them looked normal. Relieved, Jack and Dundee followed him.

After a while they came to a clearing with a pond in the middle of it, and the man, who happened to have a mini camp stove in his rucksack, cooked the fish.

Jack and Dundee settled down under the shade of a tree to watch.

'We should tell him he's on the wrong side of the Bridge,' said Jack, keeping his voice low.

'*You* tell him,' said Dundee, unwilling to upset their host.

The man appeared with the fish, which he served on a large tin camping plate. Then he dove into his rucksack and pulled out a bottle of red wine, and some plastic tumblers.

They were unable to resist the wine, or the fish, reasonably sure at this point that the man wasn't a witch or a leprechaun.

'Have you been away long?' asked Jack, when they had finished the fish, and were already on their second tumbler of wine.

'Forty days and forty nights,' replied the man, taking a small diary out of his jacket pocket to check. I can tell you this, I'll be glad to get back to the bank.'

'The Bank?' said Dundee, assuming it was where the man worked.

'Yes, the bank, overlooking the Bridge. It's a wonderful spot. Do you know it?'

'Where on the bank?' asked Jack, holding his breath.

'Number two.'

Jack was in shock. He stared at the man, unable to take his eyes off him. Dundee gave Jack a kick, in an effort to ensure he kept his mouth shut, but it wasn't necessary. For once Jack was speechless.

'I only popped out for a spot of fishing,' continued the man. 'I was looking for somewhere new, and decided to try the Wilde Blue Yonder path. I found the pond. But then I wandered on, outside the City boundaries...silly really. I must have fallen asleep because when I woke up I was in the Otherworld - at a Lake.'

'Were there any leprechauns involved?' interrupted Jack.

Dundee gave Jack another kick with his boot. 'This Lake, was it black?'

'Why yes, it *was* black,' said the man. 'I found a path, and followed it into one of those Otherworld Cities - Falias. It's a marvellous place you know, incredibly busy, full of life. I stayed there for a while but it wasn't for me. The people were wonderful, and so young. They kept telling me I could be as young as I set my mind to be, but I couldn't get the hang of it. I kept my coat and scarf on - to remind me of home.'

The man stood up and began putting away his things. 'Talking of which I must be off. She'll be wondering where I've got to.'

'Wait!' cried Jack, about to tell him he was on the wrong side of the Bridge. But he couldn't manage it. The man carried on putting away his cutlery. Jack looked to Dundee in desperation.

'You're still in the Otherworld,' said Dundee, blurting it out.

'Oh,' said the man, a little shocked. 'I think you must be mistaken. Look.' He pointed to the tree by the pond. 'There's my hat and fishing brolly, just where I left them.'

He wandered off to collect his things.

It suddenly dawned on Dundee that *he* was wrong

and the man was right. 'Oh no! We're back!'

'What do you mean, we're back?'

'We're back in the ordinary world Jack. Can't you tell the difference?'

Jack looked around. He shrugged his shoulders.

'Our thoughts must have dragged us back here! Just like Mrs D said they would.'

'You mean…we're back on the Island!' cried Jack, suddenly catching up. 'But…how are we going to get back…to the Otherworld?'

'Almost there.' The man waved to them from the other side of the pond.

They waved back.

'*He* managed it, and he wasn't even trying,' said Dundee. 'We'll have to find the path of most resistance again. Keep our thoughts on the future this time.'

'What about him? We'll have to make sure he gets home first.'

Dundee nodded.

'You do realise he's Mr Snarlington-Darlington don't you?'

'I know! What do you think she'll say when she sees him?'

'She'll go mad! He looks dreadful.'

'Is it definitely him?'

'It must be. According to her he went missing on a fishing trip ten years before I arrived on her doorstep. He always went fishing on Sundays. She told me often enough.'

131

'What age were you when you arrived on her doorstep?'

'I was two.'

'And you're thirty two now. That means he's been gone forty years, not forty days.'

'I know. Wait till he looks in the mirror.'

'Wait a minute!' cried Dundee. 'There's no such thing as time in the Otherworld Jack. It's in all the books. The hero goes off on an adventure into the Otherworld thinking he's been gone a few days, and then he discovers he's been gone for years.'

'How long have we been gone?'

'Not even a day…that's probably six months.'

'Six months!'

'Aye, we'll have to be careful. There are stories of heroes returning from the Otherworld after hundreds of years and turning to dust.'

'Are you saying we shouldn't go?'

'Nae me. What aboot you.'

Jack swallowed courageously, and shook his head.

Dundee grinned. 'We should give ourselves a time limit though.'

Jack nodded. It was a good idea. 'How long should we stay – a week?'

'It's not a holiday Jack, it's a quest. It'll take longer than that to find the Key to Stress City.'

'But what's the point of being heroes if we come back like him.' Jack pointed towards the tree where Mr Snarlington-Darlington had fallen asleep again.

132

'That's true.' Dundee thought it through. 'What aboot twelve days, that should be long enough - we'll be the same age as Brian when we get home.

'And we'll be heroes.'

'Let's hope so. We need to start acting like heroes Jack. Forget all aboot the idiots we were in the past.'

'They're forgotten.'

'Heroes then.'

'Heroes.'

They shook on it.

'I need a drink,' said Dundee. 'There's another bottle in here.'

'What is it?'

'I'm nae sure. It smells like whisky.'

They raised their tumblers, took a gulp, and were out for the count.

Jack and Dundee must have been a long time dreaming - for they were all grown up. Heroes, capable of great courage and self-sacrifice - a little crazy perhaps, compelled along the forest path by some higher purpose. They arrived, at last, at the Lake at Black Rock. A curtain of vines separated them from their comrades. They drew out their daggers to pull back the vines, and were about to step forward, when there was a loud rustle in the bushes. They turned to face what they assumed was their enemy, and awoke with a start.

They were back to their old selves again, lying down in the dirt, their mouths dry and stained from the wine.

Before they had a chance to pull themselves together there was a rustle in the bushes. Just like in the dream. Something was hacking its way towards them. Something big and it was getting closer. They backed away towards the vines, still on their behinds. Whatever it was, it was almost upon them. They opened their mouths to cry out but nothing happened.

'Ah, there you are,' said Mrs D emerging from the bushes with Echtra, and without further ado she walked straight past Jack and Dundee, drew back the curtain, and stepped through.

Chapter Nine

Fianna

Their journey to the Lake had not been easy. Jack looked as though he had brought half the forest with him. Dundee was in a similar state, his suit covered in dirt, his jacket torn at the sleeve. Echtra's white vest and black trousers were streaked with the dust of the road, and Mrs D's summer hat was beyond repair.

At first they struggled to see anything. The Lake was in darkness, the sun, its only source of light, momentarily hidden by a passing cloud. Then the sun's rays swung down through the gaps in the vined ceiling, and suddenly there they were, like Gods in the wild, stretched out on huge rocks around the edge of the Lake, as if they had been waiting for them.

Nothing could have prepared them for coming face to face with the Fianna. Never before had they seen such startlingly beautiful people. The power of their energy, within the confines of their vined surroundings, was so overpowering that for a moment their spirits, which had been cramped up for so long in human form, rose up and had a good stretch.

Finn was the first to come forward. He stood over

seven feet tall, and was almost twice the width of Jack and Dundee. He was conventionally handsome, his eyes a glorious grey blue, and his hair, which fell in great waves at his shoulders, matched the colour of the sun, and was so bright it was almost blinding.

'We heard you shook the City awake,' said Finn, addressing the lady in charge.

'I ruffled a few feathers,' said Mrs D, who had to put her sunglasses on to look at him.

'What news of the Fairy Queen,' he enquired.

'She's missing, unprotected,' replied Mrs D. 'And there's another problem. The Key to the City is gone.'

'Yes, we heard,' said Finn. He gave her one of his sunny smiles. 'Don't worry. We'll find her, and the Key.'

That was it. Finn had agreed to join them. Mrs D smiled her thanks. The quest had begun.

Finn greeted Echtra, who he clearly knew, and when he had finished giving the ladies their due attention, he turned to Jack and Dundee.

'It is good work,' he said, as if they had achieved something of great worth. 'Good work indeed.'

As Finn spoke he placed his huge hands on their shoulders, and they could feel the warmth of his nature. It was as if they had come home. Tears sprang to their eyes which they were unable to hold back. It was an overwhelming moment they were at a loss to understand.

Then they heard someone laugh. It was Fergus, the poet. He was coming towards them with Diarmait, who had the beauty of a girl. The sight of them up close took their breath away. The warriors threw their arms around Jack and Dundee like they were long lost brothers. Mac the giant appeared behind them, which was a shock, then Diorruing the Seer, who had been keeping his distance. Diorruing waited until the camaraderie had died down and then ushered them away like a princely guide towards the left of the falls where they joined a secret path that led into the Fianna camp.

Jack and Dundee stumbled into the camp like children who had inadvertently fallen into the pages of a story book. The mythical warriors were real - fiction had become fact - and all the facts they had been told before were now completely fictitious!

In the clearing were at least twenty men in combat, some were attending to their weapons, others were returning from the hunt. Each man as fine as the next. Some of the warriors wore the jewels of their forefathers - rings of gold on their fingers and at their ears, jewelled belts around their waists, and bracelets at their wrists.

Finn's favoured hounds bounded forward to greet them. Dundee recalled their names, Bran and Sceolang, from his books. The dogs raced ahead into the centre of the camp where the visitors were met by a team of men and women who had been with the Fianna for centuries. They sat on giant logs around a camp fire where they were served food from the spit and given copious amounts of red wine, which the Fianna seemed to have in limitless supply.

It was sometime after supper, and the night had drawn in, before Finn spoke of the quest.

'Have you any idea where your friend, the Fairy Queen, may have gone?'

'No, but she would never abandon the inhabitants of the City,' said Mrs D, taking out one of her fancy hankies to dab her eyes. 'She believes in them you see. Knows all their dreams by heart.'

'Do you think she stole the Key?' asked Diarmait, once Mrs D had managed to compose herself.

'I cannot say for sure,' replied Mrs D, truthfully. 'She's certainly not the type to hatch a plot. Then again, if an opportunity to seize the Key presented itself outside her bedroom window, then she would likely take it.'

'Aife is set on finding her, whether she has the Key or not,' Finn reminded them.

'Perhaps someone else has taken both the Key, and the Fairy Queen,' suggested Fergus.

Finn nodded. 'It's possible she may have been taken hostage.'

'Hostage?' gasped Echtra.

Even Mrs D looked worried. There were a whole host of possible suspects, none of whom anyone in their right mind would wish to spend any length of time with.

'She's perfectly safe,' said Diorruing, fed up being ignored. 'She's taking tea on Scathach Island.'

Finn patted him heartily on the shoulder, and Diorruing managed a slight smile at the crumb of attention.

'Diarmait,' ordered Finn. Diarmait was up before Finn had finished the sentence. 'Get word to Angus, we'll meet him at the Bridge at dawn.'

There were no sleeping quarters in the camp, but Mrs D insisted that she and Echtra were given a windbreak, out of sight of all the male hormones. They chose a spot nearest the horses, which left Mac out on a limb. Mac, who was permanently on duty as Protector, settled his bear-like body close to the fire by Jack and Dundee, and promptly fell asleep.

Jack and Dundee, who had been given Mrs D's tartan rug as a blanket, were wide awake, drinking wine, and staring at Diorruing, who was the last to leave the fire.

Diorruing simply refused to conform to the elements around him. He was dressed for the palace as opposed to the wilds of the forest. His hair was short, smart and shiny. The collar of his white shirt was fastened high at the neck. His jacket was silken gold, embroidered with the symbols of the Seer. His lower half was in keeping with the rest of the men, the high boots of a hunter, his calves and hips bound by leather straps for the purpose of carrying weapons, even though he had none.

If the Fianna had all the virtues then Diorruing had all the faults. He was vain and arrogant, impatient with lesser beings. Dismissive and ungrateful to his comrades who had a tendency to be over protective of him - his second sight often blurring his vision, making him the most vulnerable.

Dundee, who knew the Fianna by heart, had brought Jack up to date with everything he knew about the warriors, including the visionary abilities of Finn's royal looking Seer.

Jack was in awe of the warrior prince. He had never met anyone as high and mighty as Diorruing before, and was just building up the courage to ask whether he could see into their futures.

Dundee however, who was anxious to learn everything he could about their new world, dove in first.

'Who is Angus?'

'Angus is a God,' said Diorruing, omitting to give Angus his full title. 'He looks after all twelve regions in this realm - the realm of 'Struggle and Evolution,' added Diorruing, before they could ask. 'The Fianna defend the borders. Angus and his entourage will be touring the realm just after dawn tomorrow. *They* will fly us out to Scathach Island.'

'Fly!' exclaimed Dundee.

'Yes,' said Diorruing bluntly. 'As I said, Angus is a God.'

'Where's Scathach Island?' asked Jack, desperate to say something to Diorruing, ignoring Dundee who had turned pale.

'Scathach Island lies outside the border of this realm, at the edge of a huge chasm. It is the dwelling place of Scathach, an Amazon Queen who happens to be Aife's nemesis. We'll be quite safe there.'

Diorruing then rose up, intent on bidding them good night.

'Can you see into our futures?' asked Jack, blurting it out before Diorruing could leave.

'It is impossible to say,' said the Seer, backing away from the fire. 'One day it is one future, the next day another. You are without purpose. If we are without purpose then we shall be blown around, like the wind.'

Jack fell asleep almost at once, but Dundee was tossing and turning, his mind racing. He had always been fascinated by the stories of Finn and his Fianna, and now here he was, amongst them.

'It was like being with old pals. Old god-like pals,' thought Dundee.

Seconds later someone entered the camp.

The horses reared up, almost trampling the windbreak and the ladies, alerting Mac. The other warriors flew across the camp, completely forgetting they had visitors. Jack took a kick in the back from someone's boot running into him. Dundee tried to avoid another, but rolled into the fire, setting his hair alight. Jack grabbed hold of Mrs D's rug, threw it over Dundee, and began rolling him around like a tartan sausage roll. By the time Dundee had emerged from the blanket the panic was over and the intruder, who had burst into the camp on horseback, had dismounted and was waiting for the approaching Finn.

Dundee pulled himself free of the blanket, elbowed

Jack out of the way, pushed the singed hair out of his eyes and looked up. It was a young woman - one he would never forget. Fresh and wild from her gallop through the trees. Her cheeks were flushed, her eyes dark blue and fearless, her hair as long and black as the mane of her horse. She turned to Finn and uttered the dreaded words.

'They're here.'

Chapter Ten

The Amazons

They flew in over the Bridge. Flocks of raven haired beauties - winged jezebels - born from the loins of the finest warriors. They landed in the woods in small groups and set up camps, feasting on animals and birds. One group was less than half a mile away from the Fianna camp and they had catch - three young men who had been frolicking on a grassy meadow in some far off land, and had been plucked from the ground by what they assumed were winged demons.

The young men lay in the dirt, untethered but paralysed with fear at the edge of the camp. The Amazons fed as their young captives were dragged into the centre, and under the light of the fire they were stripped and bathed in strange scented oils by hand maidens who were adept at using their skills to stimulate them. It was a ritual for all male captives. But these were ordinary men, unworthy of the attention of the Amazon warriors. Fit only as food for their servants the Baobhan, hideous succubus, with brown bird-like bodies. And as the hand maidens drew back the Baobhan moved in. The young men lay naked and helpless, their loins on fire, their minds recoiling at the monstrous reality of their plight. And they knew they were about to die, horribly.

At the Fianna camp news of the Amazons arrival was being imparted to Finn.

'Scouts,' said the young woman, her mouth still dry from her gallop through the woods. She was given water and took it gratefully before continuing.

'Twenty or more, they're close, and they have captives.'

'Then we must go to their aid,' said Finn.

The girl nodded, leaping effortlessly onto her horse as they prepared to leave the camp.

Finn headed towards the horses with Fergus and his Seer. 'Diorruing. Take the ladies with you. We'll meet at the Bridge.'

There was no time to lose. Mac, who was in charge of the new recruits, beckoned Jack and Dundee forward and, grabbing hold of their collars like they were rabbits, he hurled them onto the back of the nearest steeds, before mounting his own. And they were off.

They hurtled back along the same path that the young woman had come in on, then took a short cut along a narrow winding track, where they spent most of the time with their heads down, trying to avoid the low overhanging branches. At one point they were forced to stop where the path had been blocked by a fallen tree, and Mac was called forward to clear the way. A task he enjoyed in the same way an ogre might enjoy clearing the back garden by hurling everything over a neighbouring fence.

Whilst they waited for Mac to clear the path Dundee took the opportunity to study the girl at their lead. She was the double of Ann Angel, and Dundee was doubly smitten.

'Her name is Echraide,'said Fergus, who had been watching him. 'It means horse rider. She's one of our messengers.'

'She too bonny to be a warrior.'

'Ah Dundee, you've lost your heart already,' laughed Fergus. 'And us only a moment into the adventure.'

They had almost reached the Amazon camp when there was a huge roar of wings above them, as if every bird in the forest had taken flight. It was followed by an eerie silence.

'They've gone,' said Finn, stopping to dismount.

'That's good isn't it?' asked Jack, hopefully to Fergus, who seemed the friendliest.

'No.' said Mac, bluntly.

'It means Aife their Queen is on her way in,' explained Fergus.

'Then why are we stopping?' asked Jack, as Mac dragged them off their horses.

'We're stopping to check that the men we came to rescue are dead.'

'Dead!'

'The Amazons hunt only with the intention of

progressing of their race. Only warriors are spared for their seed, held captive sometimes for years while the Amazons have their wicked way with them. Then they are executed.'

'What a way to go,' said Dundee.

'Not really,' said Mac, pointing to something on the ground that no man would wish to be without.

The fear of the victims and the end they had endured still lingered in the air as they entered the camp and it hit them like a hammer to the stomach. The remains of the feast lay all around them – blood, entrails, flesh and feathers. Every instinct in their bodies was telling them to flee. Somehow Jack and Dundee managed to hold steady until Finn, satisfied there was no-one left to save, called them in.

But Mac had spotted one of the Baobhan at the edge of the camp still feeding on the remains of a hand. She drew back her wings when she saw him, as if she meant to fly.

'No!' cried Finn, realising Mac's intent. Mac flew at her in a fury and killed her with his first blow. Her body shuddered as her spirit left her and it called in the rest. They felt the tremor in the air.

'Move!' cried Finn.

They were back on their horses, hurtling through the woods at an incredible pace. Jack and Dundee somehow managed to keep up, but they lost the Fianna on a turn, raised their heads, forgot to duck, and both of them hit the ground. They picked themselves up and ran back to the path where the Baobhan found them.

Mac heard them fall. He swerved his horse to the left, drew wide and was back on the road behind them in seconds. Jack and Dundee were frozen to the spot. The Baobhan were landing on the path ahead of them, one by one - and they were seriously hideous – brown, like birds, with pointed faces, tiny black eyes, and beaky mouths dripping with blood. This was it. They were going to be eaten - by blood sucking bird-women! Just in time they were grabbed by the collar and lifted off the ground. They struggled as they flew through the air towards the Baobhan who were kicked aside by Mac's giant boots, and they were through.

There was no time to stop. Mac carried them in his fists all the way to the Bridge. The others watched from the railings at Mac's incredible feat of strength as he hurled them onto the wooden planks.

Jack and Dundee scrambled to their feet, their eyes fixed on the forest, expecting the Baobhan to appear. It was a while before they realised everyone else on the Bridge was looking in the opposite direction, and they turned around.

It was just like the picture in the sitting room at the cottage - a huge dark weather cloud - and it was heading straight for them.

'The Amazons,' said Echtra, as Jack and Dundee appeared by her side.

Mrs D folded her arms and tutted loudly, muttering to herself.

'Where *was* Angus. He was always late.'

Chapter Eleven

Scathach Island

It was true. Angus *was* always late but to be fair he was rather busy being a God, and had never quite gotten the hang of moving between the timelessness of the divine and the restricted time frames of the non-divine. Anything he couldn't take a good run and a jump at made him feel quite claustrophobic. Angus needed space.

God of love, youth, beauty and anything else that took his fancy Angus was one of the more unusual gods, preferring a pin striped suit with matching waistcoat to fancy silken robes, and had recently taken to carrying a briefcase. He would have fitted in rather well in Stress City if it hadn't been for his overzealous attitude and the width of his entourage.

Angus's entourage was over a mile wide. It consisted of four swans, who had been with him from the beginning and always circled him in flight. His soul mate Caer a swan maiden, who he had seen in a dream and insisted upon having. Hundreds of musicians, make-up artists, camera men, sound light and heating engineers, and on occasion Angus's warriors who carried out heroic deeds in Angus's area of responsibility; Regions one to twelve.

In addition to being a God Angus was also protector to a great many heroes, and stepfather to Diarmait, who, like most sons in bother, had called on his father for a lift. Angus was more than happy to help out. He adored Diarmait, and Finn and his Fianna. In fact he wouldn't have minded hanging out on Scathach Island himself for a few days, but his Regions were out of balance again and he had a number of quests to fulfil before lights out.

'There they are,' said Caer, swooping up behind him.

Then she fell back with the rest and Angus opened himself up to the light. To achieve this he had to ditch his film star ego and his entourage who would only weigh him down and might break the connection mid-flight. It wouldn't go down well with Diarmait if he dropped them.

Back at the Bridge everyone's eyes were focussed on the dark Amazon cloud, apart from Dundee, whose fear of heights had kicked in, and Jack who was trying to pry his hands away from the railings.

Dundee had frozen. It had happened before, when they were in the North on a guided tour of the Abbey with the Cormacs. Dundee had been gripped with terror at the top of one of the towers, and had to be carried out, and across the road to the *Hootsman* to be defrosted.

Dundee had always had trouble with heights, anything higher than the third floor and he was looking for the exit.

Mrs D stood next to them, rummaging around in her giant handbag. She pulled out a couple of scarves, handing one each to Jack and Dundee. Then she pulled out another for Echtra, and finally a much larger one for herself. She replaced her summer hat with a thick woolly one, which was also old yellow, and pulled on a pair of matching winter mittens.

Mrs D hated flying. It was always cold, regardless of the weather, and extremely inconvenient when it came to spur of the moment landings. Anyone who hadn't flown before had no idea how uncomfortable it was. No idea at all.

'If only we could fly like the birds,' *Emma's* customers were fond of saying. 'Wouldn't it be fun.'

'Not with a North Easterly wind blowing up your summer dress it wouldn't,' she would reply.

The customers would laugh out loud at her sparkling wit, but Mrs D knew what she was talking about! If she had to fly then she always flew alone, and with as many hot water bottles as she could carry.

Mrs D spotted the break in the clouds before anyone else and was not in the least bit surprised when the sun dropped down, undercut the Amazon cloud, and headed straight for them.

A flock of heavenly geese that had passed through Region one the previous day with no more than a passing glance at the weakened state of the spirits below found themselves illuminated in an Arc of Divine Light as

Angus made an open attack on the gravitational pull of the earth. The earth fought back. For a few moments nothing happened. Then gravity, a little shocked by the sudden turn of events, let go.

Region one was the lowest Region in the first realm, at the centre of 'Struggle and Evolution' where the level of gravitational pull on physical form was at its highest. In the second realm, 'Triumph over Evil,' gravity was far weaker, which was why Scathach had located her Island there, in full sight of the border, so that warriors who had heard the call might chance a leap of faith across the great chasm. Some died trying. Those who succeeded were trained in ancient martial arts. Scathach turned warriors into heroes.

Only the chosen few were able to access Scathach Island via the front entrance, and as Scathach Castle faced the sea, this was only possible by flying in. A white square had been built for that purpose in the grounds, between the Castle and the sea wall. Ordinarily it was used for training but today the white square and Castle grounds were warrior free. Scathach had important visitors.

Scathach Castle was the tallest, fairest, rudest castle in the Otherworld. Outrageously so when it came to common blood, sometimes refusing to show herself at all, which was rather odd if you were expecting to see a fairy tale castle and were faced instead with an empty space. When it came to visiting Gods however she was out, in all her glorious splendour. Pale grey in colour, with twelve cylindrical turrets that were so high the tops hit the clouds. It had four towers at each point of the compass, and a glossy red door in the middle, which was never used. Access was reached by a wide stone staircase to the right of the building, which had been adorned that morning with a sea of green vines and red roses.

In the square a hundred of Scathach's highest ranking females were preening themselves, watched over from the edge of the woods by the rest of Scathach's army. Each girl was as stunning as the next: small, slim and barefoot, with innocent blue eyes and short cropped golden hair, almost angelic, but for their battle scars. Scathach's girls were no angels. They were Amazon bred, highly skilled in the ancient martial arts. All held the mark of the dragon - a blue tattoo which ran from their necks to the base of their spines, the tail end sweeping around their hips, ending way below the navel.

Scathach, their Queen, had no such markings, and her skin was battle free. She was however female and like the rest of her army she had been at her dressing table for most of the morning. Angus was well liked.

The whole of the West tower had been adapted for Scathach's personal use. Like the three other towers, it was cylindrical in shape, but with a romantic interior - pale blue, with matching furniture, and a spiral staircase with gold trim that ran all the way up to the top of the tower. This was closed off to visitors. Some say this was where Scathach held the men who bed her. She was after all an Amazon Queen.

Scathach checked her reflection in the mirror.

Her bedroom was on the third floor, the only room in the tower with a balcony and French windows. There were three hounds at her feet, who would do anything to please her, and only ever saw her sweetest disposition, unlike her army who periodically experienced the worst. Scathach was seldom gentle with her girls – yet much revered, and courteous to her friends of course, and divine guests.

She was about to draw away from the mirror to check on their progress, when the shadow of a man flew across the glass.

'Dark, but fair reflected,' thought Scathach. It changed her mood. Then the dogs leapt up and bounded out onto the balcony.

Angus had entered the region.

They had been warned to expect a bumpy ride. Smooth flights and safe landings were beyond the comprehension of an egocentric, self-obsessed, red hot personality like Angus whose godly mind was capable, at the flick of a switch, of locking itself into the thrill of the moment thereby blocking out whatever dangers lay behind, before, above or beneath him, hence the need for his entourage who always watched his back.

Angus maintained their position in the heights above the clouds until they had passed over the border and then he dropped down suddenly, so that their first sight of the Castle was without preamble - a kick in the eye. He hovered there for a few moments in the breeze allowing them to take it all in, then he lit up his cigar which was a sign they should prepare themselves for landing.

They hurtled after him, pulled along effortlessly by the magnetism of Angus as he threw them into a dive.

They almost hit the sea!

Caer had to pull them up at the last minute forcing Angus to bump land them onto the lawn. Then he veered sharply to the left, somehow managing to avoid the front of the Castle altogether, and grabbing hold of one of the turrets to change direction, he continued on, towards the East.

The dumped passengers lay motionless on the lawn for a few minutes, enjoying the feeling of being back on solid ground.

Mrs D would happily have stayed there all day if it hadn't been for Finn and his warriors persuading her to her feet. They drew Mrs D and her brood; Echtra, Jack and a frozen Dundee, towards a sunny spot by the sea wall where Diorruing was waiting for them, looking very relaxed having spent most of the flight elsewhere with his eyes shut.

A few feet away in the middle of the white square one hundred golden haired females were on their knees, heads bowed to the ground in reverence to Angus who had continued on his way without so much as a by your leave.

Dundee could feel himself beginning to thaw - and it wasn't just the sun. This golden army would have stirred the loins of any man, free or devoted. Scathach's barefoot warriors were at the peak of their sexuality, and whilst their preference was usually towards the female of the species, it was not unheard of for them to feast on male tastes. They held their positions, eyes to the ground, their golden heads shining brightly in the midday sun, awaiting the arrival of their Queen, who suddenly appeared behind them on the vine covered steps at the side entrance to the Castle.

Scathach came towards them without pomp or ceremony. Her hair was short and gold in colour like that of her soldiers but it grew in tiny curls, cut back high above the brow, her beauty in no need of the shade of it. She was so incredibly striking that Jack and Dundee were unable to take their eyes from her. She wore no jewels or crown, for those that reach the heavenly heights have little need to show it. Her eyes were of the lightest blue, like none they had ever seen before, her skin pale and flawless, her cheeks and full lips rose stained. She was dressed like a tom boy, although she was clearly a woman. Her vest clung tight around her breasts and her slim black slacks, which covered her length from waist to heel, did nothing to hide the shapeliness of her hips and legs.

Mrs D quickly pulled off her old yellow woolly hat which was miraculously still on her head after the flight and stepped forward. Jack and Dundee were shocked to see the Amazon Queen bow in reverence to *her*. Then Scathach rose and led Mrs D away towards the Castle, indicating to Echtra and Echraide that they should follow her. When the women were safely inside Scathach Castle shut its doors, scattering the golden army into the air, leaving the men alone.

'What happened?' cried Jack in dismay.

'No men are allowed inside the walls of Scathach Castle,' explained Finn, mounting one of the horses that had been left for them at the edge of the woods. The other warriors followed. 'This is Amazon territory. Men are considered lesser beings, fit only for the expansion of their race.'

Jack looked surprised, even though they had already been told this.

Mac looked impatient.

Jack quickly mounted the nearest horse before Mac could man handle him onto it. Dundee followed and they set off through the woods.

'Why did Scathach bow to Mrs D?' asked Dundee, as they drew away from the Castle.

'D is a Goddess,' said Finn.

'A Goddess!' cried Jack and Dundee in unison.

'The Goddess of Destiny,' said Diorruing, surprised they didn't know.

'You must be exhausted after your flight,' said Scathach, addressing Mrs D as they entered the inner sanctum of

157

the West tower. 'Your rooms are ready. Shall we have tea before retiring?'

The question was clearly rhetorical. Scathach swept off along the corridor, past the elaborate spiral staircase on the right, through the pale blue double doors on the left, and into a large sitting room.

Mrs D, Echtra and Echraide followed her through the double doors and across the sitting room to two huge windows which overlooked the grounds. The women watched as the men took to their horses and disappeared off into the woods.

'Shall we sit?' offered Scathach, indicating towards the seating.

They searched around. The furniture seemed tiny and too fragile to sit on. In the end Mrs D chose a two seater antique blue velvet sofa facing the fireplace. It creaked as she lowered her behind, but held steady. The two young women, who had taken to being at her side, chose matching chairs either side of it.

Scathach chose a golden armchair at the corner of the hearth which matched the colour of her hair. Almost at once an army of girls rushed in. The fire was lit and a banquet of delicacies placed before them.

As they took supper Scathach and her honoured guest discussed the issues of the day.

'The Fairy Queen of dreams *was* here...' said Scathach, in answer to an earlier question. Mrs D had enquired as to the whereabouts of her friend as soon as they had entered the Castle.

'But she left the Island this morning... said something about going to visit her husband in Falias.'

'Her husband?' asked Echraide, looking to her new friend.

'The Dollmaker,' replied Echtra, with a smile.

'He may be her husband but he never leaves that shop,' said Mrs D, struggling with the dainty tea cup and saucer. She managed to take a sip. 'Thankfully they're at the stage in their marriage when they can live apart, and still be together.'

Echraide looked surprised. She hadn't realised there was such a stage.

'His shop is in Falias isn't it?' enquired Scathach politely.

'Yes, it's on Old Street. Would you believe it, we were in Falias this morning. I suppose we should head back there,' said Mrs D, thoughtfully.

'At least we know the Fairy Queen is safe and hasn't been taken hostage,' said Echtra.

Mrs D smiled. 'That's true. In fact she doesn't appear to be on the run at all. I don't suppose she mentioned a Key?'

Scathach shook her head. 'You should stay here tonight and rest, in the morning you can resume your search refreshed.'

Mrs D agreed. She was exhausted. She picked up her giant handbag and heaved herself up off the sofa.

'I hear Aife has the City heavily guarded,' said Scathach, rising from her chair, keen to hear news of her nemesis before Mrs D retired. 'Does she still have the net?'

'No. She has a Governor. Addison Bruce.'

'A man!' Scathach was shocked, it was unheard of. Then she remembered the image she had seen in the mirror. 'Is he fair headed?' Mrs D nodded.

'I had a vision of him this morning. He has a dark side. A Shadow,' warned Scathach.

'Yes. We all do my dear, and one day we shall have to face it.'

Mrs D was escorted to the third floor by an army of girls. She was offered a choice of bedrooms and chose the nearest, which happened to be the smallest. For once she dispensed with the need for her curlers, and was asleep as soon as her head touched the pillow.

Echraide took the room next to her, ignoring the female escorts who had been sent to her aid. She shut the door, and threw herself on the bed, anxious to be on her way. More used to a bed of moss than a bed of feathers and was expecting a sleepless night. But she had forgotten about the magic of Scathach Castle where it was possible to relive a whole lifetime in just one night, and before she knew it she had drifted off into memories of a distant past.

She had been born the daughter of a King, at a time when the notoriety of the Fianna was at its peak. Her beauty and bounty were limitless, and for this she was greatly envied by the people of the Kingdom, who considered beauty and riches to be the key to happiness. But Echraide was not happy. She was bored. She had been bored since the day she was old enough to walk - the day the palace had been turned into a battleground, her father almost broken from the strain of continually having to rein her in. But she was not to be tamed and by her late twenties was worse than ever. The King was glad he'd had the good sense to arrange her betrothal at birth to a King from a distant land. Her father had since discovered that the chosen groom, the King of the Cormac's, was legendarily bad news. But as the King had told the Queen at the time, he had no intention of stopping the marriage now.

Then, on the day before his daughter was due to meet her betrothed, Finn and his Fianna arrived at the palace. The King welcomed them with open arms, for a sudden visitation from the defenders of the realm was considered a sign of great fortune. They dined together that evening in the great hall, their table, already set for the finest nobles of the land to celebrate the festival of *Samhain*, now extended to cater for a further thirty men at arms.

The Queen sat to the King's right, beautifully dressed in her finest garments, calmly conversing with their honoured guests, as if dining with thirty heroes was

Samhain: ancient festival 31st October/1st November – end/beginning of the Celtic year.

the norm. A few hours earlier she had been lying on the floor in a faint, surrounded by her ladies in waiting, who, whilst empathising with the Queen's dilemma of having to rearrange the seating plan with only three hours to go, did not believe the problem to be insurmountable, and were desperate to return to their quarters to make ready for the army of eligible men. Their levels of frustration and desperation for male company had been heightened by the fact that all the eligible men of the kingdom had been killed in a battle several years before, and their closets were filled to the brim with dresses and shoes that had never seen the light. It wasn't just the fact that the Fianna were male, or eligible, or rumoured to be handsome. It was that up until now no-one had ever actually seen them. Their reputation was legendary - Finn's was almost god-like.

Echraide sat on her father's left, in silence for once, completely in awe of their guests. She had almost fallen over her mother earlier, strewn across the floor, and had enquired what all the fuss was about. When the ladies told her about the last minute arrivals she had adopted her usual 'so what' approach and had purposefully chosen the drabbest dress she could find in an act of defiance. Now the great Finn himself was beside her and she was embarrassed. The giant warriors towered over her, and everyone else, filling the great hall with their strength of purpose, and fine characters. News of the arrival of the Fianna at the palace had spread like wildfire - the nobility of the land had been given plenty of time to compose themselves, but still they were unprepared. Their usual arrogance and haughty manners cast to the wind.

It was a very special evening and the Queen, who was delighted that her daughter had behaved so graciously towards their guests, informed the King that she believed Echraide had finally turned a corner.

By the morning Echraide was gone. Her heart set on becoming one of the warriors herself, she swore her allegiance to the Fianna alone in the forest before dawn, then she headed North for Scathach Island.

When she reached the edge of the border and saw the great chasm her heart sank. It was a leap of faith. One she did not feel ready to attempt. But as she had left her old self back at the kingdom, and had no wish to don that deathly form again, she stayed where she was at the edge of the chasm. With the high turrets of Scathach Castle in view, she set her heart on being there, with no other thought than this.

Over the years Scathach's army grew used to the sight of her. In the summer months Echraide spent every day at the chasm, leaving her post only to hunt for food or take shelter from the rains. But in the winter weather she was forced back into the woods. At first Scathach's girls considered she might be one of Aife's spies. Her hair was dark, her body slender, and her mood solemn. But it was clear she could not fly and Aife's girls would not have dared to come alone, so close to the Castle. They informed Scathach who gave instruction that she was to be watched. They did as they were asked. First out of sight, from the heights of the trees, watching over her as she slept through the night, but as the months drew on they came closer, bolder in the summer warmth. At times they forced themselves upon her and she would awake to find herself in a hot sweat, her body burning from the touch of her fairy-like lovers.

Scathach waited, until the girl was almost dead, and then she took her. Echraide remained at the Castle for many years until Scathach, who worried the girl might live out the rest of her days on the Island without any adventure at all, began to send her on errands under the guise of messenger. But Echraide would always return. She was happy on the Island, her ambitions to become a part of the Fianna almost forgotten, until the day Scathach called for her to take a message to Finn. He was not easy to find. She began by calling on all the great kingdoms of the land but no-one had seen sight of the Fianna for years. Then she recalled their passion for hunting and took to the forests - yet still there was no sign of them. Then one day, having ventured too far into the deep undergrowth, she stumbled into a vined clearing, and there they were, Finn and his men relaxing around the edge of a black water Lake. The first man she saw was Keevan of the curling locks, and it was clear from his expression that she had been expected.

Echraide opened her eyes, half asleep in the bedroom. There was a light shining in under the door and footsteps on the stairs. She turned away towards the window, and fell back into the dream.

It was Scathach descending from the top floor where she had just left Echtra asleep. She had insisted that her handmaidens assist the girl in undressing. Scathach had watched - keen to see the body of the doll herself. She was not disappointed. The doll's body was more perfect than Scathach's own, every arc, curve and chamber, sculpted to perfection by the Dollmaker. As Echtra slipped in between the bed sheets Scathach was tempted to slip in and spoil her. But instead she turned, and swept out of the room.

The men headed deeper and deeper into the forest. The Fianna warriors never tired, and no matter how hard they tried to keep up, Jack and Dundee kept losing sight of them. Diarmait had to continually gallop back to urge them on.

'Are we there yet?' asked Jack, for the umpteenth time.

'Not far, it's up ahead,' said Diarmait, amused.

'What's so special about this lake?' asked Dundee, who was just as fed up as Jack, but was trying not to show it.

'It's got Scathach's golden virgins in it,' said Diarmait laughing when he saw their faces light up. 'It's tradition. A warriors' welcome.'

'What sort of welcome?' asked Dundee, feeling flushed.

'The friendship of their thighs.'

The Tattooed Dragon

A hundred golden headed virgin warriors descended into the white square. They jostled for position as the last few stragglers fell in, like golden haired fairies fluttering down from the darkened skies to join the rest. They settled into silent meditation. A ritual before the dance they would perform in honour of the Tattooed Dragon. The dance was long and slow with periods of great stillness, for it was in the stillness that some passed into the being of the other.

'The snake needs virgin breath to stir it, and the heat from their throats to raise its wanton head.'

'Lift me up!'

The Dragon rose and held the air, then flew off towards the lake.

Chapter Twelve

Donn of the Dead

'Och, ma heed,' said Dundee, attempting to sit up. It was too much. He fell back down to earth again, hitting Jack who was curled up next to him with his eyes shut, trying to hold on to the memories of their night of overflowing wine and virgins for as long as possible.

Dundee checked their surroundings from his position on his back. The two of them appeared to be in some sort of clearing, although he had no memory of how they had ended up there, the alcohol having dulled his brain.

The sun was out. The birds were singing. He tried again, and this time he made it.

'Jack,' croaked Dundee, dehydrated from the drink. 'Jack.'

Jack covered his ears. He couldn't see what was going on but he could tell by the tone of Dundee's voice that it wasn't good.

'Jack. Jack. Jack!' Dundee's voice was low but insistent.

'What!'

'We're not alone.'

168

Jack opened his eyes. They were surrounded by small men with round glasses and round faces. They were all wearing the same dark suits, and were grinning at them like maniacs.

Jack grabbed hold of Dundee's arm in a panic. They scrambled around in the leaves for a while, attempting to run away whilst still on the ground. Eventually they found their feet, and ran.

'Quick!' said Dundee, leading the way out of the clearing onto a dirt track. They raced through the woods for what seemed like forever but it was only a few hundred yards. Jack began to slow, his hangover kicking in.

'They're right behind us!' cried Dundee, sensing something at his heels.

But Jack had given up, the searing pain in his head overriding his fear of the men. 'It's not them.'

'What?'

'It's not the men. It's a dog!' yelled Jack.

Dundee turned his head to check before slowing to a stop. It was definitely a dog. He put his hands on his knees and bent forward trying to get his breath back. The black Scottie with eighties sideburns, raced towards him and sat down obediently as his feet.

'You gave me a right fright...' said Dundee to the dog.

Jack sauntered towards them, his hands on his aching head.

'That's weird. It looks just like that black Scottie at

home.'

'What black Scottie?'

'Have you nae seen it? It's been hanging around the City.'

'It's off!' cried Jack, as the dog suddenly skirted around Dundee's feet and ran off along the dirt track.

'Quick. Follow it. It could be our only way out of here.' They were off again at a jog.

They followed the dog in the hope that it would take them back to the Castle but instead it led them into a Labyrinth, and they were so busy following the dog they didn't realise they were in it until it was too late. The sides of the Labyrinth were incredibly high, giant hedges which were twice the height of Jack and Dundee, and they were unable to see anything over the top of them. Even if they had it wouldn't have done them any good. They were lost in the forest, in the middle of a Labyrinth, and they had lost sight of the dog. Could it get any worse?

'I hope those weird little men didn't follow us,' said Dundee, checking behind them.

'I know! Did you see the Tupperware they were carrying?'

'Tupperware?' asked Dundee, assuming it was a nickname for some sort of weapon he hadn't heard of.

'Tupperware. You know. The plastic boxes you put sandwiches in.'

'That's even worse.' Dundee looked seriously worried. 'They were trying to poison us!'

'What do you mean?'

'That's the sort of thing that happens over here Jack. The hero is tempted into having something to eat or drink, like the leprechauns in the story.'

Jack wished Dundee would stop going on about leprechauns, he was getting spooked.

'What should we do? Should we keep going?'

'I don't know. We could be heading into a dead end, or some sort of trap.'

'Should we head back then, the way we came in?'

'I don't know where we came in Jack!' cried Dundee, frustrated that he always had to take the lead whilst Jack wandered aimlessly around. 'We're lost!'

Dundee used both his hands to push the hair back out of his eyes, an indication that he was losing his temper. 'Unless you left any crumb trails or some string we could follow,' he added sarcastically.

A vision of the little men standing at the entrance blocking their way suddenly popped into Dundee's head. 'Let's carry on for a bit, see what happens.'

They followed the path until the circles got so small it felt like they were standing in one spot but still going around, like a spinning top.

'Och, that's it. I've had enough,' said Dundee, collapsing in a heap on the ground, his head pounding, his stomach rumbling.

'We can't stop now. You never know what's round the next corner,' said Jack, using one of Mrs Snarlington-Darlington's favourite sayings.

171

'Oh aye. That's what you said at the last corner.' Dundee was unwilling to move.

Jack left Dundee where he was, and carried on until he ran out of corners. He had reached the centre.

'Ah, there you are,' said Diorruing, who was standing at the most central point of the Labyrinth with his arms folded and his head in the air, looking like a prince who was waiting for a couple of idiots.

Jack had never been so pleased to see anyone in his life. He staggered towards Diorruing as Dundee popped his head around the corner of the hedge.

'Did you find the Few?' asked Diorruing.

'The Few?' said Jack and Dundee in unison.

'Yes, I sent them along with your breakfast and directions of how to get here.'

Jack gave Dundee a look and shook his head. He was fed up with Dundee's paranoia. Now they had missed breakfast. Dundee's stomach grumbled his response.

'No matter,' said Diorruing indicating they should follow him.

It suddenly dawned on Jack and Dundee that there *was* no centre, no end to the maze. It just carried on and on in huge spirals deep below the earth.

'Where are we going?' asked Jack, dutifully following the Seer.

'To see Donn of the Dead.'

They walked a thousand steps or more, until they were dizzy. Then the earth ran out and they found themselves in mid-air at the top of a gigantic staircase. Dundee froze, and grabbed Jack's arm, in a vice like grip, but Jack was having none of it. He had seen the fires below, and was convinced they were descending into some kind of hell. There was no way he was losing sight of Diorruing now. But in his eagerness to follow the Seer Jack tripped up over the top step, and with Dundee still attached to his arm they hurtled down the giant staircase together. They missed hitting Diorruing who was three steps ahead of them and continued on, at an incredible pace. It seemed there was no end to it. Then they hit a flat bit at the half-way point. Jack managed to grab hold of one of the banister rails, leaving Dundee to continue his way down to the bottom.

Jack peered over the bannister. From his vantage point on the stairs he could see they were descending into some sort of town.

'Is this hell?' asked Jack, as Diorruing caught him up.

'No.' replied Diorruing.

'What about the fires and the graves?'

'They're just for effect.'

They continued down the second half of the staircase together until they reached the bottom where they found Dundee tending to his bruises.

The staircase ended in the middle of a perfectly normal street. Diorruing checked behind the giant staircase for cars and pedestrians before leading them across the road to a tree lined pavement.

The houses were hidden from view by a wall which had tiny wooden doors set into the brick, providing privacy for the Few who lived there. They continued along the pavement, and stopped half way down when they came to the largest door, which was open, and was being painted dark green by one of the Few who let them in.

Donn's house was a two storey old fashioned tenement building that had seen better days. The house was on their left, the garden on their right - an overgrown square of grass with a clothes line hanging over it and a few rusty pegs. A thin metal staircase faced them, and was the only route of access to Donn's door which was on the second floor at the top of the staircase.

Donn preferred to live in isolation, as far away as possible from the rest of the Gods, and so he had created a town for himself and the Few. The Few, who worked from home, were responsible for keeping the records of every soul in the Otherworld. Each man had his own personal library to maintain which housed the lifetimes of all the souls he had been given to oversee. The Few were record keepers, not decision makers. When a soul was up for review it was Donn who made the call. The Few never judged. The good, the bad, the indifferent, it was of no matter to them. A job was a job. And it was a good one at that. Of course they did work extremely hard. There were a never ending number of souls, culminating in a never ending amount of paper work. When the work became too much for them they replicated themselves. It was a simple process. Every Few was male. And every Few was a mirror image of himself, and all the other Fews.

The man who had opened the door led them up to the top of the metal staircase and indicated to the left, with a wave of his arm, that they should go straight in. The front door was open and Diorruing walked straight into the hallway, but Jack and Dundee hung around outside for a while. From where they were standing they could see into the gardens of the houses below where the Few were going about their daily chores. They were very business-like in their dark suits and round glasses; gardening, cleaning, hanging out the washing and fixing things on the lawn.

Eventually Jack and Dundee got bored and stepped into the hallway. By that time Donn and Diorruing were already chatting in the front room and so, unsure of what to do for the best, they hung around in the hallway listening in.

'It's hellishly difficult trying to balance the books,' said Donn, complaining to Diorruing over afternoon tea.

'We're always in the red. It's the karmic debt from the past weighing us down. And nobody's willing to take up the slack.' He helped himself to a custard cream.

'Present company excepted of course,' added Donn, referring to the great deeds of the Fianna.

Diorruing nodded in response, smiling politely at his host.

He had heard this many times before, Donn was apt

to repeat himself, but he had great sympathy with the God knowing only too well the burdens of the great. Diorruing was a regular visitor, preferring Donn to some of the other Gods. Like Angus who did everything to excess. Donn was far more down to earth. Not the sort of God to beat around the bush.

In the hallway Jack, who always had difficulty keeping still, had spotted a grandfather clock and was standing in front of it watching the hands which were moving backwards. He put his finger on the glass to show Dundee, and as he did so the hands stopped moving backwards and started moving forwards. Dundee quickly pulled Jack away from the clock before he could do any damage. Thankfully he was not responsible for the change in direction. The hands of the clock swung to the beat of the Gods, who were neither behind nor ahead, but were always languishing around, somewhere in the middle.

As they turned away from the clock towards the door of the sitting room Dundee caught a glimpse of Donn's bedroom and was shocked by the dainty décor, which in his opinion was far too delicate for a God of the Dead. But as he told Jack later, he suspected the housekeeper was probably responsible for all the lace.

They stood at the doorway and peered in.

The front room was no better. It was the sort of sitting room you would expect your grandparents to live in. It was small and square, with a window on the left, a picture of a black Scottie dog on the ledge, an old fashioned kitchenette on the right, and a fireplace at the far end. In the middle, taking up all the space, was an oblong table which had been set for mid-morning tea, and behind that a mantelpiece which had lots of photographs of Gods and Goddesses going about their godly duties, and several huge glass jars filled with notes.

'Come in. Come in,' said Donn, who had spotted them. He stood up as Jack and Dundee entered the room.

Jack and Dundee were completely in awe of Donn. They hadn't expected him to be friendly, and they certainly hadn't expected him to be covered in tattoos. He was huge, and had the longest shoes they had ever seen - black patent with pointed silver tips. His legs and arms were long but firm. He had huge biceps and fists with silver rings, a square head, a chiselled jaw and thick jet black hair that grew straight up, like grass.

They sat at the table filling their faces and staring at Donn. When they had finished someone scuttled into the room and cleared the table. They later discovered that this was Donn's housekeeper Aribellina, who had taken on the mammoth task of housekeeper for every house in town and could lay a table quicker than a mortal eye could come into focus.

'The Fairy Queen of dreams *was* here,' said Donn, returning to the conversation he had been having with Diorring. 'But she left the Island this morning - said something about going to visit her husband in Falias.'

'We've just come from there.'

'Yes, I see,' said Donn, who wasn't really listening.

177

He excused himself from the table, his attention caught by a bee that had suddenly hit the window.

'It's good to see you,' Donn was now staring out of the window with his back to them.

'It can get a little dull around here. Sometimes we watch the bees but most of them are repeats.'

Donn watched the bee who was struggling for survival down below on the lawn.

'Sorry,' he said, turning his attention back to his visitors. 'Did I say bees? I meant lives. Sometimes we watch the lives but most of them are repeats...'

Donn took a seat on his rocker chair by the window, and faced the television in the corner which was incredibly old fashioned - dark brown, with a long speaker at the bottom, a tiny screen, and three huge dials.

Jack was about to ask if they could watch some of the lives, but Donn was still in flow, and it was bad karma to interrupt a Deity.

'...Of course we keep a close eye on the Celts. Not all of them you understand, just the ones where we hold promissory notes.'

Diorruing pointed to the huge jars full of notes on the mantelpiece for the benefit of Jack and Dundee.

'It was the Druids who came up with that idea. They argued that heroes who were forced to do evil for the sake of the common good should be able to postpone their karmic debt, until some future good deed in the next life outweighed it. I agreed. Two thousand, three hundred and twenty two misdemeanours were wiped out in favour of these promissory notes.'

Donn began swinging backwards and forwards in his rocker chair, forgetting they were there for a moment.

'Of course they were never paid off,'

'Actually that's why we're here,' said Diorruing, a little embarrassed about the favour he had come to ask on Mrs D's behalf.

There was a knock on the door. 'Come,' said Donn.

It was one of the Few. Jack and Dundee immediately stood up, partly out of good manners, and partly because they wanted to see the little man close up.

The man came forward, ignoring the visitors, his eyes on the Deity in the rocker.

'Here are their records,' said the man, who was no higher than Donn's waist. He passed the files over then left.

Jack noticed Dundee's file was thicker than his.

'Burn them,' instructed Donn, passing the files over to Diorruing. 'Their past misdemeanours will be wiped out and they will be born again, as the men they once were. But with one caveat - if they do anything remotely un-heroic they will be thrown back onto the Island of Destiny, as idiots.

Diorruing took the records and nodded gratefully.

'The sisters will take you through.'

Donn reflected on their visit for a few moments. Then he stretched his tattooed arm out towards the three huge dials on the television, which were clearly marked past,

179

present and future, and switched it on.

The Funeral

It was a simple service. Just Diorruing, Dundee and Jack with no onlookers. Diorruing considered saying a few words on their behalf, but there wasn't a lot to say given that Jack and Dundee had always gone out of their way to avoid any acts of great purpose. Instead he maintained a respectful silence whist their records burned against the headstones.

Diorruing took a cup of good wine and poured it onto the earth, an ancient ritual to honour the spirit present at the time of their passing.

And they left their old selves behind.

Chapter Thirteen

Donn's TV
Flashback – 12,000 years earlier

There was no avoiding the man on the Bridge - his body strewn heavily over the railings, his head and neck dangling over the water, like some lovesick swan.

The girl considered staying where she was, but she was late for a meeting, and so she made her way towards him, as quietly as she could. The wood was worn and creaked beneath her feet, yet the noise did nothing to stir him.

She was almost at the other end, intent on walking straight past him, when suddenly his hands, which had been clamped around his head to alleviate the pain in his heart, slid onto the railings, and he turned around to face her.

'Is it you?' he asked, his vision temporarily blinded by the overhead sun.

'Who?' she replied.

'I thought you were someone else.' The man was clearly disappointed.

'Who?'

'What do you want?' he demanded, arrogantly,

ignoring her question.

'Want! I don't want anything.' She passed him by.

Fearful he might be left alone again Keevan grabbed what was left of his charm and threw it at her feet, but she saw the insincerity of his words and cast them aside.

'Don't go,' he begged.

'I'm in a rush. I'm late for a meeting.'

'What sort of meeting?'

'None of your business!' she cried, and without further ado the girl flew down the embankment and into the woods.

Keevan made his way back to the railings and adopted his previous position but it was no good, she had broken his concentration.

'Visualise the good and the bad will recede.' The elderly Seer had told him at the Inn that morning. Well he had tried that and it hadn't worked. He had sold his sword to pay for that bit of useless advice.

'If the God of the Seas has a mind to hold you here then there is nothing you, or the Gods, can do to change it. Manannan is the oldest of all the Gods – he rules them all.' The Seer had informed him earlier that day, failing to hold back his displeasure whilst imparting the news. As far as the Seer was concerned Keevan was beyond redemption, having recently been kicked out of the Fianna.

'Perhaps love will save you, when you have finished your selfish seeking.' The Seer had called out after him,

deciding at the last minute to throw him a bone.

But Keevan was finished with love.

It was love that had got him thrown out of the Fianna, love that had found him, then drowned beneath the waves, love that had gotten them thrown into captivity.

Well, not love exactly, the King. It was the King's fault. He should never have followed him to the Land of Promise. Surely he must carry the karmic debt of every one of his rotten ancestors. The man was cursed! They had taken away their names this time - their names! And thrown them onto an Island that even the Gods had forsaken.

Keevan paced the Bridge, almost willing Manannan to take him. Then he headed off into the City. He was beginning to wish he'd stayed with the King and his cousins after all. Curse or no curse, he felt sure they would have escaped the Island by now.

But the King and his cousins, the Cormacs, had not escaped. They hadn't even tried to escape. Exhausted by one of the most perilous adventures they had ever undertaken the King decided they should lay low for a while, hoping that if they disappeared for long enough Manannan might forget about them altogether.

They stayed at their Abbey on the East coast, which had been built in the centre of town by the townsfolk and subsequently stolen by one of their ancestors who had burnt out the inhabitants and declared it a sanctuary for the clan.

The interior of the Abbey was a reflection of their plight, dreadfully dark and a little bit scary. The door to the main entrance had been stolen. The halls and many rooms were bare, the furniture, doors, even the windows had gone. Thankfully the walls were still standing, singed black from the fires of previous runaways, but dry, providing ample shelter from the harsh gales and dark rain that blew in off the sea.

In the mornings the King, his twelve cousins and their depleted army of twenty eight men, prepared their arms. In the afternoons they trained, and in the evenings they toasted all the days they had been together, until they had forgotten every bad thing that had ever befallen them, and were ready to ride out again.

First Brian, the King's messenger, was sent forth to check the lands for avenging Gods.

It was expected he would be gone for some time but he returned a few hours later to inform the King that there weren't any Gods on the Island.

'No Gods!' cried the King, surprised but relieved.

News travels fast when there are no panes in the windows and by the time Brian had imparted the news to the King and his cousins, the men were already crowding the street with their horses and swords, anxious to get going.

They waited in silence. The men who rode with the Cormacs, whilst reasonably talkative in the company of their kin, spoke very little outside their inner circle. The

King's messenger, Brian, however was like the croaking bird of doom and there were times when the men would have gladly ripped the beak off him. But the King would have none of it. He knew Brian was dour, as his ancestors had been before him, and so the men were forced to sit and listen to Brian as they waited for the King and his cousins to join them.

'Steer well clear ma mother warned me,' said Brian, his freckles were out and his red hair which was matted from the wind was standing on end.

'The Cormacs are cursed. It's a fate worse than death riding out with them.'

The men were apt to agree but held their tongues.

Brian had inherited the title of 'Messenger to the King' from his forefathers. An enviable position of high rank and reasonable pay, but employment with the King was fraught with danger. Throughout the kingship of the Cormacs all the King's messengers and all the King's men had met with dreadful ends. So dreadful that the tales of their demise were never told, and the Messengers had been given the burden of carrying them through time. And so the King made allowances for Brian's grim nature and, despite having overheard his low opinion of him through the open window, the King had taken it in his stride, giving Brian a friendly cuff about the head which sent him careering into the Abbey wall. Then he took up his steed and led his cousins and their army of men out of town.

'Was there ever a'body so dour?' said the King.

The King was a brave and cheery soul who relied upon the blood of his ancestors to stir him into battle. The clan's only purpose was death. Their murderous reputation having followed them throughout the ages and so the King had no choice but to go with the flow, although he had introduced a number of changes. First they had a cause, and a heavenly one at that. This had a positive effect on moral giving the men a feeling of justification when it came to swiping the heads off their enemies. Secondly the King always tried his best to keep the men alive. The ancient fathers had given little thought to the well-being of their armies, often boasting themselves victorious despite the total slaughter of their kinsmen. And finally, the Cormacs were always prepared. In all the days of their confinement at the Abbey the men did not lay down their arms. Every day was battle day for the Cormacs. An enactment, where any lesson learned might be the one that saved them. In this they never faltered - for they knew that if they gave doubt a moment defeat would surely claim them. Freedom had its price.

Unfortunately they were a long way from it. The ancient ancestors had sold them down the river, binding the sons of the future to promissory notes from the past - karmic debts that would take a lifetime of heavenly deeds to wipe out.

But these karmic debts were nothing compared to the *Geis* - strange injunctions invoked on the King and his cousins by the Druids at birth. So many it was

187

impossible to remember or follow them. 'Never to kill a bird, or hunt on a waxing moon, or eat the meat of a certain animal depending on what land they were in, always to defend a woman, yet deny others, depending on the colour of their hair…etc.' To break a *Geis* was to incur some dreadful misfortune and so death and destruction sort of followed them around.

'This was the curse of the Cormacs.'

Their last adventure in the Land of Promise had been so disastrous the King was relieved when they were only exiled. He had been hoping that after several days in hiding they would be able to sneak off the Island without drawing too much attention to themselves, but apparently Keevan had been spotted on the Bridge trying to throw himself off it.

'Och, he's taken it worse than I thought,' said the King, when he heard the news.

They headed South, towards the City.

It was the following day before Keevan saw the girl again. He had been wandering the streets behind the Goddesses' Theatre and had discovered a cobbled passageway hidden behind a wall. He was about to make his way down it when he spotted the girl at the bottom, heading up with a spotty young man in a poet's tunic. Keevan settled himself down on the pavement to wait.

'Look!' said the young poet, throwing his hands towards the beggars at his feet in a dramatic fashion.

'Humanity in despair. Our streets are simply littered with the evidence of it. Must I clamber over a heap of defeat just to get to my own doorway? Surely the Gods have failed us. They have fled - and we have been left to fend for ourselves. What are we to do? Who will guide us? Are we to guess our own destinies?'

'We cannot always be guided by the Gods,' replied the girl.

'Then by who?' asked the poet. 'The Druids?'

He was about to launch into an attack on the Druids when he spotted a warrior up ahead, who was so fixated on his female companion he decided it would be best not to linger, and so he backed away.

The poet bade the girl farewell in the turn, but she did not hear him. It was as if he had disappeared in a puff of smoke.

Keevan took the place of the young poet and accompanied the girl, who was called Echtra, through the square. She said very little. Still, Keevan kept up the charm, insisting on escorting her home, which he discovered was a cottage overlooking the Bridge.

They walked the forest path together, the sun playing hide and seek with them through the gaps in the trees. Sometimes Keevan was at her side, sometimes he bounded ahead, walking backwards to keep her in sight. He found that if he got too close she pulled away. Even the slightest shift in his position could cause her withdrawal, and it held his childish fascination. He kept up the game, until they were almost at the crossroads,

189

unsure as to whether he was welcome. Then he drew in, and as the sun's rays hit the path, he put his hand to her arm. She blushed.

Later, when he was alone and had time to reflect, he found he could think of nothing else - which was just as well for he had no wish to recall his past. The shame of his exile from the Fianna, the disastrous days that followed - it was as if some greater force than his had decided his life should take a turn for the worse, and in the turn he had lost himself, and his fine companions who were his joy. Deeply wounded by this sudden change in his fortune Keevan had drifted away from the path of heroic deeds and into unknown territory which was how he had bumped into the King and the Cormacs.

Like the Fianna, the Cormacs had pledged to fight for the benefit of the Universal good. Their methods for fighting the Universally bad were a little more extreme, but their hearts were in the right place. Keevan had joined the King in the hope he might redeem himself with Finn, but in the middle of a quest that should have been their making they had inadvertently drowned a Princess. Finn would never take him back now. And if truth be known it was this that had caused him such distress on the Bridge.

That evening Keevan had returned to the Inn intent on drowning his sorrows. He was in good company. The Inn was full of men like him, men who had fallen by the wayside. Men who drank like the worst was yet to come, and it was. Keevan soon discovered that the God of the

Seas was the least of their worries.

After sharing every detail of his misfortune with a couple of warriors at the bar, Keevan, who could never tarry long on the subject of defeat, enquired as to the possible routes of escape.

'Surely by now someone has managed to escape this God forsaken Island?' he enquired, raising his voice in the hope that someone might come to his aid, but instead everyone in the bar turned on him.

The masks were off and it was not a pretty sight. It was his cheery hope that soured them. They had lived without it for years and it was no longer welcome.

'You're wasting your time,' said a thin mean looking man, pushing his way into the conversation. An exiled Druid, and there were plenty of them. This one was as old as the hills and his skin was so flaky and dry that whenever he touched something he left a part of himself behind.

Keevan tried to back away without making it too obvious but the Druid kept coming, until Keevan's back was fast against the bar.

'There's no escaping this Island laddie. This is mortal land - stolen from the Gods by Mortal Kings. That sea out there is Manannan's Sea. It's impassable. You're trapped here, like the rest of us.'

There was silence in the bar, all eyes upon the Seer, as he voiced their plight.

Keevan looked suitably depressed but the Druid wasn't finished. He ran his tongue over his dry lips before imparting the next bit of bad news.

'That's not all laddie, rumour is it that Aife…'

Keevan had his blade at the Druid's throat within seconds. 'Aife?'

Keevan wished he'd worn his gloves. The Druid's neck had shed a layer of skin onto his hand. He shook it off in disgust.

The Druid's eyes almost popped out of his head. He assumed Keevan had swiped a blow at his neck. He coughed and spluttered, his beady eyes streaming with tears.

Keevan kindly withdrew the knife and handed over his own whisky.

The Druid meanly drank it all and placed the empty glass on the bar.

'Aife has her eye on the City,' said the barman, retrieving the empty glass. 'Word is, she's on her way here, with her Northern army.'

The barman was kind enough to pass the information on before having Keevan thrown out into the rain.

If Keevan and the King were looking for something to spur them into action, a suicidal leap of faith across the Bridge for example, then Aife was it. Aife and the Cormacs were mortal enemies. The ancient ancestors had gotten into the habit of catching the winged jezebels and herding them through the forests like cattle so that they could practice their death swings whenever the mood took them. It was this sort of callous disregard that had given the Cormacs a Universally bad name. The ancients had bordered on psychotic. They had no enemies, having slain them all, and their reign of terror had ended when the Gods decided they should be cast out to some eternal place of exile. But not before they had sired an extensive brood, and so the Cormac line had continued on.

The modern day Cormacs however were no match for the Amazons, and Keevan, who was guilty by association, was no match for them either.

Keevan had allowed himself to be dumped on the doorstep of the pub without bothering to raise a finger, deciding it wasn't worth the effort. A dark cloud that had been waiting patiently overhead for his arrival opened up when it saw him and a torrent of rain flooded the street. The wind flew up and hit the sign above his head which was highly appropriate. *The Hell and High Water.*

That evening Keevan had sat on the sodden step, placed his head beneath his arm, and with a tear in his eye he had called out to Finn. And Finn must have heard him, because the following day he had met the girl again, and through her he would discover his true destiny.

'She's not here,' said the Fairy Queen of dreams, calling through from the kitchen of number seven to the visitor in the hallway who was struggling to find a peg for her hat and coat.

The visitor, who was extremely important and not used to being abandoned in hallways, made her way through to the sitting room and took a seat by the hearth.

Knowing it would take the Fairy Queen at least another ten minutes to suggest it she made herself at home, settling back into the sofa and placing her feet as close as possible to the fire which was on its way out.

'Make yourself at home,' said the Fairy Queen, eventually.

Minutes later she appeared in the doorway with a heavily laden tea tray at her breast and after a slightly shaky start, she began the journey from the kitchen to the hearth, serving the Goddess, before taking her seat on the sofa opposite. The sofa the Goddess had selected was the best in the house, so much firmer than its twin, that had lost most of its stuffing from a split in the seams, and so when the Fairy Queen lowered her behind she found herself automatically deflated to an appropriate level of subservience. This did not disturb her in the least, for it was not in her nature to be so disturbed. In fact it was not in her nature to be anything other than cheery, and at that particular moment she was simply grateful for the chance to sit down. The Fairy Queen of dreams, favoured friend of Gods and Goddesses, and loyal wife to the Dollmaker, had been at it all morning. Dusting, wiping, scrubbing, sweeping. Every inch of the cottage had been seen by the broom. Unfortunately her spick and span version of cleanliness had fallen way short of the Goddess's standards but she had run out of time, which was one of the problems of living in Region one - there was never enough of it.

'She'll be back soon,' said the Fairy Queen, referring

to the absence of her charge. 'I did tell her you were coming but you know what it's like with these lost causes, they're so incredibly difficult to abandon.'

The Goddess of Destiny nodded, remembering some of her own.

'You said there was a problem with her,' enquired the Goddess, getting straight to the point.

'Yes…that's right. She appears to have developed a will of her own.'

'A will of her own?' said the Goddess, surprised.

'Some flaw in the mechanism. I'm sure it can be easily fixed….but there's another problem,' said the Fairy Queen, anxious to reveal it.

The Goddess raised her eyebrows, hardly surprised.

'It's the Chiefs of the South, the ones who control the City. They're saying there's no such thing as the Otherworld.'

'No such thing?'

'Yes, I'm afraid it's affecting the inhabitants. They've stopped believing…in the Gods.'

'Stop believing!' said the Goddess, incredulous. 'How do they think everything got here!'

The Fairy Queen stared awkwardly into her tea cup.

'Well,' said the Goddess, leaning back into the sofa, offended. 'That *is* a problem. As you know the Chiefs of the North are due to return, at my request, to ensure the dolls have safe passage out of here. They were hoping to liberate some of the inhabitants at the same time.'

'We can't force Deliverance on the people,' muttered

the Fairy Queen.

'No, indeed,' sighed the Goddess. Then she noticed an envelope on the mantelpiece.

'Is that for me?'

It was clearly a recently delivered item for it was dustless, marked for the Goddess's attention and written in the sort of handwriting that was difficult to ignore.

'Yes. It came for you this morning,' said the Fairy Queen excited, having recognised the handwriting of Manannan, the Gods of the Seas.

The Goddess skimmed through the first page of the letter which was godly gossip for her eyes only and then slowed down when she got to the important bit on the second page.

'What is it?'

'It's a Prophecy.'

'A Prophecy?' said the Fairy Queen surprised, for Prophecies were incredibly difficult to orchestrate. 'We haven't had one of those in a long time. What does it say?'

'It says, *When the Gods are expelled from this Island the people will cease to see the Celestial. They will forget the Gods and deny their existence. This City will be taken by Shadowy forces. Hidden behind the veil, 'they' will govern the thoughts of the people. Few will escape the fate of an early death. Cut off from the spiritual their bodies will wither and die, and they shall be born over again, in like mind.'*

'For how long?' gasped the Fairy Queen.'

'*Twelve thousand years.*'

196

'Twelve thousand years!' she cried, throwing herself back into the sofa. 'Does it say anything else?'

'*The dreadful state of the weather…floods…*The sort of thing you would expect from the Gods of the Seas….and then *Deliverance. The return of the Gods, led by 5 and forty who have paid an enormous price,'* concluded the Goddess, shocked by the Prophecy. She passed over the second half of the letter to the Fairy Queen.

'The 5 is written as a number. Is that important?'

'Heroes and Heroines are always written as a number,' replied the Goddess, taking a box of biscuits out of her handbag and offering them over.

The Goddess of Destiny always carried a box of custard creams whenever she was visiting the Island. The food in Region one was always dreadful.

The Seer was walking through the square when he encountered the Cormacs. It was not a pleasant experience. He had always considered the fallen heroes at the Inn to be unsavoury, but when it came to the Clans it was clear they still had a fair way to fall.

'The Bridge is the only way off the Island,' said the Seer, anxious to be on his way.

'I've already told this to the other warrior,' he added, hoping to gain the King's favour by giving them some additional information.

'Whit other warrior?' asked the King, grabbing hold of the Seer's hood.

'Did he have a heed like Medusa?' asked the King's

first cousin, grinning into his face like a maniac.

The Seer tried to answer but the bottom of his hood kept cutting into his throat, interfering with his breathing.

The King reluctantly let go.

'Yes,' wheezed the Seer, trying to catch a breath.

They left him in a heap in the middle of the square. The King wasn't a great fan of Seers. It seemed to him they only told you the good when you were up to your neck in the bad.

They headed out towards the Bridge at a gallop. The King positioned himself on the embankment with his messenger Brian as the twenty eight men and the King's twelve cousins searched around for Keevan.

'He's nae here,' called the first cousin, from beneath the Bridge.

'Crivens, he must have jumped,' said the seventh cousin, who was above him, hanging over the railings.

'He's nae jumped,' said the third, who was standing next to him. 'He's hasnae got the bottle."

'He'd be brave enough to jump if he had the mind to,' said the King loyally. He was about to call his men back in when a head appeared from the door of the cottage behind him.

'Excuse me,' said the head to the King. 'You wouldn't by any chance be 5 and forty would you?'

Echtra tried to lose Keevan at the crossroads – some important visitor at the cottage, the need for privacy. But there was no getting rid of him, and by the time they reached the embankment she could see there was no need.

There was an army of men on the lawn, and the cottage was full of warriors. The King was in the sitting room on the sofa next to the Fairy Queen. His face lit up when Keevan entered the room. He stood up, and the cousins drew back to let Keevan and Echtra through.

Brian was bumped off the opposite sofa in favour of Echtra. The King made room for Keevan, and passed the letter over, before resuming his conversation with the Goddess.

'This letter seems to suggest that the 5 and forty heroes come later.'

'Twelve thousand years later,' added Brian, from the floor.

'There's no time, just the present.' reminded the Goddess.

'What do we have to do?" asked Keevan, skimming the contents of the letter.

'Stop the Amazons taking the City,' replied Brian, hoping it would put him off. The last thing he wanted was another Godly mission. He was hoping to get home for a rest and put his feet up for at least the next few hundred years.

'Where does it say that?' asked the first cousin, grabbing the letter from Keevan.

'It's not in the letter!' said Brian, who was fed up having to explain everything to the Cormacs. 'Aife has her eye on the City. Everyone knows that.'

It was an impossible task. Aife's Northern army was reported to be three hundred strong. They could fly, and they were deadly. An unbeatable foe and a heavenly cause - for the King, Keevan, Brian and the Cormacs it was just another day at the office.

But devising a plan to defeat the Amazons was easier said than done. They had been having a strategy meeting on the lawn for the last two hours and were still no further forward, partly because of the continual interruptions from the Cormacs who, as far as Brian was concerned, were all brawn and no brains.

'I'm just saying. Aife's army is three hundred strong. We're outnumbered,' insisted Brian.

'Aye, I know!' said the King, getting frustrated.

'We'll take them, nae bother,' said the first cousin, who was the eldest.

'Aye!' cheered the cousins.'

'We can't take them all!' said Brian.

'Oor ancient ancestors could have taken them all, nae matter how many Amazons there were,' said the second.

'Aye,' agreed the cousins.

'The ancient Cormacs were psychopaths,' argued Brian.

'Aye!' cheered the cousins.

'And Wullie's the only psychopath round here,' said the third.

A rumble of laughter went through the ranks.

'We'll fight,' said the King, ending the argument. 'Or

end up imprisoned in the City with the rest.'

'Then we'll have to stop them at the Bridge,' said Keevan.

'And just how are we supposed to do that?' asked Brian.'

'We'll use you as bait.'

Everyone laughed, except Brian. 'It doesn't matter where we fight them. We're still...'

'Outnumbered. Aye, we know!' said the King, losing his temper with him.

And they were off again, round the houses.

The Cormacs and their army spent a drunken evening on the lawn, considering their fate. If they tried to escape across the Bridge Manannan would fill their throats with the tide and leave their souls to rot on the slimy ocean bed. If they stayed and fought, the Amazons would surely rip them apart. But they were well used to being at rock bottom, and after polishing off several bottles of wine that the Fairy Queen had found in her husband's cabinet they were back to their usual 'we'll take them nae bother' selves.

The King and Brian had hung around the embankment, continuing their discussion on strategy.

Keevan had sat alone on the bank, out of sight of the others. He had no skill for strategy, and no desire to spend what he assumed would be his last moments alive with the drunken Cormacs on the lawn.

He was surprised and greatly relieved when late into

the evening Echtra joined him. His earlier childish bravado in the forest had been replaced with a manly vulnerability. He shared his secret thoughts with her – his dread of the morning light - his fear that the sea God would swallow him up.

She revealed a secret of her own – her true identity - which was a shock. The dolls were something of a myth in the Otherworld. Keevan had always imagined them to be fair haired, delicate and feminine – the 'tied to a tree facing a dragon' types. But Echtra definitely didn't fit the bill. Her hair was dark, and cut short, more in keeping with a boy than a girl. He assumed she must be flawed in some way. 'Maybe she had been cast out like him.' The thought caused his heart to turn towards her, and when it did there was no turning it back, no matter how hard he tried - and he did try.

Having fashioned the chain of events in the mortal world the Goddess of Destiny returned to her Otherworld home. She had called them in at midnight and given instructions. The twelve dolls would leave the Island under the protection of the seven Chiefs of the North, who had just arrived in the City. Brian was to escort Echtra, the twelfth doll, into the City and deliver her to them, with a message for the Chiefs, warning them of the impending Amazon invasion. Keevan never saw Echtra again.

In the early hours the King had a dream. They were

surrounded on every side by a Celtic mist and there were demons above them. He could hear the beating of their wings. As he drew out his sword to ward them off the King felt the ground beneath his feet crumble away. He was falling.

The King awoke with a start. The sun had risen up, but had yet to reach the bank, which was enveloped in a heavy white mist. The King found his sword, and made his way blindly back to the cottage. He stood on the lawn surveying the land. It was unlike any mist he had ever seen before. It hid the Bridge and was making its way slowly up the bank, covering everything in sight.

'This was no mist,' thought the King. 'It was Feth Fiada - the Druids fog.'

That was when the idea came to him and he woke Keevan up to tell him about it.

'Sounds more like a premonition to me. A bad one,' said Keevan, when the King had explained the dream.

'Aye, maybe, but the fog gives us the element of surprise. And that's won us mair battles than it's lost us.'

The Fairy Queen appeared at the back door with their breakfast and he called her over.

'Here's how I see it.'

The Kings archers lined the bank, invisible in the fog, their arrows aimed at the skies. The King's army were behind them with their broad swords, steeling themselves for what was to come. Behind them the

King's cousins, the Cormacs, had their claymores and a crazy look in their eyes. The King and Keevan commanded the rear. With Brian gone, the Fairy Queen took the watch - from the bedroom window, as opposed to a hill. They were ready.

But when the call came it was not what they expected.

'Oh…Oh, my goodness…run!' cried the Fairy Queen in a panic, hanging out of the bedroom window.

'Whits she saying?' asked the King.

'I can't hear her from here,' said Keevan.'

'Och. I'll have to go oot and have a look,' said the King, emerging from the fog with his claymore.

'I'll come with you,' said Keevan.

It was a shock. Aife's army was like the black cloud of hell coming towards them. There was definitely more than three hundred. It looked more like a thousand.

'Whit's going on?' said the first cousin, emerging from the fog. 'Och, yer joking.'

'We've nae chance,' said the second, coming in behind him.

'If we leave now we can make it,' said Keevan. 'The Druid's fog will hide us from Manannan's sight.

The King had had the same thought. But it was seriously bad karma to abandon a quest – and a Godly one at that. Then again, how much worse could their karma get.

The King stared at the incoming Amazon cloud, undecided. As he hesitated more cousins came out of the fog, with their views, some for and some against. Meanwhile the cloud was getting bigger. Then it dipped.

'They've seen us!' cried Keevan.

'Retreat!' The King had made the call.

The King's army flooded onto the Bridge, with the Cormacs behind them, the King and Keevan at the rear. As they hit the Bridge they could hear the beating wings of the Amazons already above their heads. Thankfully the Amazons couldn't see them. But by blind chance one of the King's men was taken up into the Druid's fog. The delighted screech of the Amazons overhead was frightening. They heard the bloodied body drop. The King called to his men in a fury to take up their arms. They raised their swords, just like in the dream. And as they did so, Manannan the God of the Seas, rose up and drowned them.

Chapter Fourteen

The Gods have their own rules

Present day

'Of course I demanded an *eric*.*' Mrs D paused to take a sip of her tea.

'What sort of *eric*?' asked Scathach, curious to know how one God might compensate another.

They were sitting on the balcony of Scathach's bedroom having breakfast.

'That those I had chosen would return, at the appropriate time, in order to fulfil the Prophecy. Manannan agreed. The Fairy Queen dreamt them up.'

'You mean, the idiots?'

'Yes….Jack, Dundee, and his cousins the Cormacs. But Manannan held a grudge. He used his cloak of forgetfulness so that they would be unable to recall their true identities.'

*eric: *compensation imposed for wrong doing*

206

'Manannan is easily provoked,' said Scathach, forgetting herself. Only the Gods could judge.

There was a knock at the door. One of Scathach's messengers joined them on the balcony.

'We've had word from Falias. The Dollmaker is missing.'

Mrs D's tea cup hit the saucer. 'Then the Fairy Queen is no longer safe. We must leave as soon as the men return from the forest.'

'You have my horses at your disposal,' said Scathach, following her to the door.

As they said their goodbyes another one of Scathach's girls entered, with more tea.

'I'll take that by the trees out of the wind,' said Mrs D.

'Who is she?' asked the messenger, as Mrs D left the room.

'She's the brains behind the curtains.'

Scathach Castle by the sea is the most relaxing spot in the whole of Angus' jurisdiction, disconnected from the first realm by a great chasm, and therefore out of reach from the usual tittle tattle that pollutes the air waves. It is said, that it is the only place in the Otherworld where you can be sure your thoughts are completely your own, and so if doubt and despair happen to drift onto the fringes of your tartan travel blanket you have no one to blame but yourself.

That morning the grounds were filled with a

feminine air. The waters beyond the sea wall were calm. The mountains looked as though they had been assembled in the heavens. The wind had dropped, the sun was only just up, and a fine mist hung over the Castle turrets. Every so often a fairy-like troupe of Scathach's golden haired warriors would flit overhead, casting huge bird like shadows across the lawn.

Echtra and Echraide were sitting on the steps, outside the red front door of the Castle, enjoying the beauty of it all. Their peace and quiet was interrupted by the sudden appearance of Mrs D, who swept out of the side entrance with a team of helpers. She didn't see them. They watched as the helpers raced after her, down the steps, and along the edge of the forest, stopping when she did at a large tree, which was close to the sea wall, sheltered from the wind. The helpers waited patiently whilst Mrs D settled herself down onto her tartan travel blanket. Then they laid out her tea tray and disappeared.

Mrs D shuffled around until there was no breeze to speak of, and then sat back against the tree with a dainty tea cup in her hands. She spotted the girls and gave them a wave. Then the ladies settled in to wait for the men to emerge from the forest.

Finn was the first to appear, followed by Diarmait, Fergus, then Mac. They gathered by the sea wall as Mrs D filled them in on the latest news.

Mac, who always had his eye on their surroundings, was the first to spot Diorruing emerge from the upper part of the forest with two new companions - Keevan of the curling locks, and the King of the Cormacs. The girls made their way down the Castle steps towards them. But the heroes did not see them. They were at their beginning, their eyes only just used to the light, and the Seer was ushering them on, towards their Fianna brothers. But as they drew closer to the sea wall Keevan's eye was momentarily caught up in the fluttering of a tiny black butterfly at his cheek. It drew his attention back, towards the Castle, and that was when he saw her. And his heart drew back twelve thousand years, remembering. Diorruing caught the exchange and drew him on. As the heroes approached their comrades the sight of the Fianna Leader made Keevan's eyes water. Finn stepped forward and took him by the hand. Keevan was back in the Fianna.

They were greatly changed. Keevan no longer played the fool. The King was cheery and less troubled by external elements. There was other evidence as well. The King had a scar on his face. They were taller, and much broader.

Mac headed for the stables to fetch the horses and they gathered around Mrs D's travel blanket which had been well placed, at the beginning of the *Warriors Return Road,* a one way exit route to the first realm that would lead them back to Falias. Everyone spoke excitedly of the quest. There was loud laughter, impossible boasts, and bold promises. Then Mac appeared with the horses and Finn addressed them.

209

'The Amazons use this road to cherry pick the warriors who have been trained at the school,' he warned. 'So be on your guard.'

'We should pray to the Gods,' said Echraide, as she and Echtra mounted their horses.

'Diorruing has the foresight to guide us. Diarmait has the love to bind us. Fergus carries the power of our word. And Mac is the strength in our arms. We need no more Gods than this,' said Finn. And they were off.

Scathach watched them go. Then she turned to the girl at her heels. 'Summon the Dragon.'

Their journey along the *Warriors Return Road* was tense but uneventful. Finn took the lead. Fergus was behind him. Diorruing watched over Mrs D and Echtra. Diarmait held the centre with Echraide. Keevan and the King were behind them and Mac at the rear. They had crossed the border, and were half a mile away from Falias when Diorruing stopped them. There was something dark and alarming up ahead and it was heading straight for them, at a pace. Forewarned and forearmed they were ready. But even with Diorruing's warning the speed of the Amazon scout took them all by surprise. It came in confidently low. Mac belted it out of the way with his giant dagger. The headless body fell dead on the path. Another appeared, *swoop*, then another, *swoop*. Mac took them all out.

Then a whole flock of them flew in out of nowhere, to their left. Echraide's horse bolted right, off the path.

The King attempted to go to her aid, but she was already pulling back in. They collided. She drew in the reins but her horse lurched forward. A scout came at her. The King took it out with his fist, hurting himself. It was no joke. He grimaced as he pulled his grazed bloody knuckles back to the reins, and caught her eye. If the King was looking for a mirror, she was it. The woman that was soon to govern his heart held his gaze. The King forgot about his hand. The scouts dodged around them, taken out by their comrades, the bodies splattering blood on their romantic moment.

Then silence. They took a breath. It was short lived.

The Fianna may have slaughtered their scouts with ease, but the incoming Amazon warriors were crafty. They began dropping out of the sky. They blocked the road in seconds, spreading quickly out into the woods. Soon there would be no way round them. Finn fearlessly urged his horse forward towards the blockade, the others tight behind him. The Amazon warriors drew in, ready for a fight. Finn drew as close as he dared, then he swung off the track, through the woods, and was back on the road ahead of them. Without looking back they sped on towards Falias. But Mac was too slow at the rear and as the Amazons drew around for the chase the giant fell.

Keevan and the King felt Mac hit the ground. Their comrades were too far ahead to call back, so they turned around, and with suicidal courage, galloped back towards the on-coming Amazons, miraculously avoiding death in the confusion. They found the giant off the road smothered in a mass of black winged fiends and dove on top of them. It was a valiant effort but eventually they went under and everything turned black.

Finn drew them out with his own hand, and as they emerged from the darkness they saw the giant shape of the Tattooed Dragon above them. A thousand of Scathach's finest warriors held the air. Some had been called in from other realms to defend them, and for a while the dark retreated.

'I see you got your nerve back,' said Mac to Keevan and the King as they were helped to their feet. Then the six warriors, now horseless, caught up with Diorruing and the three ladies, and they walked the final half mile to Falias together.

This time they entered Falias through the four pillared entrance. The sign on the right said *Welcome to Falias*. As they passed through the pillars they saw four visiting Masters, spiritual teachers from the third realm, who were standing in a line to their left. Each man was over eight feet tall, and wore strange coloured robes with unusual peaked headwear. They nodded as they passed by. The citizens of Falias came out of the shops and cafes to watch them pass through. The arrival of Finn, five of his finest warriors, their messenger Echraide, the King of the Cormacs, the Goddess of Destiny, and her treasured charge Echtra, had created a bit of a stir. Falias often received the odd visiting God or Goddess. Heroes and heroines were common place. But Finn and his Fianna were legendary.

On the better side of Old Street *Emma's* was open. The music was playing, the food was ready, and all the tables were free. Mrs D's helpers stood to attention as Mrs D entered the café. She waltzed straight through to the kitchen leaving her guests to a choice of tables.

Like giants in a dolls house Finn and his warriors wandered around the café, bumping into things, finally settling down on tables one, two and three. Mac took the window ledge which was wide and flanked by flowery curtains. The others took the chairs which miraculously held their weight. Mrs D's helpers appeared from the kitchen with several trays of delights. As soon as they had finished they brought out more. Then their hostess appeared with a tea towel in her hands.

'I've spoken to my helpers. They say they heard a kerfuffle next door at the Dollmaker's shop when they were closing up last night. When they arrived this morning the door was off its hinges and the Dollmaker was gone. No-one knows who's taken him, and there's been no sign of the Fairy Queen.'

'Diorruing and I will search the shop,' said Finn, easing himself out of the tiny chair. 'Fergus, take Diarmait and pick up fresh horses.'

It was Finn's intent that Mac stay behind to protect the ladies. But Mac was feeling very uncomfortable in such a confined space. It was affecting his breathing. 'I should go with them,' he said, rushing out of the café, with the intention that Keevan and the King look after the girls.

But they had other ideas. Keevan and the King knew Falias well and their hearts were set on visiting the *Hell and High Water.* 'We should go with him,' said the King.

Echraide nodded her agreement and the heroes left the cafe.

Next door in the Dollmaker's shop, Finn and Diorruing were upstairs searching for clues. It wasn't easy. They assumed that the shop was topsy-turvy due to the fact that the Dollmaker had been kidnapped but it wasn't so. During his long absence from his wife the Dollmaker had let himself go, evidenced by all the mess. Nothing was ever put away. There were tools and shavings all over the floor, drawers pulled out and left, brooms and buckets overturned and never put upright. The only thing that had been clean and pristine prior to the intrusion the previous evening was the shop window. But this was now smashed to pieces. The Dollmaker had managed however, on his way out of the shop, to leave a clue behind. Finn spotted it amongst the splinters of wood and glass. It was an advert for Showtown - a circus bound for Finias, the second City.

Back at *Emma's* café Mrs D, who was in fine spirits, was just adding the finishing touches to a strawberry pavlova when one of her favourite tunes came on the radio and she turned up the volume. Which was a pity because she didn't hear the warning wails outside. An old crone appeared in the doorway and began struggling up the step with her walking stick. The girls jumped up to help her.

There was no-one behind the bar of the *Hell and High Water* when Keevan and the King walked through the door and so they helped themselves. As they leant at the bar the King noticed a painting of the manager on the wall above the official license notice. He looked pale and incredibly dour. The King grinned at Keevan and then leapt up onto the bar and called out.

'Brian!' said the King, his voice loud and commanding. 'We're back!'

Brian came scuttling out of the back, saw the King and beamed. 'I'll get my stuff.'

They had been inside the pub for less than fifteen minutes but when they stepped out into the street the sun had gone in. The shopkeepers had closed their doors. The pavements were deserted. Their girls were being hauled out of the café by a seven foot Black Witch, and there was no way of getting to them across the current of Banshees blocking the street.

Finn and Diorruing emerged from the Dollmakers shop to see Keevan, the King, and the newly recruited Brian trying to force their way through the tide of wailing women. Finn and Diorruing were the closest to *Emma's*, but the enemy was at its densest nearest the Witch, and they soon found themselves trapped against the door of the Dollmaker's shop under the weight of the mob. Nothing was getting through.

A black Scottie dog who had been watching the proceedings from the steps of the *Hell and High Water* padded off into the alleyway, returning moments later with a dozen wild cats he had chased from the bins, and he drove them straight towards the Banshees. There was only one thing the Banshees feared more than the wail of the Black Witch - and it was wailing wild cats. They scattered, opening up a temporary route for the three heroes to get through.

Echraide, a skilled warrior, had escaped the clutches of the Black Witch, but the Banshees had her by the hair, and were dragging her to the ground. The King leapt forward, with his favoured dagger he had retrieved from Brian, and sliced their Banshee heads off. He stood before her, like a child showing off, the wailing mouths of the Banshees he had just beheaded still open on the ground around them, expecting a grateful smile or a nod, but instead Echraide just looked annoyed. Before he had time to wonder why he realised Keevan was in trouble.

Keevan had faced the Black Witch head on - love spurring him into action. As Brian fought the Banshees circling the Witch, Keevan had edged around onto the steps of the café, and had taken a mad leap onto the Witch's back. The Witch let go of Echtra and fell backwards onto the pavement. Unfortunately Keevan was beneath her. He struggled for breath, blindly trying to reach her throat with his dagger. One of the Banshees found him, and dug her talons into his curls. Others joined gleefully in. Keevan was hauled out from under the Witch by the mob. They dived on top of him and everything went black. The wailing in his ears was deafening. He couldn't think straight. He was slowly being flattened to death.

Mac, Fergus and Diarmait suddenly appeared at the top of the street, amazed at the sight before them. They mounted the horses and, using Mac's head as a battering ram, forced their way through the mob, flattening a good number of Banshees in the process, freeing up the King and Brian who were able to rescue Keevan. Keevan and the King then grabbed the girls, and reunited with Finn and Diorruing at the Dollmakers shop.

The Witch's fury knew no bounds. As the sea of fiends headed towards them they began reversing up the street, backs against the wall, fighting for their lives. The Banshees were everywhere and this time there was no-one around to save them.

'Now what?' asked Keevan.

'We fight to the death,' said Finn.

The Witch sensed she had the upper hand. This was it. Suddenly a door opened behind them.

'Be quick,' said the young man with the celebrity smile.

The party of nine stood in the middle of the tiny book shop trying to catch their breath but their rescuer hurried them on into the adjoining room.

'Where are we going?' asked Keevan.

217

'I assume you're looking for the quickest way out of here?' said the young man, as the Banshees began shrieking outside the shop window. The King nodded.

'The best way out is through the Library of the Subconscious,' said the man, pointing to a small door at the end of the shop. 'Ask the Head Librarian to show you the door to the Story World.'

'Where will that take us?' asked Diorruing, as the man urged them on. 'We need to get to Finias.'

The young man nodded. 'It's a shortcut - to everywhere.'

'What about Mrs D?' asked Echtra, hanging back with Keevan and the King as the others stepped through the door into the Library.

'No offence,' said the man with a smile. 'But she'll be safer without you.'

'Well…erm, thanks,' said the King, offering the man his hand.

'Duggey,' said Duggey, shaking the King's hand before returning to the television on the counter, and turning it up full blast to drown out the Banshees.

They stepped through a small door and into the Library which was larger than they expected. It was split into two levels and decked in old wood. On the upper level, where they had come in, there were reams and reams of books to their right, in aisles that seemed to go on forever. On the left was a huge oblong window at street level, and a glass front door with five steps that led down to the lower level, which had a small podium where the books were signed out, and a long seat for reading purposes. At the beginning of the aisles, blocking their way, was a man with a large open book in his hand. He didn't look happy to see them.

'Yes?' said the man, with a question mark and a sigh.

He was barely three quarters the size of an ordinary man and yet he managed, due to his superior intellect, to appear taller than any of them. His face was a mixture of wisdom and sobriety and it was clear they had disturbed his peace and quiet.

Everyone stared at him, unwilling to be the first to say anything, and so Diorruing took charge.

'Excuse me. We're looking for the door to the Story World,' explained Diorruing.

'Only the characters in the stories are allowed inside the Story World,' said the Head Librarian.

'We *are* the characters in the stories,' said Diorruing, haughtily. '*We* are the Fianna.'

'I see,' said the man, unimpressed but forced to give way.

'Very well.' He sighed again, as if everything was far too much trouble. He walked slowly down to the lower level and drew out a pile of forms from beneath the counter. Then he returned to his former position.

'You'll have to complete these applications for entry, in triplicate, and sign the disclaimer at the back. In the Story World your thoughts create the world around you. Immediately. There's no time delay in there. It's

219

incredibly dangerous….'

'WHERE'S THE DOOR?' boomed Mac.

The man was clearly used to being shouted at because without blinking an eye he took his key out of his pocket and led them up one of the aisles. On the way he gave them some good advice which they never bothered to take.

'Whatever you do don't interfere in any of the stories. It could be disastrous, for the characters and for yourselves,' instructed the man. Then he unlocked the door, and after taking up so much of his time annoying them, he sent them on their way with a smile.

Duggey was watching the Wizard of Oz on television when the Black Witch and seven of her Banshees crept into the shop. She sneaked past the counter as the Wicked Witch of the West flew over Dorothy on her broom.

The Black Witch made her way into the Library of the Subconscious through the small door which had been left slightly ajar by Duggey. She found the Head Librarian, who was just about to lock the Story World door, knocked him unconscious with her walking stick, and stepped through.

Chapter Fifteen

The Best of Dreams

The King was riding in a distant land. The forest track was deep and centuries old but he had no eye for it, his heart set on the young woman ahead of him. Each time he galloped towards her she raced away. There was no taming her. It was a continual battle between them – a royal rage - and it was high time they made up.

The King slid his boots out of his stirrups and fell to the ground, landing with an almighty thud on the path. He winced as his head hit a sharp stone, but felt it would be worth the pain. His horse bolted.

She raced back when she saw it, and fell to her knees. The King was quick. He grabbed his errant wife by the arm and dragged her through the undergrowth until he found a bed of mossy ground. With little grace he threw up her skirt and bared her flesh. She arched her back to avoid the bark beneath her. He seized his chance and moved quickly in, grabbing her hips and pulling her to him, until there was no room left between them. Then he took hold of her hair that had fallen loose, pushed his hot cheek against her neck, and entered her with a royal passion.

Under the shadow of the jezebel cloud that would show Keevan no mercy, Echtra came to him. It was said that dolls had no will of their own, yet something drew her to him, some karmic memory. He felt it too, and saw his death - the end of his days in her ebony eyes. And Manannan must have slept early that night because Keevan took her virginity in the warming tide.

Keevan and the King were drowning in a sea of ecstasy. Then Brian woke them up. The dream world faded in and out for a few moments until their eyes came into focus and all they could see was Brian's dour face.

The world behind Brian looked too good to be true - as if the sky and the landscape had been painted in.

'You get used to it after a while,' said Brian sullenly, moving out of their line of vision and they realised the others were waiting for them on the path.

Nothing was brighter than that day. In the wake of Finn and his sunny disposition the visitors attracted the attention of everyone and everything that was good in the Story World. The path, which was wide enough for all, looked as if someone had drawn it, and coloured it in. The trees along the route were perfectly placed, flowers grew wild but they were perfectly shaped. The air was clean, the sky was the right shade of blue, and the sun was out.

The inhabitants came out of their towns and villages and lined the route to greet them. In the air and on the ground they were surrounded by all manner of creatures; strange looking animals and odd looking birds, all flitting about in a rush, clearly having their own stories. At one point they came upon a clearing filled with black winged horses and were tempted to take a few in order to speed their journey on, but Diorruing reminded them that in the Story World karma was quick and they would soon find themselves tethered, so they left the horses to enjoy their freedom.

Everyone was filled with the warmth of their surroundings. Everyone except Brian.

'How much longer?' he complained, dawdling at the back, uncomfortable with the joy of everything.

'We leave the path at the next bend and head West,' said Diorruing, pleased to be in charge for a change. He had taken it upon himself to take the lead, having had a vision of the exit doors early on in the journey.

Diorruing stopped at the bend to wait for them. The inhabitants of the Story World immediately gathered around him but he dismissed them with a wave, like an arrogant prince who didn't have time to be pleasant to his subjects. He led the party of nine away from the path, and attempted to hurry them on, through a lush green field, which led onto a lush green hill. But it was hard to be in a rush in heaven.

The scene that hit them at the top of the hill was even more enchanting than the one they had left behind. It had a back drop of shimmering mountains, a huge yellow sun on the right, a magical forest on the left, a giant fairy tale Bridge in the middle, and a tiny village below it in the dip.

They followed Diorruing towards the fairy tale Bridge and stopped when he did, a few feet away from it.

'*This* is the Land of the Giants of Heavenly Thought,' announced Diorruing.

Everyone looked suitably impressed.

'The exit doors lie beyond this Bridge,' he indicated with his arm towards two giant red doors set into one of the mountains, which looked as if they had been added in at the last minute.

They assumed they were about to cross but instead Diorruing led them away to the left, down a grass slope until they were out of sight of the Bridge, and in sight of the village. He indicated that they should sit down. It took a while. Finn insisted on checking the security of their position first. Fergus headed down the slope, his poetic eye drawn to the village below where everything was a different colour, including the inhabitants. Diarmait checked the Bridge, and was quite taken with it, wondering what it would look like with him on it. Keevan and the King checked beneath it. Mac wandered behind them, looking bored. Diorruing huffed and puffed, until they were finished, and he had everyone's attention. Then he began.

'In the Land of Heavenly Thought the Giants live high in the mountains, and the people live below the Bridge. The Giants are hardly ever seen. But there is one Giant whose thoughts are plagued with the doubts of love, and he comes to the Bridge every day to sing about it.

When the Giant is on his way down the mountain his foot-steps echo like thunder and the villagers rush out of the houses with their yellow buckets. When the Giant arrives on the Bridge he sings a song of sad lament and the villagers fill their buckets with the Giant's tears. When the song is over the Giant's lost love appears from across the valley. She's big. As she runs towards him the valley shakes and shudders and the villagers rush indoors to watch from their windows. The Giant lovers meet in the middle of the Bridge, kiss and make up. When they return to the mountains the sun comes out and all is fine and well, until the next morning when they have another row.'

'When the Giant's song is over, and his back is turned, we cross.'

The inhabitants of the village had heard the Giant's song a trillion times and more but still they opened their windows to it.

The visitors on the grass felt the approach of the Giant long before they saw him. He strode down the mountain side like a prince in a tale, dressed in fine clothes with blond wavy hair and a handsome face. When he reached the Bridge he stopped in the middle, as though playing a part, and waited for the music to begin. When it did, he threw his right arm up dramatically towards the heavens and sang as though he was singing to the angels. His voice soared through the air. It was exhilarating, like nothing they had ever heard before. Their spirits rose and fell with the Giant's yearning heart, and when his lost love appeared on the horizon their hearts leapt with his in delight.

When the Giant lovers had been reunited, and were far enough away, they returned to the Bridge. Diorruing crossed alone. He was followed by Finn, Fergus and Diarmait. When Finn was sure the other side was clear of Giants he called the girls on.

Keevan, the King and Brian watched from the other side as the girls crossed cautiously over the Giants Bridge. Then it was their turn. They raced on, hoping to catch the girls up, who were over half way there. They assumed Brian was at their heels. But Brian was not. He was still on the other side. Brian had convinced himself that being the last one to cross he would surely fall to his death. Finn called out to him, but Brian wouldn't budge.

The King turned, and commanded his messenger on. Brian stepped out. As soon as he did the Bridge disappeared and the King, Keevan, Brian, and the girls, dropped down into the Land of Hellish Thought.

Chapter Sixteen

I'll get you my pretties

The Witch's road was a lonely one. The Banshees were no company at all and the smell of them attracted all sorts of unimaginably disgusting flying insects. They had been walking through a darkened forest for over an hour and there was no sign of an end to it. Then at last they came out of the gloom and into the beginnings of a village.

There was a row of seven tiny cottages at the edge of the forest. All of the cottages had red doors, a front garden, a path, a gate and a wall which was low enough to sit on. The Black Witch and her Banshees stopped for a rest on the wall. A woman walked by with a basket of red apples. The Banshees hissed at her as she passed but she didn't flinch. If it had been anywhere else in the Otherworld the sight of a seven foot Witch flanked by seven white haired fiends lined up along a wall might have raised an eyebrow - but the woman didn't bat an eyelid. In the Land of Hellish Thought like was drawn to like, the woman with the apples was just as bad as the creatures on the wall, and was no doubt on her way to carry out some dreadful deed on a princess who didn't deserve it.

The Black Witch and her crew were about to make a move when suddenly the door to the middle cottage opened and a witch poked her head out. She was a lot smaller than the Black Witch and extremely ugly. Her hair was all over the place, like her face which was down on one side and up on the other, forcing one of her eyes to bulge. Her lips were blood stained, her teeth black, her skin tinged with green due to the habit she had of snacking on the frogs she used for spells, and she cackled a lot in her sleep which woke the neighbours.

She screamed at the Banshees and tried to shoo them off the wall with her witches broom but they stayed where they were and so she went back inside for a spell, leaving the door open. The Black Witch followed her into the hallway, killed her with one swipe of her walking stick and poked her head through the sitting room door.

The room was split into two. On the left was an old fashioned sitting room with patterned curtains at the window, a small two-seater sofa against the wall, and a fireplace opposite. On the right, in what should have been a dining room, the Black Witch found the witch's office. There was a cabinet against the wall with a cupboard for her potions and shelves for her books of spells. In the far corner stood a huge black cauldron with brooms stacked behind it, and a few dead birds in a budgie cage that had been there a while. The carpet was covered in blood that had dripped down from the large wooden table which stood in the middle of the room. It was full of saucepans, bowls and jars with mice, frogs and bats in them. Some dead, some alive, some with eyes and no tails, some with tails and no eyes. The smell in the room was disgusting.

The Black Witch indicated to one of the Banshees to open the French windows at the back of the room and they stepped out into the garden, which had a shed at the bottom, a deckchair on the lawn and a small cage against the fence. There was nothing of interest to them inside the cage, except for a swan which appeared to be dying and so they returned to the dining room. They were about to leave when the Witch saw something green and interesting in the fireplace.

A few hundred yards down the road Keevan, the King and the girls were picking themselves up off the grass bank, which had, until a few seconds earlier, been beneath them. Now the Bridge had disappeared, along with the Fianna and the exit doors.

'What happened?' said Brian, who had rolled further than the others and was in the middle of the village street.

'I'm not sure,' said the King. 'But we've definitely left the Land of Heavenly Thought.'

The village was still there, in exactly the same place. It was the same size with the same number of houses. It even had the same number of people in it, except everyone was in black and white. The sky was grey and gloomy. As were the faces of the villagers who were wandering up and down the street carrying buckets, hunched over and dragging their feet, as if the buckets had the weight of the world inside them.

'Where are we?' asked Brian, looking extremely worried.

'Ask him,' suggested Keevan, pointing to a man who was heading in Brian's direction.

Brian scowled and folded his arms. He wasn't good with strangers.

'Ask him about the Bridge,' The King called down.

'And the exit doors,' added Keevan.

Keevan, the King and the girls headed quickly down the grass bank towards Brian but by the time they got to the street the man had gone.

'What did he say?' asked Keevan.

'He said we're in the Land of Hellish Thought.' replied Brian, shrugging his shoulders.

'What?'

Even the King looked worried. 'Did you ask him about the Bridge?'

'He said he'd never seen a Bridge… or an exit door,' added Brian, before Keevan could say anything.

'What else did he say?'

'Nothing…he wasn't very friendly. He said he was on his way to the lake to fill up his buckets. Apparently they have to do it every morning. It never rains here, and the lake is over a mile away.'

'Does this lake have a name?'

'The Lake at Dairbhreach,' said Brian, who was good at remembering names, being a messenger.

'That sounds familiar,' said the King, trying to recall where he'd heard the name before. 'We'll head for the lake. Follow the villagers' route through the woods. There could be another town or a city close by where we can get some directions out of here.

As they headed out of the village Keevan, who was convinced that Brian's dour thoughts had landed them in trouble, tried to broach the subject with him – but the King's messenger was notoriously bad tempered.

'So…Brian, what do you think happened back there, on the Bridge?'

'What do you mean what happened? How would I know?' said Brian, immediately on the defensive. 'It's not my fault the Bridge collapsed underneath us.'

'I'm not blaming you,' said Keevan, trying to placate him. 'I was just curious. What were you thinking when you stepped onto it?'

'What do you mean, what was *I* thinking. Anyone's thoughts could have landed us here!' exclaimed Brian, his face blushing bright red.

'Oh aye, the Bridge was fine until you got on it,' said the King, laughing heartily. Then they all did, even Brian. Somehow the King always managed to remain cheery no matter what had befallen them. After all, they were heroes, and with the girls of their dreams. It wasn't that bad.

Then they met the Leprechaun.

'The top of the morning to ye,' said a voice. They almost jumped out of their skin. The edge of the forest was in sight and they had been passing by the front lawns of the seven cottages.

'Over here.' They peered over the wall.

The man was less than a foot tall, dressed in green with a pointy beard, and had one of those smiles that was trying to be friendly but was actually quite sinister.

'I saw you, dropping out of the sky,' said the Leprechaun, taking off his hat to the girls who noticed his head was covered in soot.

'You didn't see me, but I saw you.' He smiled, in a way that made them want to run away.

'I can tell you're from the Heavens because you're in colour like me. It's the ones who aren't in colour you have to be careful of,' said the Leprechaun, which was a lie. 'The black and whites, they're the worst.'

'And of course the witches,' he added.

'What witches?' asked Brian, alarmed.

'The witches that live in these cottages,' whispered the Leprechaun. Everyone took a step back from the wall.

'That's how I came to be imprisoned here in this cottage. The witch kept me in the chimney.' The girls gasped.

'She caught me fishing at the Lake,' continued the Leprechaun, another lie.

'The Lake at Dairbhreach?' asked Brian.

'Yes. That's the one. Is that where you're headed? I'll come with you.' The Leprechaun clambered over the wall.

'I thought you said you were imprisoned?'

'I was,' replied the Leprechaun. 'But the witch met with an unfortunate end this morning. Come on. I'll show you a shortcut.'

The Leprechaun smiled up at Brian, but his eyes said otherwise.

Brian wondered if the Leprechaun had killed the witch, and he was about to decline his offer of directions, but it was too late. The little man was already ahead of them scuttling towards the woods, grinning like a maniac.

'I don't trust him,' said Brian to the King.

'Och aye, me neither.'

'Nor me,' said Keevan.

They followed the Leprechaun into the darkened wood. The heroes insisted on taking the hands of the girls, for protective purposes, leaving Brian traipsing behind them.

For several hundred years the Leprechaun had been trapped inside the witch's cottage, caught in the act of trying to steal one of her spells.

When the seven foot Black Witch had swept into the cottage that afternoon and killed his mistress the Leprechaun had been as pleased as punch. He had decided to open his eyes, keen to meet her acquaintance in the hope she might free him from the Story World hell he had found himself in. The Leprechaun assumed, correctly, that the Black Witch and her fiends were chasing the people in colour. He had seen them out of the sitting room window, falling out of the sky. He told her all about them, and as he did, he could see by the look on her face that he had hit the right note. The Witch almost jumped for joy. Then she had paced around the sitting room trying to devise a dreadfully clever way of stealing the girls and killing the idiots. But the Leprechaun was way ahead of her, and as he told the Witch his plan he saw that it fitted the bill perfectly. He hoped she would remember it later when it came to his freedom.

The Black Witch could hardly believe her luck. They had dropped right into her hands. She had watched the Leprechaun's exchange with the idiots, hidden behind the curtains of the sitting room window. They looked different; taller and much broader, and their hair was longer, but it was definitely them - the two idiots from the City, with their two bonny charges. And the third idiot, the pale one with the freckled face and the hair that looked like a bird's nest.

The Witch watched from the window as the party of five followed the Leprechaun into the forest and then she turned to her Banshees who were lined up in front of the sofa.

'Just wait till they get to the Lake,' said the Witch rubbing her hands in glee. 'They'll be so surprised when they run into Aife's double.'

'The Queen?' said one of the Banshees, looking confused but managing to look cross eyed instead.

'I said her double you fool. Didn't you hear the Leprechaun? Aife has a double in the Story World. She's the wicked stepmother in the *'Children of Lir.'*

The Banshees looked blankly at the Witch.

The Witch sighed heavily. 'In the story, Aife takes her step children, a young girl and three boys, to the Lake at Dairbhreach and demands that her servants kill them. When they refuse she encourages the children into the water and uses her Druid's wand to turn them into swans. They stay that way, for nine hundred years,' cackled the Witch, heading out of the cottage, the Banshees following behind her.

'Can't you see the irony of it? They've managed to evade Aife, the Queen of the Amazons, and they're about to run into her Story World double at the Lake.' But the irony was lost on the Banshees who weren't very bright.

The path to the Lake was easy, the villagers having forged it by trudging up and down daily with their buckets. After a mile or so they left the track where the path bent sharply to the right and headed up a tree lined hill until they reached the top.

'That's the Lake, down there,' said the Leprechaun, pointing through the trees to the shore at the bottom of the hill. They looked to where he was pointing, but when they turned back he had gone.

'I told you he couldn't be trusted,' said Brian, drawing his dagger. Keevan and the King followed his lead, expecting to face a whole host of Leprechauns, but nothing happened.

Then Echraide grabbed the King's arm and pointed towards the shore. Something was happening below.

An extremely tall, dark, handsome woman in fine clothing was standing by the Lake dishing out commands to her servants. Four blond children were playing close by, a girl and three boys.

'I knew I'd heard that name before,' said the King, 'The Lake at Dairbhreach is in the story of the *'Children of Lir.'*

'Then that must be Aife,' said Brian. A coldness swept through his veins at the thought of what she was about to do to the children, and he shuddered. Echraide and Echtra looked horrified. They all did. They knew the story.

They watched from the top of the hill as Aife's servants recoiled in horror at her orders to kill them. Then Aife made her way towards the shore, encouraging the children into the water.

Keevan and the King could bear it no longer. They flew down the hill towards the Lake with Brian racing behind them.

'Wait!' he cried, 'We're not supposed to interfere in any of the stories.' But it was too late.

As soon as the heroes were out of the picture the Black Witch pounced. She swung her walking stick smack into the back of Echraide's head. The warrior girl lay on the forest floor, dazed as the Witch tethered her in thick rope

236

she had found in the witch's shed. She did the same to Echtra, who was being restrained by the Banshees. Then the Witch dragged them both down the hill until she had a good view of the Lake and insisted they watch the show.

'Look, how sweet,' said the Witch. 'They're trying to save the children. Maybe Aife will turn *them* into swans too.'

The girls looked on anxiously as Keevan and the King ran into the water and began dragging the children out of the Lake.

'Don't worry my pretties. They'll be back to their old selves again - in 900 years. But I'm afraid you won't be around to see them. I'm taking the two of you back to the Island of Destiny, where you'll die early,' said the Witch, cackling loudly, which turned into a cough that almost choked her.

Down at the Lake the heroes were losing. It was three against one, once Brian had caught them up. But Aife was incredibly strong. She swatted them with her Druid's wand as if they were flies and they fell into the rushes. Frightened, the children began backing away from the shore into the water. Aife pointed her wand towards them, about to cast the spell. But the King suddenly appeared behind her and jumped on her back. Aife screeched and tried to shake him off, staggering backwards towards the shore. The King lost his grip on her and fell into the water. Keevan and Brian raced to his aid. But before they could reach him Aife had raised her Druid's wand, and the children, and the King were turned into swans.

Horrified Keevan and Brian rushed into the water, in a futile attempt to save him. But the King was full of fear. He flapped his great wings spraying water everywhere, blinding Keevan and Brian, stopping them from getting close. Then, not one to miss an opportunity, Manannan the God of the Seas, rose up and drowned them again.

Chapter Seventeen

Suicide Bridge

Jack was on the wrong side of the Bridge when the rain stopped. He had his hands in his pockets and was leaning over the railings muttering something incoherent like…

'Ung.'

They had failed, and he was back in the ordinary world. He pulled his hands out of his pockets and placed them on his head, freeing some of the Otherworld leaves that had attached themselves to his curls. They swirled down to the waters below. It took a while. For a brief moment Jack thought he saw a vision of his former self reflected in the water, and he edged himself up over the railings to get a closer look. But there was nothing to see, just floating mud and leaves. He was about to pull himself back to firmer ground, when something flew up behind him and hit him sharply on the head.

'Yikes! I'm over!'

Seconds later the back door of number three, 'the bank,' opened and Sharon popped her head out. The rain appeared to have stopped but it couldn't be trusted and so she skipped back inside for her rain hat and coat completely missing Jack's head dive off the Bridge. By the time the swan had flown down and saved him she was already half way to the bus stop.

Shocked but unharmed Jack lay at the bottom of the grassy bank, soaking wet and covered in mud, with no memory of how he had gotten there. He could hardly breathe, something heavy was weighing down on his chest, and he thought he might have broken his ribs. He opened his eyes, still blurry from the water, and found himself face to face with a huge swan. And it didn't look very happy.

'Dundee?' ventured Jack.

It was way after nine when the bus pulled into the square and yet there were still lots of people making their way into work. Sharon jumped off the bus, the only one with a spring in her step, picked up two cappuccinos from the news stand in the square and headed off into Old Street. She was looking very smart in a black dress, red Macintosh with matching rain hat, and black high heels, which were much higher than she was used to. After almost breaking a heel on the cobbles she veered right, onto the cracked pavement which was almost as bad. When she reached the antique shop half way down Sharon stopped to check her appearance in an old silver mirror which was always in the middle of the shop window, resting on a square of green velvet. Using her painted red nails, she spiked up her new hair style, which had been cut by a real hairdresser instead of her cousin and was far more flattering. Then she added a touch of rouge to her cheeks and lips and headed into Duggey's book shop.

Sharon and Duggey had become firm friends, since Jack, Dundee, and Echtra's disappearance. She had recently fallen into the habit of popping into the shop on the way to work, and popping in again on the way home.

'Any news?' she asked, stepping cautiously over the threshold in her new high heels.

'No news,' said Duggey, giving her one of his brightest celebrity smiles.

Sharon tottered over to the counter and delivered Duggey's cappuccino with one hand whilst spiking up her new hairstyle with the other. But Duggey didn't seem to notice her hair, and because she was running later than usual, Sharon tottered out again and headed back in the direction of Stress City Headquarters.

The disappearance of Mrs D, a small yellow Café, Jack, Dundee and Echtra, three years earlier had captured the imagination of the entire City. There were rumours that Mrs D was a fairy who had spirited them off into the Otherworld. Stories of their adventures on the other side of the Bridge had taken on almost mythical proportions - stories fuelled by Duggey, written by a young journalist girl whose *'Wilde Blue Yonder - Fact or Fiction'* articles had become the talk of the town.

The inhabitants of Stress City were enchanted by the

possibility of an Otherworld, and although they had no intention of making the trip themselves, they were looking for reassurance that if there *was* an Otherworld at the end of the Bridge, it was nothing to write home about.

But it wasn't long before City Hall put a stop to it. They issued an official announcement, quashing the Otherworld rumours, stating there was no such thing, and it was about time everyone came to their senses. And after a while everyone did, returning to the business of the day.

Well, almost everyone. Duggey continued to spread the word. As did his willing accomplice, town gossip Sharon, despite the fact that her father had banned such talk from the house. And Mrs Snarlington-Darlington, who insisted the rumours about the Otherworld were true, and had taken to her bed, refusing to leave the house until Jack had been returned to her.

Duggey took the lid off his cappuccino and searched his pockets for his bacon sandwich. Then he remembered he had left it at home in the fridge.

Back on the bank Duggey's bacon sandwich was making its way out of the back kitchen of number one, courtesy of Jack who had two cans of beer and a dog bowl in his arms. He had tried to get into the kitchen at number two which he knew would have more food in it, but no matter how hard he hammered on the back door there was no answer from Mrs Snarlington-Darlington, who for some reason still had the curtains drawn at nine thirty in the morning.

Jack staggered towards the swan, still dizzy from his fall. He threw the items on the grass and went back for a bag of bird seed which he stole from the bird table of number five. Then he plonked himself down in front of the swan which was shifting restlessly from one webbed foot to the other. Jack poured the contents of one of the cans into the dog bowl. Then he opened the other for himself. The swan gulped the beer down as fast as it could. Jack took a few sips from his can and then opened the bag of bird seed, throwing a handful of it onto the lawn before taking the wrapper off his bacon sandwich.

'Whits this?' said the swan. 'I'm nae eating seeds!'

'I can hear you!' cried Jack, 'And you didn't even open your mouth. Say something else.'

Somehow the swan managed to look annoyed.

Jack reluctantly handed over half his bacon sandwich. The swan gulped it down in one. Then he added some of the contents of his own can to the dog bowl and they concentrated on drinking their beer in the sunshine for a while.

'So, how's it going?' said Jack, out of habit.

'What do you mean how's it going? I'm a swan Jack, a swan! I hate heights. I hate flying. I'm cold, I'm damp, and people keep chucking bread at me.'

Jack fell back onto the lawn, laughing hysterically. Then he sat up, feeling guilty.

'It's not my fault you fell into the water.'

Dundee padded around the lawn, looking fed up.

'Don't worry,' said Jack, trying to make amends. 'We'll get you back to normal.'

'Oh aye. That's easy for you to say. We're back Jack, back in the ordinary world. I'm going to be stuck like this, forever,' said Dundee, bending his swan neck in sorrow.

Jack felt bad. Then he remembered something.

'Why did you push me off the Bridge?'

'I didn't push you. I was trying to save you.'

'I wasn't jumping!' cried Jack, throwing his arms up, dramatically.

'Aye, I know. I was trying to warn you. The Bridge keeps fading in and out. It's been at it all morning.'

'Oh,' Jack felt bad, again. 'We'll go back to the Otherworld, find you an antidote or something.'

'How? Emma's cafe is gone. I checked the clearing this morning. It must have disappeared the day we left. And everyone in the City is on a go slow. The City is dying Jack. Just like Mrs D said it would.'

Jack stared at the lawn, unsure of his ground. He was uncomfortable being the one in charge, trying to solve all the problems. In the end they decided to do what they always did and headed off to Duggey's.

It was a strange sight for the passengers on the bus that morning; a man and a swan, walking side by side along the visitor's road, appearing to be having a conversation, and for a moment everyone was shaken out of their

Monday morning blues. But they soon sank back into them again when they got to the City gateway.

At Stress City Headquarters Ann Angel was in a meeting, her phone was off the hook, and her assistant Sharon was in the kitchen finishing off her cappuccino, with a love struck look in her eyes.

Sharon had yet to tell anyone how she felt about Duggey. Not even her mother who usually heard everything first. She hadn't told Duggey either but being the man he would be the last to know. Duggey had no idea why Sharon spent so much time in the shop and accepted her gifts of cappuccinos and bacon sandwiches with the innocence of a young fawn. Meanwhile Sharon was dreaming of the day when they would tie the knot, unaware that her relations had already set the ball rolling in the direction of Bob, a serious young man with a head for figures who had a long career ahead of him with Mrs Snarlington-Darlington's cousin, Eric at the Bank.

Sharon forced herself up off the stool, tossed the empty cup into the bin, and headed back into Ann's office. She threw herself down into Ann's fancy leather chair and stared at the phone – considered putting it back on the hook, then decided against it - unable to focus on anything but Duggey. And so she sat at Ann's desk doodling love hearts on her shorthand note pad wondering whether she should confide in Mrs Snarlington-Darlington.

Sharon had become a regular visitor at number two,

'the bank' ever since Mrs Snarlington-Darlington had taken to her bed - although she was never alone. Mrs Snarlington-Darlington had visitors around the clock - neighbours, church goers, psychics, religious gurus, café owners, shop owners, people from the Bank, and the dry cleaner who was in and out every couple of days. And of course her ladies of the week who catered to her every whim, bringing her culinary delights on their relevant days and so Mrs Snarlington-Darlington was bigger than ever, but she wasn't herself. She insisted on having the curtains drawn at all times, with a dim light at her bedside, saying she didn't have the strength to even powder her nose. She did nothing but eat and talk about Jack, who she insisted was on the 'other side,' and despite her friends telling her otherwise, and her many visitors who thought she was losing her marbles, Mrs Snarlington-Darlington was staying put until Jack returned.

'Five and forty heroes, who have paid an enormous price,' said Dundee, who had kept up an on-going dialogue all the way into the City.

'Well I've paid the price Jack. Never again. I'm telling ye now. As soon as I'm back to my old self again I'm staying here…in the ordinary world. And the next time Destiny calls you can tell her I'm oot.'

Jack kept his thoughts to himself. Dundee had a lot to get off his swan chest. But when they got to the City gateway and Jack saw the square he let out a gasp.

'What's happened to everyone
'I told you it was bad.'

Stress City had lost its fizz. Everyone ⎯
at a mechanical pace to the beat of ⎯
which was doing its own thing - so ⎯⎯ moving
forwards, sometimes moving backwards, and sometimes
stopping altogether. People kept forgetting where they
were up to, stopping in the middle of a conversation, or
repeating themselves over and over. There was hardly
any noise, and all the problems had gone. No-one
bothered to complain about anything anymore. The
weather was the weather. The job was the job, and that
was that.

Jack and Dundee weaved their way around the slow
running people in the square and headed down into Old
Street which didn't look any different, but then again
there was no-one around. They were relieved to see
Duggey, who was exactly the same, sitting behind the
counter, low in his chair, with his boots up and his eyes
fixed on the television set which was still showing the
Wizard of Oz.

'Just put it on the counter,' said Duggey, without
bothering to look up.

'Duggey.'

'You're back!' cried Duggey, jumping up off his
chair so fast it fell to the floor. He came out from behind
the counter and shook Jack's hand vigorously, patting

247

the shoulder.

'Where's the man?'

'Erm…'

'You've not left him over there have you?' Duggey laughed.

'Of course not,' said Jack, trying to laugh as well to lighten the mood.

'He's over there.' Jack pointed to the swan who was standing in the doorway with a large tartan scarf around its neck which Jack had insisted Dundee wear to make sure he didn't mix him up with any of the ordinary swans.

'Where?'

'There,' said Jack, pointing directly at the swan.

'The swan!'

'Yep,' confirmed Jack.

Duggey cautiously approached the swan at the door. 'Dundee?'

'Aye.'

Duggey flew back, hitting his head on a picture of Laurel and Hardy on the trail of the lonesome pine.

'I can hear him!'

'I know!'

'I need a drink,' said Duggey, swinging into the kitchen with a seriously worried look on his face. Jack grabbed a stool at the counter and put his head in his hands. If Duggey was worried then they really were in trouble.

Duggey played barman, listening intently as Jack

relayed the story of everything that had happened to them, including their unexpected return to the Island that morning.

'I can't understand it,' Jack complained. 'We didn't do anything un-heroic, so why were we thrown back.'

'You killed off your hero characters didn't you, which means we're all in trouble.'

'What do you mean?'

'You signed the heroes' contracts. Now you'll have to save Stress City, as yourselves. Duggey took a large shot of whiskey at the thought. 'Have you seen what's happening to everyone?'

Jack nodded.

'It's because of the missing Key. And soon we'll have no chance of getting it back. The Bridge is disappearing Jack – it's our only link to the Otherworld. Once that goes we'll be cut off - forever.'

Jack felt as though he'd been kicked in the stomach. He would never see Echtra again.

'And the dreams will go with it.'

'What do you mean?'

'The dreams of the City are locked inside the golden pillar box. They're fading away. That's why all the problems have gone. No-one cares anymore…'

Duggey's attention was drawn back to the television set as the lion in the Wizard of Oz jumped out onto the yellow brick road.

'…and you two are the only ones who can save the day. If only you had the nerve.'

249

Jack put his head in his hands and sighed heavily.

Duggey turned his attention back to the counter. 'Have you been home yet?'

'No. We couldn't get in.'

'Mrs Snarlington-Darlington's taken your disappearance pretty badly. She hasn't left the house for three years.'

'What do you mean three years? We've only been gone...'

'Three days?'

Jack had forgotten about the time difference. He jumped off the stool in a panic. 'It's definitely three years, not three hundred.'

Duggey worked it out for him. 'You spent one night at the Fianna camp, one night on Scathach Island. That's two days. You must have missed a day in the Story World. Yep, three days.'

'Dundee said we might turn to dust.'

'You won't turn to dust,' Duggey laughed.

Jack was unconvinced. He raced through the tiny door to the left of the counter and stepped into the bathroom. He checked himself in the mirror. He looked fine. Better than usual. He returned to his stool.

'You look fine Jack. If anything you look younger, and broader, maybe even taller.'

'Really?' said Jack, feeling pleased. 'You look the same as you did when we left Stress City.'

'You're whatever age you set your mind to be. I learned that in Falias.'

'Oh aye, you both look great. I'll just head off to the pond and droon myself,' said Dundee, who was fed up being ignored.

They had forgotten all about him!

Duggey rushed forward, full of concern.

'Help me put him on the counter.'

'Be careful.'

'Watch his feathers.'

'Pour him a whiskey. Use the basin in the kitchen!'

As they were fussing over the swan on the counter one of the 'well to do's' poked her nosy head around the door.

'We're closed!' said Duggey, rudely. She ran off to spill the beans.

Meanwhile, back at number two 'the bank' Mrs Snarlington-Darlington was sitting up in bed with the curtains open.

'It's just like I said,'said Mrs Snarlington-Darlington to the Mondays who were gathered around her bed like chicks to a mother hen.

'He was asleep in the forest under a tree. I knew it was him, even though he had grey hair and a long beard. When you've been married as long as I have you can recognise your own husband, no matter how hard they try to disguise themselves.'

The Mondays nodded in agreement.

'And then I saw Jack.'

'No!' said the Mondays in unison. Mrs Snarlington-

Darlington looked suitably forlorn. She had their full attention.

'Jack was in the dream too. He called out my name. I could hear him, loud and clear. As if he was standing outside this very window,' said Mrs Snarlington Darlington, wiping her eyes with one of Mr Snarlington-Darlington's hankies.

'It must be a sign,' said one of the Monday's.

'Do you think so?' asked Mrs Snarlington-Darlington, perking up at the thought.

'Yes,' said the others, relieved that Mrs Snarlington-Darlington had finally opened the curtains. 'They're coming home.'

Back at the book shop Duggey was planning their escape.

'The Bridge is far too risky…'

'What about Dundee? We have to get him back to normal first,' said Jack, who had no intention of going back to the Otherworld on his own.

They headed off into the book aisles leaving Dundee asleep on the counter having finished off half a basin of whisky. They searched through the book shelves for over an hour but found nothing.

'There are lots of spells for turning people into something, but nothing for turning them back,' said Duggey. 'We'll have to get him back to the Otherworld. It's his only chance…'

Jack sighed, and threw his head into the middle of a spell book in frustration.

'Wait,' said Duggey, slapping his forehead for being so stupid. 'You can go back through *Emma's*.'

'But *Emma's* disappeared the day we left,' said Jack, following Duggey out of the book shop.

'Yeh, but *Emma's* double is still here.'

Two doors down from Duggeys, in exactly the same place as it was in Falias, sat *Emma's* cafe, still primrose yellow under all the dust, but boarded up. They rushed back to tell Dundee the news.

'Break in,' said Dundee impatiently when he saw the boards across the door. Duggey broke in.

Inside the cafe it was like the ghost of *Emma's*. The floor, tables, chairs, cake display case and till were covered in a thick layer of dust. But the layout was exactly the same – the image of *Emma's* in Falias. They walked through the dusty café and into the corridor. As they turned the bend they were relieved to find the back larder open.

It was time to go.

'Well, cheerio again,' said Duggey, shaking Jack's hand and patting Dundee on his swan head. 'I'll catch you on the other side.'

Duggey watched them go and then he slid back into the shop and settled down in front of the television just in time to see Dorothy kill the witch.

Two doors down at the dry cleaners the nosy 'well to do' was picking up her dining room drapes.

'I saw him, as clear as day this morning walking

along the visitor's road. Everyone on the bus did. And he was talking to a swan.'

'A swan?' said the dry cleaner, carefully checking that he had managed to get the slight stain out of her pink silken drapes before placing them into the protective cover.

'Yes. A swan. It was definitely Jack because I've just seen him again in the book shop with that other layabout, *and* the swan. And they were both talking to it. I heard them!' said the 'well to do.'

The dry cleaner tried his best not to laugh. It wasn't good for business.

'Whatever next.' said the woman next to her.

The young journalist girl behind her backed out of the dry cleaners and headed off in the direction of Duggey's with her *'Wilde Blue Yonder - Fact or Fiction'* notebook in her hand.

Chapter Eighteen

Dreams refined or replaced

The High road to Finias was straight and wide, forest lined, with plenty of shade, and plenty of places to rest your weary head, yet it was rarely taken. The road was said to be haunted by lost souls - ghouls from the lower regions who hung around the borders of the higher realms, desperate to be brought back to life, finding devious ways to enter the bodies of weary travellers who would stop for a rest by a rock or a tree and suddenly find themselves invaded. The way these creatures entered the body was never pleasant so most travellers opted for the Low road, a dirt track through a fiend infested forest, where at least the fiends could be seen and you had a fair chance of beating them off.

The Adventurer and his crew always took the High road. There was little likelihood of them being attacked by anything, natural or supernatural. Their cosmic Convoy was well known - a line of seven caravans marked by the ancient symbols of the seven souls of man. At the head of the Convoy leading the horses were nine men dressed in black who were as old as the hills, known as the dragons, for their leathery skin, their spit which

255

was pure poison, and their capable aim with a tail whip. A crew of muscle bound heavies took the front caravan, the next line of defence after the dragons. Outlaws ran the Convoy on horseback protecting those who travelled with them; bad seeds, exiled shamans, alchemists and seers, magicians and sorcerers, singers, performers, poets and players. The Adventurer and his Chiefs took the tail end in the Den, a place where they undertook a variety of bad habits which usually involved an excess of something.

The Convoy had come to a halt after a report had arrived from the front of a group of horses heading their way. The Adventurer and his Chiefs disembarked, taking the news in their stride. It took a while for them to walk the line. Most of the people travelling with them came out of the caravans to greet them and stretch their legs. When at last they did come to the head of the Convoy they were delighted to see a group of young females; the Sisters, who were well known, but rarely seen. They worked for Donn of the Dead, and were a lot less holy than they should have been.

No females ever travelled with the Adventurer, he forbade it, and so almost everyone gathered around to have a good look at the Sisters, who looked more like women of the night than nuns. They had pretty faces and long hair that had been tied back beneath their black habits. They wore black leather riding boots, stockings and suspenders which were clearly on show beneath their short black dresses. Each wore a ruby ring on their marital finger, a jewel of great power which was said to guide them through the worlds, provided their bodies remained untouched by unholy hands, a fact that the men in the Convoy would fantasize about later.

The Sisters followed the Adventurer and his Chiefs back to the Den to discuss the purpose of their visit. The Den was large enough for seven but cramped with the additional five female visitors. The Sisters were offered the only two sofas in the room, which sat either side, beneath the curtained windows. The Adventurer took his seat in the left hand corner, leaving his Chiefs relegated to the floor. But they didn't mind. From their vantage point they could clearly see what was going on beyond their suspenders, and they took off their shades to get a better look.

'We bring news from Donn of the Dead,' said the eldest Sister, interrupting their fantasies.

The Adventurer sat forward, intrigued. They had never had much to do with the God of the Dead. Donn and Angus had never quite gotten along.

'It's about the Shadow,' she continued.

They were all ears.

'He's stolen some of the Few.'

'Donn's helpers?' asked the Wings.

She nodded.

'They can duplicate themselves,' said the Guardian Angel, who was sitting against the door on his own.

'If they can do that then we're really in trouble!' said the Heart.

257

'Not without the prototype,' explained the Sister. 'And *he* is well protected.'

'He'd better be,' said the Adventurer.

The Sister nodded. 'The problem is, we have no idea how the Shadow is taking the Few, and until we do there is no way of stopping him.'

The Adventurer leant back in his chair and took his shades off. His eyes were red, his skin lined and rough, and his chin unshaven. Yet somehow he managed to maintain his sex appeal. He let the conversation roll for a moment whilst he contemplated this latest news. For the sake of bygone times he had let the Shadow be. It was a mistake.

From the tales people told the Shadow's crazy circus, Showtown, was easy to track, but the Shadow was always several steps ahead of them. One day they would come face to face. It was a day the Adventurer was looking forward to.

'We need to get someone on the inside, someone the Shadow trusts,' continued the Sister.

'We know someone,' said the Adventurer, now back in the conversation. He indicated towards the wall where there was a photograph of the Rev at his best, preaching to the converted.

'We know the Preacher,' said the youngest Sister, who was the prettiest.

'We'll bring him to you,' said the eldest.

And so it was agreed. The Sisters would track back to find the Rev while the Convoy continued on towards

Finias.

It was early morning in Falias and the shop keepers and café owners had yet to make an appearance. Old Street was still warming up. The sun had yet to reach the stores on the right hand side of the pavement, and *Emma's* was still in the shadows. The sign on the door said closed. A young man passed through on a bike with the morning mail. He delivered a few letters to the shops on the left and then swerved to the right with a bundle of letters for Mrs D who was one of his regulars. He was about to post the bundle through the letterbox when he thought he heard something inside the café. He peered in through the glass door but he couldn't see anyone, and as curiosity killed more people than anything else in Falias, he jumped swiftly back onto his bike, deciding to mention it later to the lady in charge.

Jack picked up the bundle of mail and flicked through the envelopes.

'There's one here with wavy hand writing,' said Jack to the swan at his side, who was picking crumbs off the floor. 'I think it's from the God of the Seas. I bet it's about us.'

The swan began to flap. 'Don't open it. It'll be more bad news.' It flew up in the air almost attacking Jack.

'Ok, ok!' Jack placed the mail on top of the till. Dundee was getting more like a swan by the hour. The sooner he got him back to normal the better.

Jack took a cautious look out of the window. The

street was empty. He turned the handle of *Emma's* door and stepped quietly out onto Old Street. The swan followed him. Then the two of them headed up the street in the direction of Duggey's, having decided there was more chance of finding a spell there, than in the ordinary world book shop. They were almost at the door when the swan started flapping backwards.

'What is it?'

'Look!'

Jack looked. Twelve small men in dark suits with round faces and round glasses were heading towards them. Some were in the middle of the street looking around. Others were on the pavement peering into the front windows of the shops and cafes. They appeared to be searching for something. And they didn't look very friendly.

'They look just like the Few,' said Jack. 'Aren't they on our side?'

'Do they look like they're on our side?'

Jack took the next few strides in reverse. Then, before the men could spot him, he ran back into *Emma's*, and hid in the kitchen. Dundee insisted on joining him, even though he was disguised as a swan. They almost died with fright when the men, who did indeed look very much like the Few, peered through the letter box and the windows and hammered on the door. Then they walked on.

With his heart beating ten to the dozen Jack poked his head out of the kitchen.

'They've gone. You go out and check the coast is clear.'

Dundee was about to argue, then he remembered he was a swan. He waddled out onto the pavement and checked the street to the left and the right a few times, as if about to cross the road. The shop owners of Falias, who were just arriving outside and beginning to open their shutters and doors, stopped to stare at him. Even for Falias, the sight of a swan in a tartan scarf attempting to cross the road was an unusual sight.

'Jack.' Jack. Jack!'

'What is it now?' said Jack, sticking his head out of the door.

'Look who it is.'

At the top of the Street there was a man on a bike with wonky steering who was swerving from one side of the road to the other. At one point he almost hit the pavement. He was the double of Doc Spoc.

'Is that who I think it is?' Jack joined Dundee outside.

'I hope so. Come on. He might have a potion that could turn me back into a man,' Dundee almost took flight in his rush to get to him.

As they headed back up the street the man drew his bike to a stop and laid it against the door of his surgery. He took the bicycle clips off his trousers, a hanky out of his pocket to polish his shoes, his key out of his top pocket, and opened the door. Then he went inside.

They were still a few doors away from the surgery when Jack realised that the Few had turned around and were heading back up the road towards them. Jack flew up onto the pavement and into one of the shops which happened to have its door open. The swan took a moment to realise he was on his own, and flapped in behind him.

Jack moved straight to the tiny window and peered out through a gap in the curtains to watch the men, who walked straight past the shop, and then continued on into the forest. He turned around.

The shop was completely bare, apart from two men who looked exactly like the Few, but weren't, and were sitting behind a desk, like they were getting ready to read the news.

'Can we help you?' said the man on the left.

'Can we help you?' repeated the man on the right.

'Erm, we're just browsing thanks,' said Jack, looking around for something to browse at, but apart from the two men and the desk there was nothing see.

'Have you any idea what you want?' asked the man on the left.

'Any idea at all?' added the man on the right.

'Not really,' said Jack, his eye on the street outside.

'Then you'll want next door,' said the man on the left.

'You won't get to see them today though. They're incredibly busy. You'll have to make an appointment,' said the man on the right.

'Why, what do they do?' asked Jack, suddenly curious.

'They help the people who *don't* know what they want.'

'What do you do?' asked Jack, dragging himself away from the window.

'We're new. We have a plaque. It arrived this morning,' said the man excitedly, jumping up off his chair and heading for the door, the man on the left following him.

'*Dreams refined or replaced...*' read the man on the right, pointing to the sign.

Jack smiled and nodded politely.

'We help the people who *do* know what they want, but fancy a change.'

'Some people find their dreams are taking too long.'

'Some people find their destinies are too difficult.'

'We're fine with our destinies thanks,' said Jack.

'I'm not.' said Dundee, decisively. 'What do I have to do?'

'It's a simple process.'

'Very simple indeed.'

'If you'll just follow us into the changing room,' said the men.

Jack suddenly noticed a curtain that hadn't been there before.

'If you'll just step behind the curtain to change.'

'You'll be a brand new swan in no time.'

'With a brand new destiny.'

263

'But...I don't want to be a swan!' cried Dundee, backing away from the curtain. 'I want to be a man.'

'Oh!' said the men, looking flustered. This was clearly something they hadn't allowed for.

'Look. I don't mean to be rude,' said Jack, steering Dundee away from the curtain before they could get into any more trouble. 'I just need to get my friend here changed back into a man. Can you do that?'

'We can do most things,' said the man on the left.

'Yes, we can do most things,' said the man on the right.

'But we can't do that.'

'No we can't do that.'

'You'll want Doc Spoc. He's next door to the book shop.'

The surgery door looked exactly the same as it had in Stress City, except it was much fancier, and it had a sign on it.

'What does it say?' asked Dundee, too low to see it.

'All wounds healed, save that of love.'

'It's definitely him then.'

'Come in, come in,' said the Doc, who had heard the door open.

'Let me do the talking,' said Jack, as they passed by the small reception area that never had anyone on it, and the waiting room that never had anyone in it.

They stood in the doorway of Doc Spoc's surgery and peered in. It was just the same as the room Jack had been in three days earlier, except everything was on the opposite side. The surgery bed was on the right, Doc Spoc's desk was on the left, and it had a picture of the woman in blue on it! Doc Spoc looked exactly the same as his ordinary world double, although his hair was a little tidier, possibly due to the woman in the picture. He had his head down and was scribbling something in a note book. Jack tried to read his writing but couldn't. Then the Doc looked up at Jack and smiled.

'There's no antidote for love I'm afraid,' said the Doc, cheerily.

'I'm not the patient, he is,' said Jack, indicating the swan beside him.

'Oh I see,' said Doc Spoc, ushering them into the surgery. 'What seems to be the problem?'

'He's a man,' said Jack, taking the seat opposite, the swan at his side.

'And he can't seem to accept that he's a swan?' enquired the Doc.

'No. He really is a man,' said Jack, thinking he had made himself clear.

'So he's not a swan at all then. No swan relations?' chuckled the Doc, amusing himself.

'No,' said Jack, un-amused.

'And how did this happen?' asked the Doc, getting out his special glasses to have a closer look at the swan man.

'He got caught up in a spell.'

'Caught up in it? So the spell wasn't for him?' Doc

Spoc peered into Dundee's swan eyes with a small torch. 'I see. Was he in the water when this happened?'

'Yes. He was!' cried Jack, relieved Doc Spoc seemed to know what he was talking about.

'And did everyone in the water turn into swans as well?' asked the Doc.

The look on Jack's face confirmed he was right.

Doc Spoc smiled and reversed his chair, which was on rollers, back towards the desk to indicate the examination was over.

'You see, spells rely heavily on beliefs, otherwise they don't work,' explained the Doc, placing his hands behind his head and leaning back in his chair. 'You need the right setting, the right mood…'

There was a moment of silent anticipation as Doc Spoc considered the possibilities.

'Is he very superstitious?' The Doc suddenly sat up straight.

'Yes!' cried Jack, optimistic. The swan looked towards the Doc, with hope in its eyes. 'Can you cure him?'

'No,' said the Doc, bluntly. 'The only way you'll cure him is to reverse the process, surround him with swans who turn into humans.'

'And how am I supposed to do that?' cried Jack.

'You could try Duggey's next door. He's got lots of books on that sort of thing. But I think he's out.'

In the ordinary world Duggey was in.

'They were here! In the shop. Oh, I can't believe it. It's so exciting isn't it?' Duggey smiled, as Sharon gripped the edge of the counter.

'What about Echtra, is she here to?'

'Erm, no… she's still on the other side.'

'What about the Fairy Queen. Have they found her?'

'No.'

'Have they found the Key?'

'No.'

Duggey gave Sharon the highlights of Jack and Dundee's adventures in the Otherworld, omitting to tell her that the Island was surrounded by invisible fiends, a Black Witch had taken her friend hostage, Dundee had been turned into a swan, and the Governor Addison Bruce was a Villain. He didn't want to alarm her.

'They were on the Bridge. This morning! How exciting. I must have missed them. What about Mrs Snarlington-Darlington. Did she see them?' Sharon was talking ten to the dozen.

'Jack said they tried to get in but there was no answer.'

'I have to get over there now,' cried Sharon, grabbing her coat. 'Just wait till I tell her he's back. Maybe she'll get out of bed.' In her hurry to get out she skidded in her new high heels down the dip in the floor.

'Be careful,' warned Duggey, coming out from behind the counter. He grabbed hold of her arm to steady her. She caught his eye. It was a moment. Duggey let go and backed away towards the counter.

Sharon moved towards the door.

'Wait,' he called.

'Yes,' she gasped, hopefully.

'Jack's not here.'

'Oh,' said Sharon, disappointed.

'They've gone back to the Otherworld, to resume their heroic quest.

'Oh...yes of course,' said Sharon, thinking this would go down well with Mrs Snarlington-Darlington. 'Are you coming?'

'No. I'll catch up with you later,' said Duggey, shyly. Something had happened between them and he had no idea what it was.

Sharon left the shop as happy as could be, leaving a romantically confused Duggey behind.

It was Dundee's knowledge of stories that saved him. He had remembered a myth about the swan maidens who, at the end of every Celtic year, would gather together at a Lake and transform from swans to maidens. The only thing they had to do was find out where. In Duggey's absence they began searching the aisles in the Celtic Myths and Legends section. Jack was on the floor surrounded by open books with ancient text, so ancient he could hardly understand the words. Dundee was up above, pulling out any relevant books with his beak, and allowing them to fall on the floor.

'There are a few swans in this story,' said Jack.

'That's the *Children of Lir*,' said Dundee, checking the pages of the book from up above. 'We've just been in that one! Wait. I think I've found something.'

A gigantic heavy book on Irish Myths and Legends hit the floor with a thump.

'That nearly hit me!'

'Open it,' insisted Dundee, dropping to his side.

Jack opened the book in the middle, which turned out to be exactly the right place. The chapter began with a picture of the swan maidens. It was the most beautiful and sensual image they had ever seen. The swan maidens were bathing in a lake surrounded by a background of dark green reeds. Their white feathers were glistening in the shimmering waters. Some still in swan form, some in transformation, and some fully formed, emerging from the lake as beautiful naked maidens. At the bottom of the picture it said, *The Lake of the Dragon's Mouth*, and underneath that, '*Samhain*.'

'What does that mean?' asked Jack.

'Samhain is the end of the Celtic year…but it doesn't matter what day it is.'

'Every day is story day in the Story World,' said Jack grinning. 'Let's go.'

'Hold your horses. These women are naked. If this works I'm nae wandering around in that world withoot ma clothes on.'

They headed into the Duggey's dusty back closet, which had boxes of his old clothes, marked by the year.

'That looks too small. That's too old fashioned. I'm

269

nae wearing that.'

Jack was getting frustrated. For some reason Dundee was much more vain as a swan.

'There's a box over here from the seventies,' said Jack, brushing the dust off. 'Look, a black shirt and trousers.'

'They're bell bottoms!'

'They'll do.'

'What aboot shoes.'

Jack found a pair of brown winkle pickers that were one size too large.

'Och, you're joking. I'm nae wearing those.'

'Dundee! We're supposed to be saving the day. Who cares what you look like!'

Whilst they were arguing over clothes there was a loud bang next door.

'What was that?'

'Shsst,' said Dundee, who had far better senses as a swan. It's coming from the Library.

Jack picked up the clothes and shoes, as Dundee waddled off along the aisles, and put his swan head to the Library door.

'It's the Witch. She's coming out of the Story World door. I think she has the girls with her.'

'What shall we do?'

'Go get her!' said Dundee, bravely.

The Head Librarian, who was up a ladder dusting, saw it all.

Delighted with her catch the Black Witch strode confidently through the Library, dragging the girls behind her like dogs. She was still relaying her cleverness to the Banshees when the swan attacked. The Witch was thrown back by the force of the wings hitting her full on in the face. She cried out, lost her grip on the girls, and before she knew what was happening Jack had grabbed her captives and was hurling them back towards the Story World door. The Banshees were too slow to react and within seconds they were gone. But Dundee was still on the Witch's side of the door. She flew up off the floor in a rage, intent on grabbing the swan and ringing its neck, but she was floored by a giant book on gardening which the Head Librarian had accidently on purpose dropped on her head. And Dundee was through.

Back in Stress City Sharon was sharing the good news with Mrs Snarlington-Darlington.

'And they were thrown back here this morning, onto the Bridge,' said Sharon.

'Then it *was* Jack. It wasn't a dream at all. Oh Jack,' cried Mrs Snarlington-Darlington, jumping out of bed and into her bedroom slippers.

'He's not here,' said Sharon quickly. 'They've gone back to the Otherworld.'

'Gone back?' cried Mrs Snarlington-Darlington, collapsing back onto the bed. 'Oh!' she gasped, 'I'll never see him again.' Sharon dashed towards her with the

271

hankies.

'Don't worry. He'll be back again,' said Sharon, in a reassuring tone. 'Jack and Dundee are heroes now.'

'Heroes,' said Mrs Snarlington-Darlington, realising how this would sound to her friends.

Later that afternoon, when the Mondays arrived, they found Mrs Snarlington-Darlington in the sitting room cleaning the silver, with Jack's pictures lined up along the mantelpiece.

Back at the book shop the Black Witch found what she was looking for in the Celtic aisle of Myths and Legends. By the time Duggey arrived she was already on her way to the Lake of the Dragon's mouth.

Duggey hopped onto his chair, switched on the set, and settled back for an old episode of Stingray.

'Anything could happen in the next half hour.'

One hundred and fifty swans, with silver chains around their necks, flew across a darkened sky. The moon cast its light on their white winged forms, and Dundee was at the centre, a part of them all.

They settled at the Lake of the Dragon's Mouth, and wet their wings in the divine waters. Some drifted solitary and calm in the reeds, others flocked together in groups of five or six. As the water began to bubble and rise they began their transformation. Each as beautiful as the next the maidens arched back their newly formed female bodies in a groan of sexual pleasure as the swell of the warm current rushed between their legs, swirling up around their hips, and the tender points of their breasts. They threw back their heads and wet their long blond hair in the sunlit waters. Finally they lost their wings. Then one by one they rose naked from the Lake, still with their silver chains around their necks. All had tasks to perform before they came together again.

Dundee drew up his arms as if in a dream, and placed his hands on the wet hair of his human head. 'He was back.' He drew his fingers over his face, his lips, his neck, and then further down all over his body just to check he was all there. His skin was like a new born. He had muscles on his arms and chest, his stomach flat and taut. He stopped when he came to his loins and was unable to resist the urge, his manhood swelling with blood. He let out a groan of sheer ecstasy, and swam around the lake, full of energy. Then he sensed someone watching him. It was the swan maiden Caer, the girl of Angus's dreams. She was sitting on the bank, her feet dangling in the water. Dundee swam towards her, embarrassed at what she may have seen. But when she smiled he forgot it.

Caer was unlike the other swan maidens. Her hair was dark, thick cut and wavy, and fell short of her shoulders. Her eyes were blue like the divine waters, her lips full, her flesh white and her breasts like fresh pink rose buds, unlike any he had ever seen. He could see how a God like Angus would be so besotted with her. Caer was irresistible and in his heightened state of

273

arousal he felt it was best to stay where he was, beneath the water.

'We must demand something of you in return,' said Caer.

'Anything,' said Dundee, and he meant it.

'One of our youngest maidens has been taken by a Leprechaun. She fell into a trap at the Lake at Dairbhreach.'

'We've met him,' said Jack, coming out of the forest with Dundee's clothes.

They were on their way back to the Land of Hellish Thought to rescue a swan maiden. Caer's directions had been easy - a straight path through the woods. But as they drew nearer to the Hellish Land it grew darker.

Jack and Echtra took the lead, with Dundee and Echraide behind them, and they trudged on, towards the gloom. Dundee tried his best to focus on the task ahead, but with the beauty at his side, he was unable to keep his lustful thoughts from his mind.

'It's pitch black up ahead,' said Jack, assuming Dundee was still behind him. But he was not.

Dundee had held back, purposefully. His intent was clear, and before long he had pulled his warrior queen off the track and into a clearing. Dundee was at his most handsome, strong and highly charged after his transformation in the Lake. His hair still wet from the divine waters, his manhood pulsing with life again. He could hardly contain himself. But it was she who came to him. Dundee was on fire. He tore off her clothing, then his own, and pulled her to him, grabbing her hips until there was no room left between them. When he took hold of her hair she arched her back, and it was better than the dream.

He didn't notice the lone magpie above him in the tree, or the Black Witch, who had followed them. The Witch's face turned green with envy. She threw a spell over them, a bad one. Then she returned to the dimly lit trail. She could see the white hair of the Banshees in the distance and she hurried towards them.

The Banshees had been tasked with keeping an eye on the doll. But spying on her wasn't easy. The track was like a fog of gloom. The doll kept dipping in and out of their field of vision, and every so often the idiot would appear, and they had to pull back into the woods.

If it hadn't been for the Banshee spies Jack and Echtra would never have gotten together at all. The sexually unfaithful Jack was alone with the girl of his dreams, yet unable to act. He felt awkward, even shy. Dundee's sudden disappearance hadn't helped. He was far less confident without him.

Jack was walking backwards, checking behind them for signs of his pal, when he saw something white in the distance. He stopped suddenly. Without thinking he grabbed Echtra and drew her off the track into the

275

woods. Then dagger in hand, a glimmer of the hero within, he bravely returned to the gloomy trail and waited for the attack. Nothing came.

He returned to her. Jack's heart was beating fast. He felt a desperate longing, had held it all those years. He put his hand to her arm. She blushed. His lips were on hers, her mouth opened up to his, and they were caught up, in the memory of their distant past; the warm tide of Manannan's sea, her white flesh, her perfect curves, her breasts, the sound from her throat as, with expert ease, he pulled off her garments beneath the water, and found her. He was strong and held her steady, his face to hers, above the waves, and as he entered her it felt like all the stars had burst in the heavens.

The Black Witch missed their karmic coming together. She was livid. Addison's instructions had been clear; the doll was to remain untouched. She took it out on the Banshees further down the trail. Then she flew on, towards the Land of Hellish Thought, to plot Jack's dreadful demise.

Back in Stress City Mrs Snarlington-Darlington was up and about and considering purchasing a property in Old Street.

'It could do with a spring clean,' she said, wiping her finger along the counter of *Emma's*.

The estate agent, whose patience had run out several hours ago, was standing in the doorway with a fake smile

276

on his face.

'It could be a gold mine in the right hands,' said the man, who was tall and lanky, and looked like he might fall over in a strong wind.

'Don't be ridiculous,' said Mrs Snarlington-Darlington, who didn't take kindly to being sold to.

She studied the skirting boards and the corners, in a manner that suggested she knew what she was looking for, and then headed into the adjoining room with Sharon at her heels. The man stayed where he was. He knew when he wasn't wanted.

The ladies headed along the corridor, taking an age to discuss the toilet facilities, which Mrs Snarlington-Darlington felt would benefit from some flowery wallpaper and a plant. Then they reached the back larder.

'And you say this is where Jack went through to the Otherworld?' whispered Mrs Snarlington-Darlington, opening the larder door.

'Yes,' said Sharon, 'Duggey told me, and I believe him.'

'I'll take it!!' screeched Mrs Snarlington-Darlington, her voice echoing loudly along the corridor and into the café.

The man almost fell backwards out of the door. 'At last!'

Chapter Nineteen

Aife, Queen of the Amazons

'I'm sorry about the cage,' said the Leprechaun, calling over his shoulder to the swan, who had to bend her neck to allow for the height of it.

He was sitting on a deck chair in the back garden of the witch's cottage enjoying the sun and his freedom, reading the paper and drinking a gin and tonic.

'It's too small for a swan but I'm sure they'll have something bigger for you in Showtown,' said the Leprechaun.

'I hear the Shadow pays a fine price for swan maidens,' he laughed annoyingly, rocking backwards and forwards on the deckchair and almost collapsed it, spilling his gin onto the lawn.

He scampered back into the cottage through the French windows and began searching through the witch's cabinet for another drink, perhaps a fine wine. It was then he heard the voices in the front garden.

Confident, self-assured and all grown up after their love making in the woods, Jack and Dundee had spent the remainder of the journey discussing the evil Leprechaun, and what they were going to do to him when they found him. And so, by the time they reached the cottage, they had no choice but to storm heroically in. Dundee took the lead. Jack covered his back. They checked downstairs, then upstairs. When they were sure the cottage was fiend free they called in the girls from the open window of the witch's bedroom, gagging from the disgusting smell. They were still in the hall recovering from the stench, when the girls called them into the back garden. They had found the swan maiden – in a cage! It was padlocked. Dundee hammered at the chain with his huge dagger until it broke, and rescued the swan from the cage. He carried her through the cottage and out onto the front lawn where he laid her down on the grass. She was weak, but her desire for freedom overcame her exhaustion, and after several attempts to fly, she rose and flew off towards the Lake to complete her transformation before it was too late.

The four returned to the garden to check there were no other captives and then headed back into the dining room intent on leaving, but when they reached the sitting room Dundee spotted something green at the bottom of the chimney. It was the Leprechaun. And his eyes were shut.

'It's not him,' said Jack, poking the Leprechaun with his finger. 'It's just a toy.'

'It is him,' said Dundee, determined to find someone to bash. 'Try hammering his head against the wall.'

Jack picked up the toy.

279

'It wasn't me,' cried the Leprechaun suddenly coming to life, almost giving Jack a heart attack. He dropped the Leprechaun and leapt back from the hearth.

It was the Witch,' said the Leprechaun, jumping to his feet. He could tell they weren't convinced, and he scuttled off towards the sitting room door. Dundee gave him a kick with his winkle picker shoe. The Leprechaun hit the floor, but he was up in a flash.

'I'll get you back for that,' he hissed, backing away.

'Oh aye, you and who's army?' said Dundee, more confidently than he felt. The Leprechaun was really scary.

The chase began. Out of the door, into the hallway, and onto the lawn where they ran into the Black Witch and her Banshees.

A few hundred yards above the clouds Diorruing was pacing up and down in front of the exit doors, like a princely version of '*Jack and the Beanstalk,*' anxious to escape the Giants land.

As Finn and the Fianna had searched the woods for their missing comrades, Diorruing had been relegated to stay behind, in case they returned. But of course they did not, and the searches were unsuccessful. Diorruing had been unable to give them a clue as to their whereabouts, his foresight blurred by the hundreds of stories in the Story World flitting through his mind. It was giving him a headache. But even without his second sight Diorruing could sense something very dark closing in on them.

When Finn and his warriors returned for a second time Diorruing insisted that they leave the Story World. But Finn refused.

'Try again,' he commanded, and the Fianna returned to the woods leaving Diorruing behind at the doors.

Bored of pacing up and down Diorruing went to sit on the Bridge for a while. The villagers assumed it was the Giant and rushed out with their yellow buckets, delighted when they saw that it was a prince of their own size. The mothers and fathers called to their daughters, children came running out of the back gardens, aunties and uncles, grandmothers and grandfathers, and soon there was a whole crowd of people smiling up at Diorruing who was hanging over the railings looking forlorn. The sight of them cheered him up and for a few moments the unwelcome images faded out. He could see the villagers quite clearly now with their yellow buckets, and he remembered a trick he had learned from an old master. He would count the buckets. This would clear his conscious mind of the clutter, and allow his subconscious through.

'One, two, three, four. One hundred and three…two hundred and two…' The villagers kept moving around, and he was counting the same buckets over and over, but it didn't matter. 'Three hundred and four, three hundred and….' He had them! They were below the Bridge. He could see the village in black and white, the witch's cottages with the red doors….and the Black Witch. She was going to burn them!

There was no time to lose. Diorruing stood bravely alone in the middle of the Bridge and closed his eyes, willing himself down into the Land of Hellish Thought. But nothing happened. He paced the Bridge backwards and forwards, the villagers annoying him now, following him around with their buckets. He tried again, and again, dark thoughts. But it was no good. He just couldn't get there. Then he sensed someone watching him from the other side of the Bridge. It was a black Scottie dog with eighties side burns.

Diorruing recognized the dog at once – it was Donn of the Dead's.

'We'll burn him in the fire,' said the Black Witch, who was on her knees by the fireplace, two of her Banshees looking dutifully on from the doorway.

The Witch had found a mixture of potions in the dead witch's office. She had used them to ignite the fire, which was now burning madly with purple, red and orange flames. The smoke filled the room with a ghastly odour. The same smell as in the witch's bedroom.

The Banshees began backing away from it, towards the French windows.

'Here,' commanded the Witch. They stepped forward.

'Pass me that egg timer. If we burn him for long enough the witch's flames will blacken his soul, then no-one will be able to resurrect him, not even the Gods,' explained the Witch to the Banshees, as if it was a cookery programme.

The Witch had surprised them all by focusing her attack on Jack and the doll. First, she had grabbed Echtra and dragged her back into the cottage. Jack had followed them in, as the Witch knew he would. As soon as Jack was in the hallway he was hit from behind by two of her Banshees. The cottage door slammed shut. The remaining Banshees closed ranks, and Dundee and Echraide were left outside on the lawn.

'Jack!' cried Dundee. But it was hopeless. They were unable to get anywhere near the door for Banshees. They raced around to the sitting room window to see what was going on.

'They're burning him!' cried Dundee.

The Witch pulled Jack towards the open hearth by the hair. He could feel the immense heat from the flames at his head but he ignored it. His attention was solely on Echtra who was being dragged out of the room by two Banshees, intent on caging her. He suddenly remembered the story of the tin soldier.

'I love you!' cried Jack.

Almost immediately a black Scottie dog flew in through the French windows and leapt at the Witch. She fell back into the fire, shrieking as the coloured flames caught her hair and her face. The Banshees released their grip on Echtra and rushed towards her. But the fire was not easily put out. The witch's flames had already blackened her soul, and they were too late to save the left hand side of her face.

'I'm melting.' cried the Witch.

She was still burning when they dragged her out of the fireplace. Despite her ability to shape shift the Witch would remain forever deformed. And when she saw her face in the sitting room mirror her screech was so loud it was heard in both the Heavenly and the Hellish lands.

In the ensuing chaos Jack and Echtra managed to escape the sitting room and when they emerged from the witch's front door they were back, in the Land of Heavenly Thought. The witch's cottages, the Black Witch, and her Banshees had disappeared and Caer was standing there smiling at them.

'Thank you for saving her,' she said to Dundee.

Dundee nodded, unsure of what to say. She looked even more enchanting in clothes, her dress shimmering in the sun.

She stepped forward, and opened out her hand. In it was a small silver radio on a chain.

'Take this. It will enable you to call on Angus and his warriors of love, if ever you need their help.'

'I see them,' said Diorruing.

'Where?' asked Finn, assuming he meant in a vision. They had just returned and heard the news.

'There,' said the Seer, pointing to the Bridge.

Fergus rushed forward, helping Jack who had taken a real hiding from the Banshees.

'Where's Brian?' he asked, when he had caught up

with their escapades.

'We'll tell you later,' said Dundee.

'The doors!' called Finn, who was already there with Mac, Diarmait and Diorruing. Everyone was needed. The exit doors were Giant size. It took a while but finally they managed to pull them apart, just a little, and as they did the vision that had been trying to get through to Diorruing all morning popped into his head.

'No!' he cried, trying to close the doors again.

Mac, sensing all was not well, dove in. The others joined them.

But it was too late. The force from the other side was too great. They were thrown back. The doors flew open. And there, standing before them, was the dreaded Aife, Queen of the Amazons.

It was rare to see the Queen. Not even the Fianna who had been matched against the Amazons many times, had ever been this close to her. She was magnificent, more than eight feet tall in battle dress. Her long dark hair billowing out from the force of the beating wings of her soldiers, who circled around her, creating a deadening rhythmic beat. There were so many of them they cut out the light. Everything was black. Only the face of Aife was pale and perfect in the madness. Some say she stole her beauty from the girls she took to war but Aife's belle was all her own. Her face was like a divine sculpture, spoiled only by her eyes which were as black as hell, and they were staring straight at them.

The Amazon warriors filled the space between the earth and the sky. Even a bee would have had trouble getting through. Aife could have taken them all at once but instead she went for Finn. The attack on their Leader took them all by surprise. With no visible sign from the Queen a flock of warriors covered him in seconds. Finn just disappeared into the darkness. There was no way of saving him, but they tried. Whilst the Fianna were frantically searching for their leader, Aife slid out with Finn in chains, leaving the capture of the other warriors to her soldiers in command.

The warriors fought the Amazons for as long as they were able, but it was hopeless. The scouts they killed were easily replaced. The enemy persisted until the heroes grew weak and bloodied.

They backed away toward the exit doors. Mac at the front, determined to protect them, Diarmait and Fergus behind him, Diorruing with the girls, and then Jack and Dundee, who had been incredibly heroic defending their rear.

Dundee caught Jack's eye and shook his head. This was it. They were done for.

Then Jack spotted something shiny around Dundee's neck. 'The radio!' he cried.

'What?' The noise of the Amazon legions was deafening.

'Angus' radio!' Jack grabbed hold of the chain around Dundee's neck, frantically turning the dials this way and that, almost choking Dundee, who suddenly found he was fighting for two.

'Wh…What's happening?' he choked.

'Nothing,' yelled Jack.

Dundee snatched the chain back, and flicked the switch.

'Screech…crackle…crackle.'

Jack almost jumped for joy, momentarily forgetting their adversaries. Within seconds one of the Amazon scouts had Jack by the hair.

Dundee lost his temper. He head butted the Amazon fiend, and a few more besides. Then in a fury, he swung his sword up over his shoulders, like the warriors of old, and sliced off at least three heads in one go. In awe of Dundee and his heroic outburst, Jack followed his lead. The circle of the dead gained them a few valuable seconds. Dundee tried the radio dial again. It crackled as he searched for a frequency. Then it went dead. They looked up. The Amazons heavies were closing in.

Diorruing cast a worried eye over Jack and Dundee. He'd had a vision of what lay ahead for them – and it was not pleasant - the death of ordinary men at the hands of the Baobhan. He had to get them out of there.

Diorruing spoke quickly to his comrades and they drew back towards the rear.

'Do something un-heroic!' yelled Fergus, suddenly appearing between Jack and Dundee.

'What?'

'Do something un-heroic,' called Diarmait. 'Or who

will save us?'

As the Amazons rushed forward Mac hurled Jack and Dundee towards the exit doors. 'RUN!'

Time slowed a pace as they realised what they were being asked to do. But as they started towards the exit doors Jack faltered. His thoughts on the girl he was about to abandon.

Diorruing sensed it. 'Don't look back!' he cried.

But Jack had already turned, and at that moment a dagger charred black from a fire headed straight for his heart.

Surprisingly it was knocked off course by a gigantic rolling pin covered in flour.

Chapter Twenty

The Last Ray of Hope

The Adventurer and his crew had passes to the second realm, but the man at the toll booth on the Bridge didn't bother to look at them. He knew the Convoy. He had seen it many times before, and the expectant way at which the Adventurer had approached the booth had almost guaranteed their crossing. But still he made them wait.

The man at the booth was less than three feet tall, but he had an extremely tall hat. It would have been easy for the Convoy just to ride onto the Bridge, without bothering to stop at all. There was only one of him, and almost a hundred of them, not including their hangers on. But in the Otherworld looks can be deceiving, and the man at the booth could have taken half of them out with what was hiding beneath his hat. The Wings sighed heavily, and the man added some extra time onto their wait. Eventually he re-entered the booth, signed them all in, and let them pass.

The Bridge was over a mile long, with nothing below it but an eternal pit of endlessness, which was another reason why the men had avoided any trouble.

Thankfully a heavy mist usually hung below the Bridge, avoiding the temptation to look below it.

At the end of the Bridge the Convoy turned right and hit the desert road. It was usual at that point to see Finias, the City of Fire, which was elevated for the benefit of approaching dragons, and bathed in a perpetual light. But the light of the City had dimmed, more than likely due to the arrival of Showtown and the Shadow. When they were less than half a mile away the Convoy stopped. The crew gathered together by the side of the road, and waited for further instruction from the Den. Infiltrating Showtown was not going to be easy. The Adventurer hoped the Rev would be up to the job but it was a good while before he found out.

The Rev arrived in good humour, and was greeted like a celebrity by the crew of men who made a huge fuss of him, and so it was a good hour before he joined his comrades in the Den.

'Hello boys,' said the Rev, swaying merrily up the steps. He'd had a thoroughly enjoyable journey, filled with glee at the thought of everyone having to wait for him. After dousing himself in what he assured the Sisters was Holy Water, he had helped himself to the youngest, and to the holy wine from the flask she had hidden beneath her garter belt. When the Sisters had had enough of him they dropped him off not far from the Bridge. As the Rev staggered along the High road even the ghouls avoided him, as did the man at the toll booth. By the time he stepped into the Den he was in a dreadful state, covered from head to toe in dust. His lips stained with red wine, his straggly hair all over the place. His shades were off, and his crazy eyes were on show. It took a while for them to come into focus.

'We've gotta job for you,' said the Adventurer.

The Rev nodded, swayed a little, and then toppled backwards. They placed him in his favourite box and closed the lid, leaving him to sleep it off.

Then the Convoy started up again towards the City of Finias, and their old comrade the Shadow.

The top floor at Stress City Headquarters was in darkness. The shutters were down. The work areas were empty and pristine ready for the working day and the Governor's personal assistants were sitting at their desks in the gloom.

There was someone in the building. The lift started up. The doors opened to reveal a Witch whose face was horribly charred on one side. She stepped out onto the thick pile carpet covering it in flakes of black cinders, which the cleaners would later say had ruined the carpet. She dragged the doll to the place that had been made up for her - the twelfth desk next to the Addison Bruce's office. In the morning she would start up with the rest.

Three hours later it was rush hour on Main Street. Well, not rush hour exactly. The City Hall clock was still out of sync, as were the inhabitants, some of whom were still sauntering into work at half past nine. But the problems were back, along with the noise and everyone was complaining about the lack of room on the pavements again. It was almost like normal.

'Talking to a swan apparently,' said the man, who was conversing with his lady friend as he waited for his change at the counter of *Emma's*. 'Sounds a bit far-fetched if you ask me.'

It had been almost a year since the swan incident, and yet the inhabitants were still talking about it.

'It does sound a bit far-fetched, doesn't it?' said a woman, who had been listening in. She was sitting in front of the till, having tea with Miss Blunt, the retired school teacher from number five 'the bank,' who, after twelve years of hiding behind her broom, had decided to re-join the living.

'Well. You can take it from me, it is true. I saw Jack myself. He was outside my kitchen window on the lawn stealing seed for the swan from my bird table. And I can assure you, there's nothing wrong with *my* eye sight,' said Miss Blunt, in a voice that would brook no argument.

Everyone in the café was listening in. *Emma's* was small and Miss Blunt used to take morning assembly so her voice always carried further than she intended.

The conversations were about to kick off again, in light of this new information, when Mrs Snarlington-Darlington entered the room and everyone stopped what *they* were doing in order to see what *she* was doing.

Mrs Snarlington-Darlington had recently become a *cause célèbre*. And it wasn't just the fact that she had re-opened *Emma's* on Old Street, or that she had been appointed Problem Solver for the City. It was more than that, something noticeably different that no-one could put their finger on. It was almost as if she knew something they didn't, which of course she did.

'I'm sure Jack had his reasons,' said Mrs Snarlington-Darlington, giving the man his change before shoving him out of the café door. Customers had been banned for less.

Everyone looked down at their teas and coffees and pretended to behave themselves until Mrs Snarlington-Darlington had disappeared into the back. Then they returned to their conversations.

'As I was saying,' said Sharon, who was sitting on one of the tables for two nearest the door with Ann Angel, who was looking even more exhausted than ever. 'You've got a teleconference at twelve, which may be brought forward, or put back, depending on what happens with the clock, and so we may have to reschedule the one o'clock with the Senior Team. That's assuming they turn up this time. They got confused yesterday when the clock went back and the 07.00 updates were delayed.' She paused for a moment to catch her breath.

'You've got three teleconferences this afternoon, we'll have to play those by ear, and then it's your meeting with Addison Bruce at five. You don't want to keep *him* waiting.'

Ann stared at Sharon in admiration. Sharon was the only person at Stress City Headquarters who was able to manage the new flexible diary system, which had been introduced to cope with the time disorder. She knew Sharon was due some encouraging words, but she just didn't have the energy to voice them.

'It's so exciting,' said Sharon, referring to Ann's meeting with Addison Bruce. 'There's a rumour going around that you're going to be promoted to the top floor. Won't that be marvellous?'

Sharon sat back in her chair and finished off the rest of her coffee. Her mind on all the outfits she would have to buy to go with her new status. She would have full access to the Executive ladies cloakroom, and so she would need new make-up, a new coat, and a new handbag. Perhaps she should make an appointment with her hairdresser now...

Someone interrupted Sharon's day dreaming by opening the café door too wide and knocking into their table. Sharon acknowledged the apology from the customer at the door and then she realised there was something wrong with Ann. Her body looked deflated, as if someone had taken the wind out of her.

'What's wrong?' said Sharon, concerned.

'I don't know,' said Ann, taking off her glasses and putting her head in her hands, letting out a huge sigh. 'It's just a feeling that if I do get promoted to the top floor no-one will ever see me again.'

'That's silly,' said Sharon, placing her hand on Ann's.

Ann raised her head, attempting to smile. Sharon was shocked. Ann looked dreadful. Her blue eyes were dull, she was paler than ever, and her bun was coming out of her hair grips.

She jumped up and rushed off to pay the bill. Then returned with Ann's coat and helped her to her feet, deciding to cancel Ann's twelve o'clock. She looked like she needed the break.

On their way out of the café they stopped to help an old crone up the steps. Ann felt ashamed. Her own problems were nothing compared to this poor old lady who had clearly been disfigured in some sort of fire. Sharon was unfortunate enough to be on her worst side and was relieved when one of Mrs Snarlington-Darlington's helpers appeared and took the old lady off her hands, guiding her to the table that had been vacated by Miss Blunt. When the old lady was half way across the room she turned and smiled at the girls who had just stepped out of the doorway. Sharon and Ann smiled back. If they had seen her hidden side it would have given them even more of a fright.

No one bothered to look up from their conversations as the old crone was seated and served with a pot of tea and a copy of *Woman's Weekly*. She was about to turn to the recipe page when there was a tremendous thud in the back larder, followed by a loud banging and muffled cries.

Mrs Snarlington-Darlington, who had always been good in a crisis, strode calmly through to the back, took the key from her apron pocket, and opened the door.

'There's nothing here,' said Mrs Snarlington-Darlington to herself, her voice echoing along the corridor into the café.

'It must have been the wind,' she called through to her helpers.

'What wind?' said the customers.

Jack and Dundee looked confused.

'She can't see us!' exclaimed Jack.

'Quick,' cried Dundee. 'Before she closes the door on us.' They jumped out of the larder and pulled back against the walls, not wishing to bump into Mrs Snarlington-Darlington whether visible or invisible. They followed her along the corridor, almost colliding into her rear end when she stopped to pick something up off the floor.

'Another one,' said Mrs Snarlington-Darlington to her helpers who could see her from the kitchen. 'I can't believe the number of walking sticks people leave behind in this café.

'The Witch!' cried Jack and Dundee, in unison.

Forewarned by Mrs Snarlington-Darlington Jack and Dundee were half way out the café door before they stopped in their tracks.

They had just faced the Amazon army. They were heroes. Weren't they? They headed back inside to face the Black Witch of Bad Luck.

Dundee picked up two golfing brollies from the yellow bucket by the door. He passed one to Jack and they held them up in front of them, as though they were swords. The Black Witch stood up slowly. She was mad as hell. She had two huge daggers in her hands, one for each of them. They tensed up, ready for her attack.

The fall of the Black Witch lay in her extreme vanity. She couldn't resist a peak at herself in the mirror. The right hand side of her face was still pretty and flawless. But as she turned towards the glass her whole face started to blacken. She let out a high pitched wail and turned towards the mirror full on, to find her face was coming off in bits.

Unbeknown to the Witch the mirror at *Emma's* always reflected what was within, rather than without. And the Witch's soul was already black, and singed by the witch's fire. She tried to pull away from the glass but Jack and Dundee realised what was happening and rushed forward, grabbing her head and pushing it closer to the mirror. The Witch fought back, then she began to crumble in front of them until she had disintegrated into a big black mound of dust.

Pleased with themselves the heroes brushed the dust from their clothes, put the golf brollies back in the bucket, and left the café.

'Oh, just look at that!' exclaimed Mrs Snarlington-Darlington, who had heard the door slam and came

297

rushing out of the kitchen.

'A great pile of black dust in the middle of the floor. And I'm being interviewed at four o'clock.'

One of the helpers ran out of the kitchen with a large floor mop. It was the end of the line for the Black Witch of Bad Luck.

Outside on Old Street the heroes chatted away, full of beans, and didn't notice Sharon and Ann until they were almost on top of them.

Dundee's heart took a flying leap out of his chest. It was as if Echraide herself was standing before him, in a business suit and high heels.

The girls had just left Duggey's and were standing in front of the shop next door. Ann was peering in through the large oblong window. Sharon was standing outside the glass front door.

'Sharon,' said Jack. 'Sharon!' He was standing right next to her but it was clear she couldn't hear him, or see him.

'What's going on? Are we dead?'

Dundee was in a daze, his attention on Ann.

'I think it's a Library,' said Ann excitedly. 'It's full of books.' She could see that the shop was on two levels, with reams of book aisles at the back, and a podium on the lower level, with a seating area for reading.

'There's a notice here on the front door,' said Sharon. 'It says it's for sale.'

As Ann turned away from the window she had the

most amazing feeling, as if she had been enveloped in a divine wind. It was a sign.

'Ann?' said Sharon. 'Are you ok?' Ann seemed to have gone into a daze.

'I'm fine,' said Ann, joining Sharon at the Library door. 'Call the estate agent. Ask him to meet us here tonight. We're leaving Stress City Headquarters.'

'Come on,' said Jack, dragging Dundee away from Ann and pulling him into Duggey's shop.

For once Duggey was standing up behind the counter facing the door. He was looking much smarter than usual, and was wearing a black jacket instead of his green cardigan, his hair was slightly spiky and gelled, and he had shoes on – black pointed ones with a silver tip.

'Well, you're a sight for sore eyes,' said Duggey, greatly relieved to see Dundee back in human form.

'You can see us! We thought we were dead.'

Duggey came around the counter and greeted them both like long lost brothers.

'Not dead, just mythical.'

'What?'

'You've become heroes of myth. That's why no-one can see you. You even look like heroes,' continued Duggey, giving them the once over. 'You're taller than you were before, and much broader.'

'Really?' said Jack and Dundee in unison, wishing everyone could see them.

299

'We just killed the Witch,' boasted Jack.

'Ding dong,' said Duggey, returning to his seat behind the counter.

'You're out of McEwans,' said Brian, coming out of the kitchen.

'Brian!' cried Dundee.

'You're alive!' cried Jack.

'No thanks to you,' said Brian.

Ignoring Brian's dourness they rushed forward patting his shoulder and attempting to ruffle his hair which was even more matted up than usual.

'So, you're not dead then?' said Dundee.

'No,' said Brian, stating the obvious.

'Where've you been?' asked Jack.

'I got thrown back at the same time as you. I've been hiding up North. Addison Bruce was after me.'

'Tell them why,' encouraged Duggey.

'I stole the Key to the City,' admitted Brian.

'*You* stole the key!' cried Dundee, in shock.

'Yep.' Brian opened up his can of McEwans and pulled up a stool to explain, as Duggey opened a bottle of champagne he had been saving under the counter for the occasion.

'Twelve thousand years ago when the Amazons took the Island I was there. I was in the City when they attacked, and I managed to escape to the North. I kept a low profile. Spent most of my time tending bars, picking up whatever information I could, which wasn't much.'

Brian continued on for a while, a never ending tale

of doom and gloom.

Jack and Dundee were staring at Brian open mouthed.

'You mean…you've been here, all this time!'

'For twelve thousand years!'

'Yeh!' said Brian, impatiently. As if they hadn't been listening to a word he was saying. He took a few gulps of his McEwans before continuing.

'Anyway one day, while I was managing the *Hootsman*, a bunch of teenage nutcases walked through the door. It was you,' said Brian, nodding towards Dundee.

'Me!'

'Yeh, you and the Cormacs…I could hardly believe it. It was like the King and his cousins had walked into the bar.'

'I followed you here to Stress City, and when I arrived the Fairy Queen told me all about you.'

Brian stalled.

'Told you what about us?'

'Tell us!'

Duggey nodded.

'The Fairy Queen dreamt you up,' said Brian.

'What do you mean she dreamt us up?'

Brian shrugged his shoulders.

'You mean we're not real?' asked Jack.

'You're real enough now,' said Duggey, quickly changing the subject. 'Tell them about the Key.'

Brian continued. 'The Fairy Queen planned to steal

the Key to the City. It was kept under close guard at City Hall but she suspected Addison Bruce had access to it. The window round was her idea. I was there really early one morning outside Addison's office. It was dark outside. The light was on, and I saw him with his personal assistants. He was winding them up.'

'What do you mean winding them up?' asked Jack.

'Addison has the dolls.'

Jack's heart soared at the mention of the dolls.

'He keeps them on the top floor. They're his personal assistants, and they're wound by the same Key as the City.'

'I told you they were damsels in distress,' called Duggey from the kitchen.

'The Fairy Queen always suspected that Addison had stolen the dolls,' continued Brian. 'That morning I saw where he put the Key. Later that night I went back and helped myself to it...Unfortunately I wasn't the only one the Fairy Queen took into her confidence. The Rev knew all about it.'

'He can't be trusted,' said Duggey, coming through with another bottle.

'Thankfully the Fairy Queen escaped with the Key before the Rev spilled the beans to Addison. They came to get me. It was the Rev's idea to hold me upside down over the Bridge by my ankles. But it was Addison Bruce who dropped me.'

Duggey, Dundee and Jack came forward and patted Brian on the shoulder for his heroic deed and subsequent death in the line of duty.

'So you didn't jump then.' said Jack.

'Who told you I jumped?' asked Brian, looking annoyed.

'Erm, no-one. We just assumed,' said Dundee.

'Assumed what?' said Brian, his temper flaring. 'I'm not the type to be committing suicide.'

Everyone kept their heads down and stared into their drinks.

'What's this?' said Brian, picking up the dusty funeral notice that had been lying on the counter for years. 'Did I get a funeral?'

'Aye, ye did.'

'Was there many there?'

'There were loads there,' they lied.

Brian managed to look pleased.

'We'd better get going,' urged Dundee. 'The Amazons have got our girls, and our pals, the Fianna.'

Jack agreed.

'I'll get my stuff.' Brian raced into the back.

'Wait,' said Duggey, as they made their way out of the shop. 'I almost forgot. You had a letter from Mrs D.'

Dundee took the envelope from Duggey, which had yellow flowers on it.

'She says we're to meet her at the railway station. We're taking the Glory Train to Finias.'

'Well, you must have done something right,' said Duggey. 'The Glory Train is for heroes only.'

Jack and Dundee looked pleased with themselves.

'You should take the Bridge. It'll be quicker.'

'I thought you said the Bridge kept fading out?'

'It did, but this morning it was back, as clear as day. You two have become the link. The stories of your adventures in the Otherworld are keeping the dreams alive. But that means you'll have to stay in Legend with all the other mythical heroes until the Key is returned.'

'We should go,' said Brian anxiously. 'Before Addison finds us. He's having difficulty controlling himself these days.'

'Are you coming Duggey?'

'No offence,' said Duggey. 'But I feel safer without you.'

'I'll leave this here with you then, for safe keeping,' said Dundee

'What is it?'

'It's a silver radio. Caer gave it to us so we could call on Angus for help, but it doesn't work, and I don't want to lose it.'

'No problem,' said Duggey, pleased. He placed the silver radio safely behind the counter and then gave them directions. 'Turn right at the end of the Bridge. The railway station is three miles on.'

The three heroes headed out the door.

'And be sure to take the Low road,' he called out after them, but they didn't hear him.

On the way to the Bridge they discussed the odds.

'At least we don't have to worry about the Black

Witch anymore,' said Jack.

'Yeh, there's just Aife and her army of thousands, and Addison Bruce,' said Brian. 'Against us three!'

'And the Fianna,' reminded Dundee, 'We rescue them before we do anything.'

'That goes without saying,' agreed Jack.

'We'll need an army to do that,' argued Brian, 'or a bunch of psychopaths.'

As they emerged from the sunlit forest onto the bank they thought back to the last time they had been there with Mrs D. She had come to show them something, a world that was larger than life, and they had followed her out of the playpen like innocent children. This time they knew far more about the dangers of the world they were about to enter, and if it hadn't been for Brian they probably would have raced back to the nursery and stayed there forever. But then they saw the fog. Like a vision of their past. And there on the Bridge were Dundee's cousins, the Cormacs. They had come down from the North, heavy handed.

'Is that you Wullie?' asked Dundee.

'Aye, it's me right enough. Duggey said you might be needing a hand.'

Wullie stood at the head of the clan which was twelve strong. He had a mad grin on his face and half a can of McEwans in his hand. The three of them shook hands vigorously with every one of the Cormacs. Then they were off, into the mist. And as they crossed over

305

calmer waters the Bridge flowered up behind them, like the Knights of old they had become the elixir of life.

If you stand at the end of the Bridge you can still hear the distant voices of the heroes echoing across the water.

'Will there be any lassies over there Dundee.'

'They won't be interested in you Wullie. Not with your hair style, still living in the 1970's.'

'Haggis might stand a chance.'

'Aye, if he knocks them oot first wi his caber.'

Will you stop havering,' said Brian, losing his patience with them already...

Interview with a Problem Solver
Emma's café
Stress City

'Now I know what you're going to ask. Do I make any of the problems up myself? Well of course not. I can assure you all of my problems are real. Take this one for example. We can't agree on bedroom curtains. Trivial perhaps, but real. Am I normal, which is a recurring problem. His hairstyle's an embarrassment. She's out of control…'

'Erm,' said the journalist girl, jumping in quickly before Mrs Snarlington-Darlington could open any more envelopes. 'Our readers are keen to hear about your trip.'

'Tip, why yes of course,' said Mrs Snarlington-Darlington, pleased to be asked. 'Always try to be open, and keep an eye on the paintwork. Oops, sorry that's cafes.'

'Trip!' said the journalist, a little louder than she had intended, interrupting the conversations of the customers at the surrounding tables. 'Your trip into the Wilde Blue Yonder.'

'The Wilde Blue Yonder?' said Mrs Snarlington-Darlington, looking confused.

'You know,' said the girl, looking around and lowering her voice. 'The Otherworld.'

'Ah, you're getting me mixed up with the other

Problem Solver, Mrs D. She's supernatural you know.'

'I thought you were one and the same.'

'One and the same. Certainly not. There's only one me,' said Mrs Snarlington-Darlington, getting up to attend to an arriving customer.

It had been like that all afternoon – customers in and out, deliveries at the door, Mrs Snarlington-Darlington scurrying back and forth to the till, the cake display case, the kitchen and the back larder. There were plenty of helpers but Mrs Snarlington-Darlington was the sort of person who liked to keep her eye on things and was capable of watching several people at once.

The young journalist girl shuffled around impatiently on table three. She had studied the menu, read all the magazines, and played around with the triangular notice in the middle of the table which said *Emma's* could not be held responsible for any valuables, including husbands, wives or elderly relatives left at the table. Her reporters note pad lay open at the first page and was empty apart from the title. '*Wilde Blue Yonder – The Facts.*'

At four o'clock the café emptied out and when the last customer had gone Mrs Snarlington-Darlington returned to the table.

'And so you *do* believe in the Otherworld, do you?' asked the journalist, in a way that suggested Mrs Snarlington-Darlington had lost her mind.'

'Of course I believe in it. Jack's over there isn't he,' said Mrs Snarlington-Darlington, indignantly. 'And

Dundee.'

'Ah yes,' said the girl, referring to the notes she had made long ago when she had first shaken hands with them at the signpost. 'Jack's the one with the curls isn't he?'

'Oh Jack,' cried Mrs Snarlington-Darlington with a sigh. She threw her hand up to her forehead, ignoring the girl's question altogether.

'I knew he was different right from the start. The moment he landed on my doorstep. He used to wander off you know, whenever my back was turned, towards the Bridge. Even then he must have known – that there was something else out there. He would stand at the end of it, staring out into the mists, with the girl from number seven,' said Mrs Snarlington-Darlington, exaggerating.

'She's from the Otherworld you know.'

'Is she?' The journalist made a note.

'Yes. I think that's why he left. He followed her out there,' added Mrs Snarlington-Darlington, making it up as she went along.

'How romantic.'

'But then they lost each other.' The journalist gasped.

'Dundee fell in love, with an Otherworldly heroine. But they lost each other too.'

'How tragic. And when do you think they might find each other again?' asked the girl, hoping for a romantic ending to the article.

'You youngsters place far too much emphasis on

romance. We can't all have happy endings you know,' said Mrs Snarlington-Darlington, rising from the table to indicate to the journalist that the interview was over.

Half an hour later Mrs Snarlington-Darlington was in the kitchen doing the dishes when she heard the door open.

'We're closed.' she boomed.

She waited until she heard the door close, and then she returned to the dishes. The music suddenly switched to something hugely romantic and she heard a thump. Startled she flew into the café and there was her husband, Mr Snarlington-Darlington, looking incredibly smart and clean shaven, with a huge box of fish on the table at his side.

Mrs Snarlington-Darlington let out a gasp and put her hand to the pearls at her throat, glad she had made an effort for the journalist that afternoon, as Mr Snarlington-Darlington pulled her into his arms. He danced her around the café in a dramatically romantic fashion until she was dizzy with delight, then he took her home and they lived happily ever after, until the next time they had a row.

The following day the Stress City Headquarters Gazette ran the '*Wilde Blue Yonder – The Facts*' article with a photo of the Snarlington-Darlingtons' on the cover. And the gossips continued in earnest...

THE NEXT TWO BOOKS IN THE TRILOGY

Stress City
The Curse of the Cormacs

Stress City
The Adventurer's Dolls

INFLUENCES

CELTIC MYTHOLOGY

Peter Berresford Ellis - The mammoth book of Celtic
Myths and Legends 2002
James Mackillop - Myths and Legends of the Celts, 2005
Lady Augusta Gregory - Gods and Fighting Men, 1904
T W Rolleston - Myths & Legends of the Celtic Race, 2004
James Mackillop - Oxford Dictionary of Celtic Mythology
2004

FILM/TV

Tom & Jerry
Laurel and Hardy
Stingray
The Wizard of Oz

FAIRY TALES

Rip Van Winkle - Washington Irving, 1819.
The Steadfast Tin Soldier - Hans Christian Anderson,
1838.

INFLUENCES

SOUNDTRACK

I've got you under my skin (from "Born to Dance")
Words and Music by Cole Porter
© 1936 by Cole Porter
Copyright Renewed and Assigned to Robert H. Montgomery,
Trustee of the Cole Porter Musical & Literary Property Trusts
Publication and Allied Rights Assigned to Chappell & Co., Inc.
All Rights Reserved
Used by Permission of Alfred Music

MUSIC

Alabama 3

Th'Legendary Shack Shakers

IN REVERANCE

Stuart Wilde

STRESS CITY HEADQUARTERS

Logo: Brian T Stephen

Follow SCHQ: Lizzie Life, Emer Bruce @

www.stresscity.co.uk

www.facebook.com/Stress-City-HQ

@HQStress on Twitter

Contact us at stresscityhq@gmail.com